"Rand,

pets to suit your taste.
Why would I need a parrot?"

"He possesses an attribute I wish he'd teach you." As Jess's eyes widened in question, he leaned so close his hair touched the brim of her hat, so near he could smell her skin—and her fear. "He talks."

She spun and snapped up her parasol as she walked toward a copse.

He kept pace. The trees offered him seclusion and he turned her to him, her back to an old oak. "Jess, I think I deserve an explanation." He stroked her hair from her cheek and lifted her chin. "Tell me why you are avoiding me—and *this.*"

His kiss surprised him for its politeness. Her response astonished him for its fire. He understood only what he gave, she took—and when he purposely raised his mouth, she caught him back, a hand cupping his nape for another brief but brazen sample.

Her eyes were glazed, her lips wet, her breasts heaving. Her hat hung from dangling strawberry curls. "I want to be with you. I think, alone in my room at night, that I might even *need* you."

"Wonderful. Just tell me why, when, how. . . ."

Praise from booksellers for Jo-Ann Power's *TREASURES*

"Love, laughter, passion and intrigue, all brought together in an exciting tale full of wit and style. Reading TREASURES was a first class adventure."

—Holly Deems, *Book Rack*, Mansfield, OH

"I opened this wonderful book, fell right in and never looked up until I'd finished. Maybe Jo-Ann could put a few blank pages in the middle of her books to remind readers they must sleep sometime."

—Kim VerHage, *Reading Books*, Rockford, MI

"Jo-Ann has written another lovely story—one I picked up and couldn't walk away from until it was done!"

—Merry Cutler, *Annie's Book Stop*, Sharon, MA

"TREASURES is a real joy. Wonderfully refreshing. I thank you for writing this book, which brings tears and happy sighs."

—*Best Sellers*, Palos Heights, IL

"TREASURES is wonderful! I finished it in one sitting. Jo-Ann Power has staying power in writing."

—Adene J. Beal, *House of Books*, Tallahassee, FL

"TREASURES is why we read romances. . . . a treasure of a book—a keeper! One to read over and over again. This is destined to be a classic. Jo-Ann Power is a major talent. Her words have power and beauty."

—Kay E. Bendall, *The Book Rack*, Richmond, VA

"TREASURES is a treasure, sure to be a keeper."
—Sharon Walters, *Paperback Place,* Mercer, PA

"This book is another 'Power-ful' keeper! I could not detach myself from it. Sensual, well-depicted characters; rich like vintage wine! [A] five-star read!"
—Lucy H. Morris, *Lucy's Book Exchange, Inc.,* Raleigh, NC

"Jo-Ann Power has another winner. . . ."
—Virginia H. Hicks, *The Book Shop, Inc.,* Brunswick, GA

"I really liked it . . . great characters, well-crafted plot and a terrific mystery."
—Gloria and Archie Hardcastle, *The Bookworm,* Ukiah, CA

"Jo-Ann only gets better. An outstanding story with lots of action and love."
—Linda Fitzgerald, *Waldenbooks,* Richmond, VA

"Jo-Ann Power is always a delight and gets better with each book."
—Shelly Ryan, *1,001 Paperbacks,* Louisville, KY

"TREASURES is a wonderful read. I loved everything about it, the characters, the prose, etc. . . . another keeper."
—Laurie Schwartz, *Bergen Paperback Exchange,* Bergenfield, NJ

"Jo-Ann Power's best book to date!"
—Yvonne Zalinski, *Paperback Outlet,* Warren, MI

"TREASURES was great. Loved it. Keep them coming. Thanks!"
—Evelyn Layton, *Maida's Book Store,* Tampa, FL

"Warm and wonderful, a 'treasure' of a story to be cherished. Ms. Power just keeps getting better."
—Sharon Kosick, *Annie's Bookstop,* Florissant, MO

Books by Jo-Ann Power

You and No Other
Angel of Midnight
Treasures
Gifts

Published by POCKET BOOKS

For orders other than by individual consumers, Pocket Books grants a discount on the purchase of **10 or more** copies of single titles for special markets or premium use. For further details, please write to the Vice-President of Special Markets, Pocket Books, 1633 Broadway, New York, NY 10019-6785, 8th Floor.

For information on how individual consumers can place orders, please write to Mail Order Department, Simon & Schuster Inc., 200 Old Tappan Road, Old Tappan, NJ 07675.

Jo-Ann Power

GIFTS

POCKET STAR BOOKS
New York London Toronto Sydney Tokyo Singapore

An *Original* Publication of POCKET BOOKS

A Pocket Star Book published by
POCKET BOOKS, a division of Simon & Schuster Inc.
1230 Avenue of the Americas, New York, NY 10020

ISBN: 0-671-52996-X

First Pocket Books printing October 1996

10 9 8 7 6 5 4 3 2 1

Cover art by Vittorio Dangelico

Printed in the U.S.A.

To Stephen,
who finds his courage daily

Life is so generous a giver but we, judging its gifts by their covering, cast them away as ugly or heavy or hard. Remove the covering and you will find beneath it a living splendor, woven of love, by wisdom, with power. Welcome it, grasp it, and you touch the angel's hand that brings it to you. Everything we call a trial or a sorrow or a duty, believe me that angel's hand is there, and the wonder of an overshadowing presence. Life is so full of meaning and purpose, so full of beauty beneath its covering, that you will find earth but cloaks your heaven.

Courage then to claim it, that is all.

—*Fra Giovanni*

Life is so generous a giver but we, judging its gifts by their covering, cast them away as ugly or heavy or hard. Remove the covering and you will find beneath it a living splendor, woven of love, by wisdom, with power. Welcome it, grasp it, and you touch the angel's hand that brings it to you. Everything we call a trial, a sorrow or a duty, believe me, that angel's hand is there, and the wonder of an overshadowing presence. Life is so full of meaning and purpose, so full of beauty beneath its covering, that you will find earth but cloaks your heaven.

Courage then to claim it, that is all.

— Fra Giovanni

GIFTS

Chapter One

Kent, England
April 1877

SHE WAS THE ONE PERSON HE DIDN'T WANT TO SEE.

Not now.

Never alone.

He stared down at her as she patted her old mare on the neck, handed the reins over to his butler, and picked up her riding skirt to climb the stone steps to the front door of his house. Her ancient black dog plodded along at her heels as the monkey whom she and her cousin Cat Lyonns called Darwin slid from the rump of the horse. The macaque, in short pants, scrambled to keep up with her, chatting to himself as usual. Probably reprimanding her for her characteristic speed. That monkey was a menace.

But not as much as Jessica Curtis is to you, old man.

Rand dropped the velvet drapes of his bedroom window into place, shut his eyes, and told himself that was not true.

Jessica Curtis posed no threat to him now. Hadn't ever, really. Of course, he hadn't been able to see that three years ago. That June morning in Saint Paul's when he'd stood beside his friend Spencer Lyonns for his wedding, gazed down the aisle, and found a ghost gliding toward him, Rand's grief over Susannah's death had been too fresh for him to recognize that Jess was no apparition.

But time had healed his sorrow. He had recovered from his loss of Susannah—and reconciled himself to the fact that his beautiful neighbor resembled the woman he had wanted to become his wife.

Resembled, not duplicated.

He recognized that now.

Yet that day the uncanny similarities had him staring at Jess throughout the wedding reception and, later, sent him to find solace in a bottle of Benedictine brandy. Three nights afterward, when liquor only heightened his craving to go feast on the sight of Jess, he had come to his senses enough to put himself on one of his India-bound cargo ships. Out to sea, in more ways than one, he had kept going, traveling to any port in the world where he might find new textile markets and production methods, old colleagues—and temporary diversions from heartache.

He discovered them all, to great benefit. The diversions took the form of voluptuous, dusky-skinned women who looked like no one he had ever loved. His old friends and cohorts in cities from Alexandria to Yokohama provided camaraderie. They had also aided him in expanding his shipping business and tripling the wealth in his bank vaults.

During those years he visited England intermittently for a week or two at most. But when he had come home this past February after six broiling months in Siam and Annam learning silk production, he surprisingly found England palatable, a savory for which he'd lost his taste that terrible day when he'd finally tracked Susannah down to a Whitechapel tenement. The day she'd died an agonizing death brought on by too little trust in his devotion to her and too much faith in herbal remedies for abortion. To test his recovery from his grief, he had decided to remain in England for as long as the euphoria lasted. But he'd be wise. Stay mostly in his London house or at the one in Manchester near his mills, coming here to his manor house in Kent only occasionally and usually for business reasons.

This trip was no different. He'd come south a week ago at the request of the local guildsmen to discuss a new railroad line that was to cut through the town of Ashford. He planned to attend their meetings, give what help or advice he could, and leave. Quickly.

Before he could go to church or into a shop—and run into Jessica Curtis.

He reached for his morning coat and pulled it on. As he took the stairs at a leisurely pace, he admitted to himself that he felt no trepidation.

Only curiosity.

And great surprise.

Ironic, isn't it, after I spent three years avoiding Jessie Curtis and all the painful memories she evoked, she should pick the time that I recover to come running to me?

She wanted so little from him.

A few hours of his time for a few days. For a child.

Rand Templeton would afford that, wouldn't he? After all, he spent thousands of pounds each year on his orphanages and lying-in hospitals. He could share his talent with a child who needed what only he might provide.

As justification for her request, she knew that sounded good.

If only her body heard that! Then her blood would flow naturally, she'd become serene—and her fingers would stop touching his treasures.

She snatched her hand away from the cool marble bust of some dead Roman general. She gave a short laugh at her nervous habit and resumed her pacing. Darwin did his best on his short spindly legs to imitate her walk, while the dog, Bones, collapsed on the floor, with only his eyes following her to and fro.

"Will you two please stop doing that!" she reprimanded the animals. But the dog yawned, and the monkey paused to reply in simian some phrase she surmised meant no.

She threw up her hands.

Where was Rand?

It was certainly taking him long enough to come down. It wasn't as if she'd landed on his doorstep to partake of his breakfast. She had waited for a decent hour.

She paused to admire a landscape painting. "Well, all right, Jessie. Perhaps eight o'clock might be termed a *tad* early."

Hah! More like aeons!

She considered a side table topped with a collection of palm-sized jade and ivory statues, strode over, and subtly arranged the grouping with more symmetry.

She was shocked at her boldness and readjusted them as they had been, all the while preaching to herself: "Actually, Jessie, before the designated calling hour of one or two, this time is rather obscene."

She whirled to find herself before a gold Tudor mirror, rolled her eyes around its floor-length size, and leaned forward, hands on her hips, to speak to her reflection. "Well, acceptable or not, I'm here and he did tell his butler he'd see me."

Talk to me. And for more than a few blithe sentences about the weather, the local crops, the building projects for our students at the Farrell School for Young Ladies.

She set her jaw, spun around, and forced herself to note the more colossal splendors of Randall Templeton's drawing room. She'd never been here before, but she had heard of its assets. Better now to train her mind on those. And what riches this room offered!

The oval buttercup moire walls gave a glow to the English Empire furniture. With the morning sun streaming through cream voile curtains, the brasses and bronzes of India and Siam sparkled, along with the crystals of Ireland and Paris. Even the portraits of the Templetons were gay renderings of happy people, each of whom smiled down at her.

Jess paused before the oil portrait of Felicia Templeton. A woman who had gained notoriety for writing under her own name, Felicia had shocked society with the power of her arguments to improve the lot of women and children in the mills and porcelain factories.

Her work was carried on from near or abroad by her only child, Rand, a businessman and confidant of

Queen Victoria. A man who supported legislation for higher wages plus a shorter workday and workweek for the laboring class. A man who resembled his mother physically in the classic simplicity of his cheeks, jaw, and glistening black hair. Randall Douglas Templeton was the fourteenth marquess of Ashford, the scion of an ancient family so entwined with the fortunes of their country that every element here—each painting, vase, and sculpture—spoke of his predecessors' wealth and power and friends.

But Jess cared for them not so much as for the other beauties in this room. Her eyes darted to a French pedal harp and a xylophone. Both stood uncovered as testament to their recent use in a house where the master was not often in residence. Yet what attracted her most was the piano—his rare French Érard grand piano, ebony and gilt rococo, its ivory keyboard glowing, summoning her.

Her hand reached out, touched the keys. A chord resounded softly around the walls, definitive, crisp. The room's acoustics lived up to their reputation. She bent and tried a few more chords, a few bars from an étude she was teaching herself so that she could persuade Amanda to play more than scales.

Drawn herself, Jess glanced toward the closed door. Rand might keep her waiting, and this—her eyes traveled to the keys, which were her irresistible temptation—beckoned. Tossing caution away, she seated herself and began to play.

The venerable piano had more resonance, more power, than she'd heard from any other instrument. Even though it was more than a century old, it was the first model the famous French piano makers had constructed and one of only two in England. This particular piano lived up to its reputation. It *was* grand. Majestic. Sweeping the room with the force of its clarity. Different from Farrell Hall's two pianos, which now seemed too mellow for her taste. Whereas this—she let herself move into the drama of a piece by Bach—yes, *this* instrument could call from one the delights of music—its ecstasies. Its sorrows. Its—

She felt him more than heard him.

Her back straightened. Her hands stopped.

She turned. Caught her breath.

She had prepared herself so well for her speech . . . but not for him. She never had. She knew once again she wasted her hope to have tried. Every time she had gazed at Randall Templeton, she had been immobilized.

By his size. Inches taller than her own five feet eight.

By his coloring. Blue-black hair with eyes to match.

By the way he looked at *her* . . . oh, now, that did make her shiver. He always gazed on her as if she were unreal.

And that chilled her hope that he might become more than polite to her. Forced her into a flurry of activity to cover her sorrow at his dislike of her.

But she couldn't look flustered today.

Wouldn't.

For Amanda's sake.

"Good morning, Jessica," he said with politeness as he stood in one of the few shadows of the brilliant room. She couldn't see his face, so she sought other clues to his disposition. Her eyes ran down his body. The dove gray of his morning attire gloved his massive shoulders and lean torso with perfection. He appeared relaxed.

She clasped her hands together and offered him the pose she called Prunes in Vinegar—mouth pursed, head back. Her attitude was meant to curdle milk, or a student's blood, at twenty feet. But for Rand, she diluted the mix with neighborliness in her voice. "Forgive me, Lord Templeton. I love to play and—"

He took a quick step forward into a sunbeam and said, "And I have kept you waiting an interminably long time."

Gilded, he rivaled her fondest memory of him—when he attended a dinner party that Cat and Spence had given at Farrell Hall last summer. That night he had worn formal black and stark white. Today his softer hues of gray wool with pearl linen stock performed a sweet counterpoint to his bronzed complexion, and the manly contrasts undid her.

"Don't stop," he told her, extending a finger toward the keyboard. "You're wonderful. I remember hearing you after one of Cat and Spence's parties last June." He smiled with a warmth he had bestowed on countless others, never her.

The unexpected heat baked her reason, and she blurted, "But you left in the middle. I thought you hated my rendition."

She thought she'd see tolerance, hear diplomatic words for an uninspiring performance. Instead, he moved even nearer, caught her eyes with his magnetic blue ones and declared, "I was rude. But I often wished I had stayed for more. I can only apologize now and assure you that my exit had nothing to do with your talent or the piece you chose. I wrestled with a private torment which never should have affected our relationship. Yet I see, regrettably, it has. Allow me to make amends. If it pleases you to play now, after I kept you waiting far too long, I will not be the one to take you from your joys. Won't you continue? Please?"

"No. Thank you."

"But you will be doing me an honor. Few are as expert as you, and the instrument is so rarely used that it falls out of tune without benefits from a master's touch."

His courteous behavior astounded her with its novelty and summoned more bluntness. "You are being gracious, which is all well and fitting, but I really didn't come here to play the piano, my lord. I came to talk."

"Very well." He advanced and she could detect remorse in his concern. His tone and proximity made her freeze. Too close to him, she always felt light-headed. It was his extreme self-assurance. Today the cause was his charm, which he lavished on her for the first time. She felt her mouth watering as he said, "We will talk. But after these three years we have known each other, Jess, I would hope you'd call me Rand."

Lest he come any closer, she managed a socially correct smile.

His gaze drifted up from her lips to her eyes. "Can I ring for coffee, perhaps?" When she did not answer, he asked, "Or do you prefer tea?"

She would make him ill at ease again if she didn't perk up and treat him normally. He had offered an explanation for his behavior. "Private torments" might mean much to him, but she must accept it for whatever it denoted and state her business. *Far from the Prune, you're acting naive and featherbrained—qualities you dislike . . . which destroy a woman.*

"I don't care for anything, thank you. I realize I am calling at a peculiar hour of the day."

He cocked a brow at her. Laughter stood in his eyes.

The novelty of it thrilled her. Shocked her. Sent her to the edge of propriety and the point of her visit. "I heard from my butler you had come home to Kent the other day. I had to snatch this opportunity to catch you now or lose you entirely. You never seem to stay here at the Temple for very long, and I know you might think this indelicate of me to come so early and without a chaperon. But, well, *heavens,* Rand, I'm too old and too busy for such fripperies as a guardian tagging along behind me. So I hoped I might prevail upon our status as neighbors and ask you to see me. And I came so early because I wanted to be sure to get you"—*before you could find a reason to avoid me, refuse me*—"before your butler could say you were not at home."

Rand looked as if she'd doused him with ice. "Jess, I would never turn you away, but then . . . I see from the way you look at me that you think I would."

She swallowed her chagrin at her indelicate phrasing. "Not at home" was a favored expression of butlers to turn out unwanted visitors. From the way Rand had always treated her, Jess assumed she'd never be welcomed into his presence. Used to being regarded as an oddity by anyone who had a whiff of her past, she often wondered if Rand had heard whispers of her background and those caused him to be cool. She couldn't believe that he could be so small as to do that, but she'd had no other explanation for his behavior toward her. Until today. When private torments didn't bother him as they once had. And she felt an enormous wall fall at her feet as he ridiculed himself.

"Good God, I have been awful toward you. I have much to make up for. I apologize again. Come sit down." He nodded toward a gold velvet chair.

She took the chair he indicated and was pleased when Darwin came to perch himself near her legs and offer her a congenial way into this conversation. The monkey stood, arms folded, like a little man in charge. His gleaming brown eyes blinked at her in confusion, then scanned to Rand, who took a wing chair opposite her.

"I hope you don't mind that I brought them," she explained with a glance at Bones, who came to drape himself over one of Rand's feet. "They enjoy our students, but they also like adult company."

"Really?" He glanced down at the dog, who'd closed his eyes with a sigh and a smack of his jaws. "To hear Spence talk, these two don't care for his company."

For the first time this morning, Jess grinned. "Spence has an unusual relationship with them. Darwin never seems to have anything nice to say to Spence, in monkey talk or otherwise. Darwin, we think, somehow understood Cat's sorrow when Spence didn't marry her the first time they were engaged and waits to see how Spence performs as a loving husband. As as for Bones . . . well, he cannot forget that the first time he saw Spence he thought Spence was going to hurt Cat."

"And ever after when they meet again, the dog takes a piece out of Spence's ankle."

The two of them chuckled, and Jess marveled at the naturalness of their repartee, wanting more and walking down this path of mutual spontaneity to get it. "Bones used to be the track dog for the Ashford village butcher, and like the rest of us, he is at heart just a creature of habit. Thank heavens, Spence recognizes it. I think he'd be disappointed if he did come home to Farrell Hall and Bones failed to greet him by taking a slice of skin."

Rand seemed totally at ease now, and she grew more so. Enough to let her wayward eyes note how he filled the chair admirably. His long legs in the soft gray trousers stretched before her, and she had to tear herself from inspecting every inch. "The animals of Farrell Hall are very important to all of us, but they also help the students immensely."

"Oh, what do they do?"

In response, Darwin preened, grinning at Rand with bright white teeth.

Jess patted the monkey on the shoulder. "This small fellow always likes it when people talk about him. What do you offer to our girls, young man, hmmm?" The fellow chittered his explanation, and she and Rand both laughed. "They add gaiety. But more than that, they give companionship. A quiet acceptance that's very important to any child but particularly to those who feel different and therefore separate from others."

"Unconditional love is important to everyone. Even adults. But so few find it anywhere. If you can give it to children, I think their chances for a happier life are greater."

"That's what Cat and I thought when we opened the school three years ago. Very few institutions in England educate girls. None existed for those who were overly active and talented in special ways."

"You and Cat have made a success of the venture, too."

"Very much so! I never dreamed it could be this wonderful. We've got numerous investors and teachers from here and abroad clamoring to join the faculty. We have twenty-seven girls enrolled this year. Next term, the newest hall should be finished and we'll be able to add another ten students."

"Ten? From what Cat told me when last I saw her and Spence in Richmond, that new hall should house twenty-five more girls."

"Yes, eventually it will. But I cannot expand too rapidly. I must take on more staff, buy more classroom equipment. And to be financially responsible, I cannot do that all at once."

"Certainly. I understand." His dark blue eyes, usually so blank when they looked at her, twinkled in admiration. "The growth of a business must be managed as skillfully as its birth. And since Cat is now expecting twins and retired to Richmond, you are alone with the administration. But you appear to weather that well, too."

"Thank you. Running the school alone these last few months has been a challenge. I welcome the responsibilities. I'm no stranger to that, but . . . but I do miss talking things over with Cat. I won't bother

her with details. Not now. Twins are so rare, and I know Spence is very concerned."

Cat Lyonns had been delivered of a healthy little boy almost two years ago. Victor Lyonns was then and remained now a hardy roly-poly child. So months ago, when Cat's doctor proclaimed that her second pregnancy would bring twins, the man had declared that she needed to be more careful and take longer bed rest each day. Spence had immediately retired Cat and his son to the Red House in Richmond for the duration of her term. Jess had assumed the role of headmistress, and she was certain that after the birth of these two new babies she would remain solely in charge for quite some time to come.

"Cat is very healthy," Rand stated.

"I don't think anyone need be concerned," she continued his logic, but knew she consoled herself. "Vic came into the world without any problems."

"Cat recovered quickly, though Vic was extremely large."

"Yes, but the doctors remember how big Vic was at birth and wonder if Cat will deliver two babies of similar size. They want her to be careful, eat well but not too much, and"—she nibbled her lower lip—"I worry about her."

"But she is following doctors' orders, Jess, and the twins will come into the world safely and soon drive us all as mad as Vic does, with their curiosity and their antics. Meanwhile, you have been working yourself very hard. You do look tired."

That he would notice such a thing about her warmed her more, and to her surprise, she shared more of her personal thoughts with him. "I want Cat to feel comforted when she returns that I left no stone unturned to run the school well." She gave a rueful laugh. "I won't say it's been easy. I have never worked so hard in my life. But I love every minute. I would toil night and day, go anywhere, do anything to help any student." She had reached a point where she might explain her purpose here this morning, and she poised, ready to launch.

But with his eyes flowing from her hair to her mouth, he declared, "It shows," and robbed her of reason. "Despite the need for a bit more sleep—or is it more fun?—you look so much more fulfilled than when I saw you at Cat and Spence's wedding."

That made her stare at him, astonished at the perceptiveness with which he had observed her, thought about her. "It's true," she admitted. "Over these three years I have become more confident, decisive."

"Each time I have seen you—at Vic's christening and at that dinner party last June, you have been more sociable. More . . . content," he confirmed with a truth that had her tilt her head at him. "You love what you do, a sure key to happiness. And the success has been transferred to the school. It's a legend in London. Elsewhere, too." He beamed. "Why, last month, when I was in Vienna, I went to a supper where the topic of dealing with overly active children included a discussion of the Farrell School for Young Ladies."

"Is that right?" Jess asked, still shaken from the knowledge that he had assessed her growth over years when she was certain he had only found reasons to dismiss her.

"They wished to know more, and I found myself telling them what I knew. Unfortunately, that isn't more than a few minutes' worth, and I'm afraid I did not do you proud."

"You spread our reputation and that's more than we could want from you or even ask." Yet she was here to request help for a student.

"You're very polite, Jess. But honestly, I think you'd do yourself and the school some good if you thought about spreading its reputation yourself. Perhaps a lecture or two in London to educators and certainly to physicians who treat those similar to your students."

His businesslike approach intrigued but appalled her. "No." She could never speak in public. "I have too much work here in Kent."

"But it's often done, especially by experts like you and Cat. Such exposure could do wonders to establish the school as the credible institution it is."

No one who took the time to discover her background, her family history, would value her words. Society did not smile on children of scandalous parents. She knew that firsthand. No one, no matter her topic or her success in educating students with behavioral and learning difficulties, would come to hear her. Jessica Leighton-Curtis giving a lecture? She'd be laughed off the dais. "I couldn't."

"Why not?"

"I'm terrible in public."

"No, you're not," he shot back sweetly. "You have now become as gracious and delightful in public with strangers as with your students. As accomplished in a garden as at a piano."

"You have seen me with those whom I know well. But with others . . ."

His gaze fell to her clenched hands. "You are at ease in your skin with all but me."

"But you always treated me as if I had the plague!"

He gave a shocked laugh, which quickly died to sorrow. "Oh, Jess, what I've done! I'll tell you now what I couldn't say to anyone then, not even to myself. You resembled a woman I wished to forget."

She stared at him, jealous. Furious at herself for such madness, she felt more ire that some woman could be so important to him that she would obliterate any other from his sight. "I see. Have you forgotten her now?"

"No."

Her hope died. "That doesn't bode well for this discussion, does it?" Her fingers plucked at the fabric of her riding skirt and, appalled that he should see her undone, she began to rise.

He shot forward, like night enfolding day, and blanketed her hands with his. The shock jolted her. The iron strength soothed her. Stunned, she looked down at their flesh. The heat . . . the friendliness of it was so astonishing she had trouble focusing on what he was saying.

"Jess." Rand said her name in a deep appeal. "Jess." He lifted her face with fingers beneath her chin. This close, she couldn't avoid his eyes . . . and didn't want to. They were larger, blacker than she'd thought, more lushly lashed, kinder . . . and sultry. *Jess,* he made no sound with his lips but she loved the way they shaped her name. His thumb came up to trace her lower lip. His eyes watched what he was doing to her, and his face took on a look she would have termed yearning.

She turned away.

"Please don't go. Listen to me, Jess. I have done you and me, I think, a great disservice. I want to change that. Let me. Let me nurture our relationship with an objectivity I did not possess until recently. Three years ago, bare months before I met you at Cat and Spence's wedding, I lost a woman I cared for dearly. She died in horrible circumstances, and I found her too late to save her. Afterward I couldn't part with her memory, because I thought I might have prevented her death if I had been more dedicated to her. Then when I saw you in Saint Paul's, I could not bring myself to terms with how you looked so much like her. I have spent years mourning her, and now I find to my surprise that I am done. Let me assure you now, she was very different from you, except that a few of your features are the same."

His gaze traveled to her hair. "She had these extraordinary strawberry-blond curls, like you. And eyes of aqua. Her complexion was as fair but not as perfect as yours. She had freckles and a funny upturned nose. Not your classic profile, Jess. Not your delicate porcelain appeal. Won't you accept my faults as human ones and allow us to start anew?"

Suddenly it seemed so simple. So normal. He had never thought her odd, but similar to someone he had loved. The idea provided comfort, which she'd always craved with him. "I would welcome that, Rand."

This time, when he smiled, no shadows lurked in his marvelous midnight-blue eyes. He took his hands away, and sat back in his chair, leaving her with more than solace—a new excitement.

"Rand, I came to ask for your help."

"You have it."

She blinked. "As quickly as that?"

"Unnamed, it's yours. I have hurt you, and I want to make it up to you."

"It's not a small favor."

His mouth lifted in a comforting way. "If it were, your hands might not be so cold—and my wish to make them warmer might not be so hot. Tell me what you want, Jess."

"You." He grinned while she wondered where her mind had fled that she should be so curt. So suggestive. "I need you for an hour or two. For"—she waved a hand, licked her lips—"a few days, which I hope will do the trick. Whatever time you can spare for a child. A student. A twelve-year-old who was remarkably talented at the piano until she was thrown from her horse in a riding accident. When she fell, she landed on her head, and her ability to play the piano, among other skills, was affected. She was a wonderful musician. I heard her play once, when her parents first applied to enroll her, months before she suffered the blow. Now that she is with us, I have tried to get her to play again, but I do not have the expertise to lure her to try more than scales. I have heard you play, Rand, after supper parties and Vic's christening. You have the ability to evoke sentiments from a piano that I never will."

He shook his head, rueful. "I am amazed you believe I have something to give this child. Every time

I have played in these past three years, I have done it to pour out my bitterness. At Vic's christening, I was in a black mood. I tried to emerge, but think I must have played a dirge."

Her heart ached for him. She too knew how to take her emotions to a keyboard to play out her agony and joy. "You performed a waltz by Liszt that brought tears to my eyes."

"You are kind."

"And you are talented. That's why I need you. Amanda requires someone who can inspire her to play. Someone who feels the music—sees the variations possible, as she used to. With heart, not just mind."

"You do."

"Oh, no." She smiled sadly. "I try. But I am too much heart at the keyboard. I cannot find the discipline necessary to bring order to my chaos."

"Perhaps I should use my so-called skills to inspire you as well. Help you realize that you have the ability to master anything you set your mind to."

"Thank you, but no. I have learned that lesson sufficiently by mastering my own challenges."

He quirked a brow, his polite query about her past one for which he would not get an answer from her.

"Rand, you cannot help me. I know my limitations. I live with them. Please understand that I want you only for my student. If you'll come, I will be most grateful that you could help her. I am an entirely different story."

"So I see. Well, then, we will have to try to discover new avenues to progress, won't we?"

Chapter Two

RAND TURNED HIS BLACK STALLION DOWN THE LANE TO Farrell Hall from the main road and felt so right about what he had agreed to do.

After all, what was it? Just a few hours of his time.

Bah, his conscience warned him now as it had two days ago when she'd sat so near him in his drawing room and he had traced her lower lip. *You know what it really means.*

Yes, he did. He'd be spending a few hours with a student of Jessica's.

And if you're very fortunate, with her.

And with her.

The very thing you told yourself you would not do. Ever.

The very thing he found he could do. Because, after his avoidance of her for her looks, he had discovered in that intense half hour with her that Jessica Curtis was distinctly her own person.

So near to her, as he had never allowed himself

before, he had felt such a revelation. She was more than a bundle of energy. She was strong. With a resilience that put him in mind of the purest china. Opal skin. Swirls of red-blond curls he longed to set free from their pins and drape over her shoulders. But the most appealing of all her assets was her full pink mouth.

He shifted in his saddle at the luscious memory.

He had told himself after she returned home that he had noted all those attributes of hers before. Not that first day in Saint Paul's, of course. But the next time he saw her. The afternoon two years ago during the Lyonnses' christening party. By then he had gained some circumspection. Enough to become intrigued by her physical differences from Susannah. He had abruptly left, set off for home, and gone to his study. He took up pen and ink and sketched her face and form, looking at the proof that Jessica Leighton-Curtis was no Susannah Gage. Never had been.

But it had taken him yet more time to come to terms with the knowledge that Susannah was gone from him permanently. So much so that in all of his subsequent encounters with Jess, including the one last June when he'd fled Farrell Hall as she played the piano, he had indulged himself in the habit of leaving whenever he found he could not bear to be near her.

Today, though, he could see Jess for who she was.

Jess was tall and sleek, stunning, arresting eye and breath. Susannah had been shorter, as slim, but pretty.

Jess was English. Titled but not wealthy, and so she was a woman who worked. Who was ambitious.

Accomplished as a pianist. Modest. One who would not go in public even to promote her own school. That made him shake his head, and he wondered why an intelligent woman with so many admirable attributes could immerse herself in her work and never come up for air. Never leave the country.

Yes. Jess was definitely different from the gregarious Susannah Gage.

Jessica Curtis fascinated him. For her dedication, her love of children and animals. Her speed. Her urge to move, act, touch things.

So when she asked him this small favor, how could he not give her what she wanted? The beguiling answer came as another question: How could he stay away now that he understood in every corner of his being that Jess was a delicate woman with sensitivities attuned to him?

He had felt it.

In the moments when he had taken her hand, raised her chin, outlined her lovely lower lip, he had discovered it. And it was as if his entire past had died. Ashes gone in the wind. Leaving him to admire the living beauty of Jessica Curtis.

Demanding he control this mad desire to touch her mouth again.

With his.

Compelled by astonishment—and enjoyment—at this rampaging need, he had agreed to come here and help Jess with a student.

He stared up at Farrell Hall. His reverie had brought him to the steps of the stately Restoration relic, which always made him feel nurtured. That feeling must have come from all the ivy and wild white roses climbing up the bricks to the balcony. Such a cozy difference from the Temple, his grandfather's Palladian manor home created eighty years ago when the man was far from young but still in love with life, mad about architecture and a woman he had waited decades to marry. Grandfather was so unlike the rest of the Templetons who, family tradition said, fell in love so instantly that they married in haste, regardless of subsequent rumor. Rand chuckled to himself. *We Templetons want our pleasures immediately, especially the women we adore.*

He dismounted, looped the reins around the post, and took the steps. He lifted the knocker, and soon the front door opened to him.

"Good morning, my lord." Pool nodded his glossy bald head and boomed at him in his stentorian voice. "Marvelous to see you, my lord! You look well. May I take your hat and gloves? Lady Curtis has told me to see you to the music room. She is detained by unexpected circumstances. But she wanted me to assure you she will be with you as soon as possible and wants you to make yourself comfortable."

"Thank you, Pool." He handed over his accoutrements. Despite the coolness of the April day, his ride in the sun had warmed him. But not as much as two days of anticipation at seeing Jess again.

"This way, sir." Pool led Rand down the hall, past paintings and the gun cabinet sporting the famous Beretta flintlocks and Spanish pistols of one of Cat's ancestors.

Pool opened the door to the music room. The sienna of the ancient oak walls bathed the room in a honeyed gleam. Rand had had the good fortune to be in this room often and loved its very air. Now he would be spending a lot of time here. Days. Or weeks. As long as necessary to help a child . . . or as long as he could use the excuse to find and enjoy the uniqueness of Jessica Curtis.

His eyes trailed from the mélange of kettledrums and harp, violas and lutes, to the cello and, at last, the grand piano.

"Do play, sir." Pool had read his mind. "It is a wonderful instrument. An original Pleyel. Brought from Paris by Lady Lyonns's maternal grandfather. He was a friend of Frederic Chopin, who is said to have debuted many of his creations only on a Pleyel." Pool offered a smug smile. "We're very proud of it. One of our treasures."

"Yes, Pool, I love its sound. I'm grateful for your offer, but I'm not really in the mood to play just now."

"Ahh, well, then, my lord, may I get you anything while you wait? Tea, perhaps?"

"Thank you, I am content for only a little while, Pool." *But please bring me Jessica Curtis. Quickly.*

Jess had been dreading or cherishing this moment for two days. Now he was here, beyond that door. She could hear him. More, she remembered his touch. Exciting. Nerve-racking. She crossed her arms, closed her eyes, and let his music caress her instead.

Her fear dwindled as it had the other day. Rand had agreed so readily and without question to her request to help Amanda that Jess had found herself discarding her prepared arguments for the more interesting and surprising discussion of the local May Fair and the lecture series at the village guildhall.

Throughout their banter, she and Rand had conversed with a growing familiarity that beguiled her while it tempered her fear of him. Rand Templeton. The only gentleman she'd glimpsed in her twenty-four years, aside from Spencer Lyonns, whose attitude toward women spoke of his respect for them as equals. Though Rand's grief had barred him from showing that quality to her directly, Jess had seen him display it to others and wished it for herself. Now that she had it, she reveled in it.

And she wanted to enjoy it—and him—now.

She thrust open the doors and stood rooted to the floor when he instantly met her gaze but continued his rendition of a Liszt étude. Awash in sound, she experienced the same euphoria she felt whenever she heard his marvelously elegant hands extract emotions from a piano.

She examined him in the light of their growing friendship. Patrician in line, he possessed stark brows and cheeks and a rugged jaw, but with a generous mouth that now smiled at her. Large and long of limb, Rand Templeton could rob a woman's reason just as his music did.

Enchanted, she surrendered to the aura he created. He could not know how she admired him . . . no, she corrected herself . . . how she found him quite simply devastating. Too handsome. Too urbane. Too successful. Wildly rich. Often acclaimed by villagers and local gentry for his concern and aid with local issues. Praised by Spence for his unfailing friendship in troubled periods of Spence's life.

She went to him.

He never stopped but consumed the sight of her, from the hem of her gown to her upswept hair.

Her heart crashed to a halt at his thoroughness. And his hot appreciation.

Branded by it, she recognized that this was what she had wanted from him for years, what she had craved again for days. But to have it put so sweetly before her meant she had to respond with more than this panic, and she simply did not know how. She had never cared for any man. Never desired any attention or welcomed it. Until she met this man—and did not get it.

She had it now. Rand's eyes delved into hers, and his mouth softened while his hands continued.

The music he made drowned in the chanting of her brain. *Don't be a fool. He's here to help you, not entice you, or enthrall you.*

As if he heard her, his brows rose infinitesimally. A question sculpted his features.

She discarded her reticence and welcomed him with a smile. A polite but friendly smile.

One of his black brows wrinkled.

She despaired that he could so easily penetrate her facade. She swallowed painfully.

He watched her throat, and when his eyes returned to hers, they bore more than the heat that undid her. They held an empathy for her discomfort.

She froze. He had burned away her pretense. The very veneer of nonchalance she dreaded he would detect.

She was thankful when he turned to focus on finishing the piece. She forced herself to appreciate his artistry, the way his fingertips summoned such beauty from the instrument until he struck the last chords and echoes resounded through her chaos.

Suddenly, silence filled the space between them.

His hands went to his thighs. He faced her, and his knowing gaze met hers. "You liked that." He had only to murmur in the solemnity of the spring morning. "Shall I play it again?"

She shook her head. "No, thank you, it was wonderful, though. Your skill leaves me . . . breathless. Always."

Those expressive brows widened. "Another, then?"

"I wish it were possible. But you have so little time and"—she offered an apologetic look—"this morning it is I who have kept you waiting far too long."

Compassion—that emotion she now concluded he possessed in terrifying abundance—colored his expression in sweetness. "I have the morning to give to you and your student. Jess"—he noted how her hands had clenched—"what bothers you?"

As if he had cloaked her naked emotions in a mantle of propriety, she sailed toward him. Her fingertips going to the cool piano, she looked at him with the familiarity three years of genteel acquaintance allowed. "I cannot persuade Amanda to come down."

Humor lit his features. "Good God, Jess, what did you tell her about me?"

"The truth."

"Well, *that* obviously convinced her," he scoffed good-naturedly. "What did you say?"

His congeniality was contagious—and so startling that she grinned. "If I tell you, you'll be too flattered."

He went quite still. "For a woman who I thought eschewed coyness, you appear to be flirting with me."

No other words could have turned her to stone. "I never flirt."

"I know."

He'd watched her that closely?

Flattered, she battled delight and wished she could run from him. But if she did, she would never live it down. Never be able to look him in the eye. *Never* help Amanda.

She lifted her chin higher and avoided his issue for hers. "I told Amanda that you liked children. That you had fought for the right of girls as well as boys to be educated. That you help raise funds for new hospitals where mothers might birth their children in clean conditions."

"Why is that important to a young girl?"

"She likes babies. Her mother lost a young child two years ago. Last week when one of the Ashford village mothers had a daughter down with the whooping cough, Amanda offered to sit with the toddler and give her her medicine while the parents worked the fields. I permitted her to do it, recovering though she is herself from an accident, because I thought it beneficial for her to help others. It was the first occasion when we saw Amanda express an interest in someone or something. So you see, you and Amanda have much in common."

"You know a lot about me."

"You are modest but famous for your interests, Rand. I told Amanda what everyone else knows, as well as what few don't—that you are the finest pianist

I have ever had the honor to hear, that you are renowned for your abilities, even if you call yourself an amateur."

"That is complimentary, and I thank you, Jess." He rose. A titan, he stepped toward her. The breadth of his shoulders in the superfine fawn wool cut off the sight of anything else, and the height of him forced her head back as he came so close she could feel his body heat sizzling her nerves. He pinned her to the spot with the power of his blue eyes—and the magic nearness of his mouth. "Was there more you told her?"

Finesse fled. "That Spence said you would readily agree to play for Amanda, because you adore children and they adore you. Cat convinced me that, no matter your schedule, you would carve out the time to help me—*Amanda,"* she corrected quickly.

"I *am* gratified," he declared while his gaze fell to her lips. "My friends speak well of me. And with more facts than bravado." With the slightest brace of his palms to her elbows, he steadied her on her feet—and then he was gone from her. Across the room. Gazing at her harp. Plucking a string. Sending a note into the thick air. "So then, assurance that I like children hasn't done the trick, odd as that seems. How then shall we proceed to convince Amanda I am no ogre?"

That would never be difficult. "I wondered if you might stay for her group music class. I'm the instructor, and it starts at ten o'clock. That's another hour for you to spend here, but I don't know what else to do. Amanda has always attended, and if you played, if you'd consider it—"

Rand spun slowly to face her, concern in every line

of his magnificent body. "I am here, Jess, for as long as you want me. As often as I can help."

She clasped her hands together. "Oh, thank you! I hoped you'd say that!"

He took in her joy, his lips spreading in pleasure. She suddenly wondered how they felt. Firm? Tender? Beneath her fingers, would they part? Against her mouth, would they respond? Want?

Struck by the illogic of her mind, she forced herself to speak. Of anything. What? He came close again, confusing her more. Her old head injury disabled her from changing subjects easily when a straight line of thinking was what she dearly wanted. *Amanda,* whispered a portion of her brain bent on reason. "I should tell you more about her."

"I would welcome any information that might help me forge a relationship with her."

"You would do that, wouldn't you?" Her whisper was no question.

His answer was in his hands. As they enfolded hers and gave her a warm squeeze that sealed their alliance in a tactile way words had not yet embraced, she drifted backward to place objectivity between them. "Let's see. I did tell you she's twelve. Before her accident, she was a lively minx who would have come here to school because she was overly active, like the other students. Like Cat—"

"And you."

He didn't seem put off by that. In fact, he smiled more broadly and said, "Tell me more, Jess."

She licked her lips, tasting hunger for more of his sweet regard. "Amanda used to write poetry. Flowing verse that stirred the senses. She loved to perform at the piano, especially Mozart and Chopin. She liked to act, and her renditions of Desdemona and Juliet, her father says, thrilled her household. She is quite a beauty. With a great wealth of hair the color of rosewood and eyes as blue as a summer sky. Fragile but, underneath, quite tough."

He nodded. "I have seen such women before."

Why did she sense he meant *her?* No, no. She had to ignore that compliment for this . . . this offering of his time. She had to show him she valued his help. She had to inform him, interest him, keep him. . . .

For Amanda.

And for herself?

She walked around the room, touching the instruments, telling herself to let her mind fill with Amanda and *her* needs. Her hopes. Her terrors.

"Amanda is a broken child," she told him simply as she felt nothing but her anguish over this girl she had to save. "She came here in January. Her father enrolled her now because she seemed ready to go out in the world again. She walks, talks, and shows an interest in a few of her old pastimes. But her father also brought her to us because he is at his wit's end with her. That's not unusual for loved ones of those who have incurred such injuries."

Rand scowled. "Patience is not a virtue he could cultivate for his own daughter?"

"I think, from what he told me about their relationship, he cares for her and has tried to help her. But he, like the rest of us, knows little about what damage may have occurred in Amanda's fall from her horse. Someday we might have a way to see into victims' brains, but for now we can only deal with each injured person as if she had a condition we've not yet defined. Life with such persons can be volatile because their behavior can be very unpredictable. Amanda has outbursts of anger. She cannot concentrate on any task for long periods of time, cannot do two things at once, and as a result, she often becomes so frustrated at her inabilities that she does nothing. Worse, she cannot express emotion. She does not cry or laugh. She does not grieve, either, and that must become part of her recovery because, you see, Rand, in the same accident, her mother died."

"My God. That's hideous."

Jess nodded. This was difficult for her to discuss. The similarities to her own accident were so numerous. "Amanda and her mother rode out one day last June. Oddly, they decided to race in a rainstorm. God knows why. Her mother's horse failed to fully clear a jump, and Amanda galloped too close behind. The two animals tangled and threw both riders. Amanda's mother died immediately. But Amanda . . ." Jess recalled her own agonies after her mother's death from a fall off a horse. "Amanda was in a coma for hours, and when she emerged, she could not speak or move. Nor did she remember what happened. That's normal, of course, with an injury to the head."

Jess watched Rand carefully and noted that he believed her. "Amanda has recovered her motor abilities. She walks now with some grace. She can bathe and dress herself, though she has trouble with buttons and laces. But her clumsiness makes the sounds she produces on the piano less than fluid."

"So she needs help refining her use of her hands," he concluded.

"Yes. The small muscles and bones so vital to playing the keyboard need to be retrained."

"And you think she is physically capable of that?"

"Definitely. She has no injuries to her fingers or hands or arms. I have taught her finger exercises and encouraged her to practice her scales and tried to get her to play her favorite pieces. She moves easily, but she stops because she recognizes that her renderings are less than perfect. So it is here"—Jess pointed to her temple—"where Amanda has the injury, and here"—she pointed to her heart—"where she must want to play again."

"Has she told you this?"

"No." Jess noted his confusion and told herself she had to reveal her own past for him to fully understand her knowledge of Amanda and the child's condition. She hated to impart the tale that might make her appear different to him.

"Yet you know a lot about this condition. Why is that?"

It was all she could manage to face him, but she had to go sit at the piano to do it. Without thinking, she began to play her mother's favorite song. "Für Elise." Above the melody, Jess told him what he came nearer to learn. "I suffered a blow to the head when I was thirteen."

"I see," he said as if she'd told him any fact, as if she were whole, hearty, unaffected by any disaster. "Did you have the same reactions Amanda does?"

"All of them," she knew she said too quickly.

He did not move. "Forgive me. I never knew."

"Cat does me the honor not to speak of it."

"And you don't like to."

"Never." She kept playing.

"I don't doubt," he replied with another apology in the timbre of his voice. "But you will do it to save a child."

"The effects of my injury are still with me, though I have recovered much more than anyone ever predicted. I want the fullest recuperation for Amanda. The richest life."

"I'd say, then, that you are the expert here. What is the best way to win her over?"

That made her stop. In his eyes she saw respect.

"Play for her. For the other girls. Inspire them."

Jess heard the sound of laughter floating down the hall toward them. "Here they come. We'll observe the normal class routine. Structure is very important to those with brain injuries as well as to overly active children."

"Any child, I think."

"Yes, but our girls, with their bubbling nature, cannot sit still—quite literally—for a lot of idle gab."

He burst out laughing.

"It's true!" she told him, breaking into a broader grin. "As a teacher, I am precise, exacting, and yet I try to nurture the artistic temperament. I may look like a starched shirt, but I do like children."

"I knew that two years ago when I saw you holding Vic and cooing to him at his christening," Rand told her with sad eyes. "It blinded me how much you loved him, and I could not bear to watch."

His revelation of such an intimate secret caused her to gape at him.

"That you could love him so much and yet you were not his mother was simply devastating to me. I tried to regain my composure, but couldn't. That vision of you was another reason I left when I did, Jess."

Sorrowing for him, she waited as he struggled with the rest of his explanation. "The woman whom I said you resembled . . . lost our baby before it was born. I wanted that child. Wanted them both." Rand threw back his head and blinked hard. "That day I wished you were Susannah and Vic was a baby I never got to name. I think all children need a chance to live—and do it with good health and a decent education."

She stood and covered his hand with hers. "It shows in everything you do, Rand."

The students gathered, giggling and talking at the door.

Jess tore her gaze from the wonderful sight of Rand Templeton grateful to her. "We'll begin now," she said and turned to let her class in.

"Come in, girls. Come in. We have a surprise for you this morning. Hello, Louise, Dora. Good morning. Yes, take your seats around the piano. Well, Rose, it is so nice to see you up and about again. Sniffles all gone? Yes? . . . I'm glad. Cook's strong tea and currant scones help, don't they? Good morning, Ann, Belle, Corinne . . . Amanda."

Jess sank back against the door. Her eyes fled to Rand. Across the expanse, now filled with the excitement of youth, Jess saw in his expression a reverence that thrilled her. She bristled with the certain knowledge that he had watched her, heard her with her students. He recognized she was not merely his neighbor. Or his best friend's cousin by marriage. Or a spinster. She smiled at him in gratitude for his appraisal, his patience, and his merciful nature to offer her his time and talent for a child who meant so much to her. A child whose welfare meant as much to him, because he understood how deeply it cut to have lost one.

The girls took their seats, the older ones with eyes only for the tall, dark stranger standing within the bow of the grand piano.

Jess knew how they felt. She wanted them to enjoy his talent. His verve. She glanced at Amanda, so demur but striking in her terra-cotta dimity with polka-dot pinafore. Beside Corinne Marlow, who had become her closest friend, Amanda took a chair in the second row nearest the hall door. It was her usual seat. The one Amanda and Jess had agreed she should take, lest Amanda feel the need to leave. To walk or to plant seedlings in the vegetable garden, the only activity that kept her rapt for more than ten minutes at a stretch.

Jess walked to stand near Rand in the curve of the piano. "I am pleased this morning to present to you a friend. This is the marquess of Ashford, Randall Templeton, our neighbor whose house you've admired and whose—"

"Horse," came one girl's undertone, "Tara admired too much last month."

Rand shot an amused expression at Jess.

She stared at him, surprise foiled by embarrassment.

"What's this, Lady Curtis?" he asked, one brow arching and his mouth forming a grin.

A girl's voice explained. "Tara Doherty, one of the upper form students, was truant one day last month."

A few giggles ringed the room. "She snuck off to your stables and absconded with your black, sir. To the village. Bareback."

By now Rand was silently chuckling and looking at the young woman who dared to be so bold as to reveal this novel intelligence. "I thank you for the information, Miss . . . ?"

"Marlow, my lord. Corinne Marlow."

"Corinne, it is wonderful to meet you face to face at last. I know your parents very well."

"Yes, sir. They have told me much about you."

"Well, then, do tell me, Corinne, did Tara enjoy her outing on my horse?"

The thirteen-year-old's cinnamon curls bounced with her gleeful nod. "Definitely, sir. She says your stallion is faster than her father's prize stud. Tara claims her escapade was worth every minute, until Lady Curtis called her on the carpet for it."

Rand swung around to face Jess. His blue eyes danced. "Do tell me what was the outcome of this, Lady Curtis?"

That he was so accepting about it made her find humor in it, too. "I instructed Tara in the finer points of ownership and confined her to her dormitory for the next weekend."

"I see. Do you think she'll perform such feats again?"

"Lord, I hope not, Rand," she said with such earnestness that the use of his given name slipped by her.

A few of her students coughed.

The room filled with silence.

Someone cleared her throat.

Rand purposely blinked.

"Ah, yes." Jess felt an embarrassed flush creep up her face and turned to the audience. "So!" She clasped her hands in a good Prunes in Vinegar pose. "The marquess is a pianist—"

"Amateur pianist," he corrected as he smiled out upon the gathering.

"Amateur pianist, who has agreed to honor us with his presence this morning, and if we are kind, perhaps he'll come for a few more mornings." Jess saw Corinne Marlow lean over to whisper to Amanda and hoped it was encouragement to stay. "Please welcome him."

Jess clapped with her girls and took up a post along the wall. From her vantage point, she could not only view the expertise of Rand but also see Amanda. The child sat sweetly shy, polite. Stoic. But she was beginning to fidget.

Jess focused on Rand and prayed for speed as he moved the piano bench away from the instrument to accommodate his long legs. He sat while he contemplated what to play. She assumed he'd pick a piece by Mozart or Chopin for Amanda.

Rand placed his hands upon the keys, but as he began Jess heard no Mozart or Chopin . . . only Beethoven.

She frowned.

Why that composer? Why this selection?

Jess stared at Rand as he entered the piece she herself had once adored and now abhorred. . . .

The room grew stifling, an inferno of bad memories.

She hated this sonata. This ceaseless torment.

That's what it was. Agony put to music.

Precisely how her mother had played it.

Always. Night and day. Before she died, her mother had played the damn thing until Jess thought she'd scream from the repetition.

She shrank against the wall and somehow survived the melody. Thanked her stars she was not in the line of view of any of them.

Except Rand. Rand, who played but stared straight at her. Rand, who flowed with the sorrow of the music. Rand, who had a terrifying question forming in his eyes . . .

Until he began another piece. Some music safer for her sanity. Chopin.

Then a moan made them all spin around and gape as Amanda rose to her feet, tears streaming down her cheeks. With a crash of her chair and a bang of the door, she ran from the room.

Chapter Three

DROPS OF RAIN HIT HER NOSE AND EYELASHES. JESS paused as she and a few of her teachers emerged from the forest trail near the stream. Bones loped along behind her. She raised her face to the whirling clouds of a midnight storm, fearing this would bring the end of their search for Amanda. At the sound of footsteps, she despaired when Rand appeared once more with a dejected expression. Behind him came members of his staff and hers with a few of the villagers.

Rand walked toward her, his lantern aloft and sputtering in the wind. His eyes just as bleak as her old Labrador's. She hadn't seen Rand in hours. She wished she didn't now.

"Nothing," Rand murmured to her. "And you found no clues either, did you?"

She shut her eyes to the weariness—and the futility.

"Don't," Rand whispered as he drew near with his warmth. "Bones, if no one else, would have found her if something awful had happened."

She clamped a hand over her mouth to stop the terror from escaping her. If she let it out, the hideous possibilities she'd kept at bay could come true. Amanda might be hurt, sick, cold—

She sneezed a few times and dug a handkerchief from her cape pocket.

"Jess, come back to the hall." Rand stepped close while the search party gathered around them. "You're only going to get wet and catch pneumonia."

"I can't leave, Rand." Tears blinded her.

"You won't gain a thing by staying out here." He circled his arm about her waist. Disregarding what others might think, he pulled her securely to him. His body became a tower of comfort. His mouth buried in her hair was sweet balm, the only affection she could accept while she endured this hell of not knowing where Amanda was.

"If I give up, I'll never forgive myself."

He raised a hand to comb her hair from her cheek. She saw nothing but his compassionate eyes. "Amanda has not gone into the woods or the village. She has not crossed the stream or fallen into it. We have covered that area at least three or four times since this morning. Jess," he pleaded, "no child her age on foot can escape a herd of her friends, twelve teachers, Bones, *and* the village watch. She must have gone someplace she knows is secluded." He lifted his head, listening to the subdued voices of more tired men coming toward them from the forest.

"Lady Curtis." The Ashford village constable Jack Higgins approached her, leading his friends who'd rushed to Farrell Hall at Rand's summons this morning. "We're not doin' a bit of good and won't, now that a storm is stirrin'. We'll start again at dawn."

Jess wanted to scream at him to stay and endure whatever hardship to find this child. "But, Mr. Higgins, the rain will obliterate any tracks."

"We never found any to begin with, milady. Wherever she's gone, she's tight into it, I'd wager. An' with this rain, she'll be tuckin' in for the night." He looked remorseful.

Rand's arm tightened around Jess. "Constable, I think we must persist. Those who need to go home because of infirmity should do so. I'm taking Lady Curtis back to Farrell Hall, but after that I'll return to my house to get umbrellas and heavy coats and a supply of Wellingtons for any who'd like to join me and continue."

"I'm with ye, yer lordship," George Donner, the elderly innkeeper, piped up.

Donner's best friend, Harry Morgan, sniffed. "So'm I, sir."

Rand gave them a wan smile. "George, Harry, you should go home to bed. You've helped us greatly, but this is turning into a rugged endeavor. Why not join us in the morning?"

"I'm goin' on, sir, I am."

Jess objected. "But your rheumatism, George—"

"Ah, *his* aches 'n' pains," groused Harry with a dismissing hand, "are warts compared to a child's fright in a storm such as this one wants ta be. We'll both be stayin' with ye, yer lordship." He crossed his arms and sealed his promise with a deep nod.

George looked none too pleased to be outdone by

the largesse of Harry. "I want ta get me own coat 'n' hat. My boots've been through every snow since the blizzard o' forty-nine. Best Wellies a man could have. I also 'ave a ripe aged brandy that begs to be opened for just such a good cause as this. I'm goin' to bring it ta share, sir."

Usually, Jess was amused by these two friends who she'd bet had chided and barked at each other since long before she'd come to live in Kent five years ago. But she wasn't cheered tonight. "I am very thankful to both of you—" she began but had to stop to sneeze again.

Rand took her arm. "I am taking you home now. For those of you who wish to continue, I'll meet you at my stables in an hour. We haven't yet tried the south road and the underground caves between Farrell Hall and the Channel."

"Right you are, sir," George agreed. "We'll be there, and we shall find her yet, ma'am." He turned to four other men who had sidled up next to him and agreed.

"Sounds to me," Jack Higgins sniffed, "like we go on." His sorrowful eyes poured over Jess. "You get a good night's sleep, if you can, milady. We'll find her. She can't be far. We just haven't found her cubbyhole yet."

"At dawn I want all of you to come to Farrell Hall for breakfast and strong tea," Jess told them, and they muttered their appreciation as they offered small signs of farewell and scurried away, some to the village, others to Rand's household, and the rest to the Farrell School. Her throat closed at the sight, and she coughed

"Jess, you're catching your death out here. Come with me." He drew her hood up over her hair and brushed raindrops from her cheeks and eyelashes. Then he grasped her hand, and the two of them ran down the hill through the steady rain toward the garden and the music room where this morning Amanda had left them all in shock.

Rand flung open one of the double glass-paned doors against a gust of wind that sought to tear it from his grasp. Pulling her closer, he escorted her inside.

"Spring storms," he said worriedly as he carefully shut the door behind her and Bones. He pressed her to him from torso to thigh. She shivered. He avoided her reaction and her eyes to slide off her hood, unbutton her cape, and remove it from her shoulders. In seconds, he discarded his own coat. As if he understood her body's crying need, he turned back to her and engulfed her in his embrace.

"You're frozen," he said against her hair while his hands massaged her back.

"Numb," Jess ruefully corrected him, her memories returning in a flood now that they were no longer actively searching for Amanda. Jess's own irrational outbursts during the initial days of her recovery from her fall had been different from Amanda's today. She had not run from rooms, but ranted at her father. About anything—and nothing that made sense to her or anyone else.

Why had Amanda fled? Was it the music that disturbed her? Could Amanda hate Chopin the way she herself hated Beethoven's Moonlight Sonata? And for similar reasons?

That made her tremble.

"Jess," Rand entreated as he examined her with alarm, "Pool has built a suitable fire for you."

Bones had already found it. Standing on the hearth, the dog shook himself so that water splattered in rolling showers. He sank to the stone as Jess dropped into a wing chair and Rand went for the bellpull.

She seemed capable only of watching the blaze behind the grate.

Her hope of finding Amanda was much like those flames, wasn't it? Hot and fierce, but going up in smoke. Why had she thought she could draw Amanda out of her shell?

Because she is so much like you. Because she lost her mother. Because she has not grieved properly for her. Because she needs a friend. Someone strong, knowledgeable about such injuries to the head and the heart.

Jess drove a hand through her hair. She was confusing Amanda's accident and loss of her mother with her own fall and its repercussions. Only a few of the circumstances were similar.

Amanda Emory's catastrophe was *not* an exact replica of her own childhood tragedy. No scandalous rumors went around about Amanda's parents. No ulterior motive drove Amanda's father to seek the child's complete recovery. Harrison Emory sought only to see his daughter come to terms with the loss of her mother, suffer her grief, recover as many of her abilities as possible, and then go on with her life.

Jess covered her eyes. She needed Cat. Someone to talk with. One person who understood.

"Here." Rand circled his fingers around her hand and drew it to encompass a glass. "Sip this." As she did, Rand said, "Oh, good, Pool, I'm glad you've come. We need a few things."

"Yes, sir. Food among them, I should think. Cook and I took it upon ourselves to lay out a bit of supper for you. Won't you come into the dining room?"

Jess could deal with such a minor issue as this. "Rand, please do have something. You must be starving."

Before Rand could answer, Pool protested. *"Neither* of you ate much supper. Cook has some cold roast beef and a bread pudding, which would do you both well."

Jess closed her eyes and shook her head.

Rand stepped over to her chair. "Thank you, Pool, nothing for us to eat. But please make a pot of tea for Lady Jessica and put a warming pan in her bed. She's sneezing and needs a little extra warmth. Also, please inform Cook that the search party will come in around sunrise and Lady Curtis would like a buffet laid for them. Something hot and quick."

"Of course, sir. I'm coming out with you."

"Thank you, Pool. Dress for it."

"Yes, sir. Do ring me again when you are ready to leave and I'll have the stableboy saddle up your mount."

"I won't be long. You may have him do it now."

The butler tarried. "Milady, is there anything else?"

Jess shook her head.

"Don't worry, Pool. I'll see she goes up to bed immediately. See you in a few minutes. We meet at my stables."

Jess heard the click of the latch as Pool departed.

She took a large draft of the liquor. Smooth and strong, the liquid burned a trail of fire that soothed her throat but little else. Rand left her line of vision, only to return with a glass of his own and take the chair opposite her.

She noted his mud-splattered shoes and trousers. His body was taut with concern. She didn't have to look him in the face to know he had nailed his eyes to her profile.

When her consideration of the fire fell to the depth of her brandy, she said, "You've been wonderful to stay. It's far more than you ever needed to do, and I am—"

"You need not thank me, Jess."

"But I do."

"I know how you appreciate what I've done by the way you accept my touch." And when her eyes shot to his, he added, "By the natural way you respond to me."

She sat, stunned that he would put to words this truth, which she had tried to ignore for days. "That's not . . ."

"Ordinary for you?"

"Not proper for anyone."

"I'd venture 'acceptable' is the word you really want."

To tell him otherwise would be to lie. And she couldn't do that.

"Drink your brandy, Jess. I'm not leaving until you've emptied that glass. Do it quickly and I'll see you off to your bed."

"Rand, really." She sagged. "Don't feel as though you have to stay with me. I won't fly apart."

He gave her the ghost of a smile. "Obviously not. You keep your feelings too far inside. Locked away. Exhibition is not a quality you prize."

Her nerves sizzled with his boldness and she fought for some acceptable way to order him to cease fire.

"I'll call the truce myself, Jess. I'm not interested in hurting you or offending you. It's my way of saying I understand you, extraordinary as that may seem for a man who has been in your presence such a short time. Rest easy, my dear. I'll be leaving"—his midnight-blue eyes sank to her glass—"soon."

Defiant, she took a swallow. He narrowed his gaze in appreciation. The resulting languor felt disarming. Even welcome.

"Amanda is not far," he said. "And she's somewhere safe."

"You sound certain."

"I spend quite a bit of my free time with the children in the orphanages I support. Amanda is how old? Twelve? She's been here for three months and has not been very active. Where would she go? From what you've told me, she knows only the school grounds, the main road, and the village. She has not lost her power of reason. No child in her physical or mental condition goes exploring. She seeks a place that is significant to her—and to her heart's recovery. She has gone somewhere she knows is physically and emotionally safe."

"But Corinne Marlow, who is Amanda's best friend, should know where that might be, shouldn't she? Yet Corinne's suggestions have brought us no rewards. We know that Amanda likes to read Dickens and Scott in the tack room of the stables. That she enjoys no horses except our aged mare, Dahlia, and she loves music. Piano music, especially. But obviously not Chopin. Not as she used to when I first met her before her accident."

Rand swirled the liquor in his glass. "I gather you suspected nothing of her sensitivity to Chopin."

"If I had, I would have told you not to play that piece," she breathed and took another drink.

"Why do you think she cried?"

"That waltz you played is a stunning creation. Very romantic."

"Not like the Beethoven I played before it."

The Moonlight Sonata. She stiffened. "No. That is full of the drama of life."

"Love and loss, I'd say."

"Heartrending," Jess managed and found her throat closing. Air dwindling. Panic rising as memories loomed of her mother—and the lady's love of the haunting melody.

"So Amanda has never cried before?"

"She has stood up, muttered a few words, then fled a room, but she has not cried any tears since her accident."

"Then this is a positive sign of her recovery."

Jess regarded him gravely. "You are a wise man."

"Perhaps, only because I listen to men who know more than I about children. I told you I employ a battery of doctors for the orphanages I run. The one in London is the largest. As of last month, we had fifty-six children. Every one of them needs a doctor to cure not only the ills of the body but also the ailments of the mind. One doctor, a jovial man from Munich, has taught me more about the mental condition of deprived children than I ever cared to learn."

Jess's admiration before was minuscule compared to the gargantuan delight she felt for Rand Templeton at the moment. "You are right. Amanda's flight from the music room means her emotions are returning. But not necessarily her memory of how her mother died. Nor is this the beginning of her grieving for her, either."

"You think, then, her reaction to the waltz could mean anything?" Rand asked.

"Yes. She could recollect it from some point in her life before the accident. Or perhaps the sounds seemed discordant to her. While we might hope that would be a good indicator of the return of her memory, I cannot be certain. Only she can tell us . . . or I hope she can."

"Yet she has heard other pieces, even the Moonlight Sonata," Rand said, watching her reaction closely, "and not burst into tears."

"That's true," she said quickly. "According to her father, Amanda has been exposed to advanced compositions since she was a baby. Her mother was an accomplished pianist. Her mentor. A woman who encouraged her daughter in all her artistic bents. Their other shared passion was horses." Jess could have been speaking of her own mother and herself, the similarities were so precise.

Rand frowned. "So Amanda does not go near any of the ponies. Only old Dahlia, who goes nowhere fast and who is no threat to her."

"Yes, and she'll read. She'll play scales on the piano. She'll even listen to other musicians. She'll visit the stables, talk to the ponies."

"But ride only Dahlia," Rand concluded. "None of which requires any skill. Or investment of emotion. Until this morning when she encountered an element she could not predict or control. Is it possible she has chosen to remain unaffected? Cocooned, more accurately, from her tragedy?"

"I doubt she has."

"However, you cannot be certain."

That made Jess set aside her glass. "No, but I suffered the same injury, and I can tell you that Amanda cannot even speak fluidly now. Her sentences are simple declarations, stilted. Flat in tone. She cannot create riddles, Rand, because she cannot think that way!"

Jess shot from her chair. He was touching too many of her nerves. She wanted to inform him about Amanda and her condition only, but that seemed almost impossible to separate from her own. "A blow to the head often jumbles up your thinking. Enough so that it often requires great effort to perform one task and think of one thing completely. Therefore it becomes impossible"—until much later when one is more fully recovered—"to deceive another person."

Rand's expression mellowed. "I don't mean to imply that. But, Jess, no two bones break alike. Neither can two heads—or hearts. How can you say you know what is in hers?"

"If she has *chosen* to ignore her past, she may do it as a means of self-preservation."

"Her instinct is operating, then."

"Yes . . . maybe."

"To lessen the pain of her mother's loss?" He sat forward, his elbows on his thighs, his eyes more consoling than his words.

She sought motion, as if activity would keep the ghosts of her personal hell entombed. She ran a hand along the chimneypiece mantel and over the brass buttons on the upholstered chair as she circled the room, touched the harp, fingered the drum. With each move, she separated her own trauma from that of Amanda Emory.

"Amanda could be dealing with her mother's death or coming to terms with her own loss."

"I don't understand."

"The Chopin may have brought a rush of grief over her mother or a sudden recognition that Amanda is not the person she once was. She may despair that she never will recover all her faculties enough to play the Chopin as she once did. She may also worry that she may not be considered healthy or normal by her peers. That's an awful burden for a child to bear. But she must, and in the only way she can for now. Amanda may be like so many other children who can hide emotions, particularly things they fear or hate."

He sat back, examining her every impulsive move about the room. "I have eyes to see, my dear. What I am rather certain I saw this morning on Amanda's face when she jumped up to flee was sorrow. Jess. Stand still a minute and look at me, will you, please?"

She could barely draw air but did as he asked.

His eyes grew mellow with affection. "What I saw on yours when I played the Beethoven was fear and hate. So be at ease. I am not asking about you, Jess."

She shuddered, crossed her arms, and whispered "I know" to the floorboards.

"You and I will nurture our friendship with honesty. Though one day I may be tempted to ask you to explain your reaction to the sonata, I hope that a time will come when you will tell me of your own volition. I shall work for that, Jess. In the interim, won't you please educate me about Amanda—and about head injuries?"

How could she deny him? She dropped her arms and flung them wide in a gesture she recognized as surrender. Then she paced as she told him what he needed to know.

"Those who have recently suffered a blow to the head recuperate like any other convalescents. They are weakened by the trauma and need peace and quiet. A regulated atmosphere. While most people never recall their accidents, they do, within days or weeks, recall the details of their lives. In the most severe cases, some memories never return. But with the fortunate, as the body heals, the brain seeks clues to survival. The patients recall their names, their likes and dislikes in food or clothing or people. But they may not be able to do the simplest tasks."

She turned to him, so attentive, so sweet to sit there rapt upon her words, his eyes offering solace. How had he become so dear to her so quickly? Because he was the most generous man she had ever met. Gentle. Kind.

She forced herself to continue her discourse. "Patients like these need to learn how to wash their faces, bathe, dress. No task, however small, can be ignored. Routine comforts them and provides its own security.

Within such a framework—a cocoon, I think you'd say—such people learn to function again."

"What of their functioning intellectually?"

"That is different with every person. You were right when you said no two injuries are alike. If they recover their physical stamina and can perform the basic tasks of self-care, then the next task they confront is to rediscover their intellectual skills. The best route is to give them short bouts of reading, writing, and arithmetic. This process of recall can take weeks or months. Years, for some."

"What is it in Amanda's case?"

"She comes along beautifully. I had a long talk with her governess when Amanda's father enrolled her here in January. The woman told me details about Amanda's knowledge of subjects. I took notes and worked from them."

Admiration lit his features. "Smart of you."

"It is what we do for our girls. Most of them have had a difficult time of it, not because they have head injuries but because they are too active for their families or schools to understand."

"But Cat and you are able to help them change their behavior because you know how to curb your own impulses."

She arched a brow at him, her impetuous behavior a point that he had so recently found disruptive. "Nervous Nellies are the best at teaching others like them."

His eyes ran down her form, and as she bristled at the fierce esteem in his gaze, he pursed his lips. "I saw you as energetic, yes. Devoted, certainly. Unnerved by me because I was so rude to you."

"Thank you. I'll take that not only as a compliment but as proof I have come far from the behavior of my childhood."

He stilled. "Yes," he murmured, "I'd say that's true."

She stared, blinked. "I don't understand."

He rose, put down his glass, and while compassion gloved a shrewdness that made her shiver, he strode closer to her. Before her, in all his masculine might and beauty, he reached out a hand and, with his fingertips, he lifted her face. "Tonight you are struck with terror. But I have seen you before. Watched you." He threaded his fingers into her hair. His touch made her hum silently in the back of her throat. "Three years ago you were shy of people. Afraid, even. But you've grown accustomed to the peace of Farrell Hall and reveled in the joy of what you do. You've risen to the challenge of running the school without Cat's daily presence. You've gained confidence. It doesn't simply show—it glows on you."

"How could you know me so well?" she managed.

"I told you. I have watched you. Closely. Against the best rules of etiquette. In spite of my firmest resolution to avoid you. And now that the woman I see is you, just you, I am intrigued and drawn to you. I'm not going to stop looking at you, Jess."

"You should."

"Why?" He narrowed his dark blue gaze on her. "Is there another man you care for?"

"No. Never before," she shot back before she caught herself.

His mouth curved in a sympathetic smile. "I didn't

think so. You cannot turn away from me, can you? Nor will I from you. There is too much to discover about each other . . ." He let his sentence drift, leaving her anticipating his foray into truth, driving her breathless to whatever new shore he chose. "We'll save that for another day. Another time. You are overwrought with worry. And I would be less than a gentleman—and even less true to Pool—if I did not do my duty by you." He ran his hands down her shoulders, and though she had the wild expectation that he might do more, he merely clasped her fingers and moved toward the door.

She dug her heels into the carpet. "You must not think I'll encourage you. I can't."

Though he had taken a step away, he turned back to her. The action brought him dangerously close.

She could not move. She could not breathe. Only enjoy the heat of his body. The aroma of his cologne.

The fingers of his free hand slid across her cheek, her ear, and into her hair. He took one loose curl and drew it down her throat to tantalize her with its texture. To tempt her with the fire of his admiring gaze.

"Jess," he called her name as if it were enchantment, "you need not do a thing to encourage me. Just be yourself. Compassionate, intelligent Jess. So beautiful, sweetheart . . . so arrestingly lovely I want to wrap you up and take you home to simply look at you until I lose all my senses in you. But I won't do that until we know each other better. . . . Ah, no, you can't leave until I finish. I know you won't allow me closer any time too soon because you are a sensitive young woman whom no man has ever touched . . . and who, until now"—he lifted his hand away to display it for her, palm open—"wanted no man to even try."

Ecstatic, horrified, she took a step around him.

His fingers circled her wrists like iron cuffs and halted her. "There is no harm in it, Jess. Men and women touch often. That's how the human race gets on. But you, my dear, shut yourself off from that possibility. While I, enthralled as I am by your grace and wit, am enraptured by your devotion to the children. Yet I sense—as well you know it these last few minutes—that you show me a veneer. A mask for a woman who conceals a loving but very lonely heart, darling."

The endearment made her yearn—and quake. "I think you must go home—"

"Yes, but you don't really want to drive me away. So let me have the last word tonight. Let's call it your good manners and my lack of them." His brazen eyes sparkled with mischief and not a little objectivity. "Just imagine, if you take all night to think how to reprimand me, you can rant and rave at me with eloquence and a certain air of . . . justice."

"You're outrageous," she told him, unable to find a more articulate rebuff.

"Your pulse tells me just how outrageous." He squeezed her wrists and gave her a consoling smile. Then, disregarding propriety, he kept hold of one hand as he led her from the music room, along the hall into the foyer, and up the curved staircase. At the top, he paused to question her with a tilt of his head, and she knew he sought direction.

She took the lead, never dropping his hand, and

strode to the center door, where she spun back against the molded frame. "Good night."

He towered over her, his eyes delving into hers. "Sleep well," he whispered and lifted both her fists to his mouth. His firm lips pressed kisses on her knuckles. "Recover your health. Rest. We'll find Amanda soon. I promise you."

Turning on his heel, he left her.

Long afterward she stared into the night.

Unclenched her hands.

And concluded she had discovered one man who gave his word, kept it, and then offered more than was ever asked of him. She marveled that she had been so fortunate as to be his acquaintance, his neighbor. She wondered what else she might become. Down that road of thought lay possibilities she had never considered. Not with any man. But with this man she felt hope gush through her body that she might find . . . what?

A friend, her weary mind suggested.

Much more, her heart rejoiced.

But she quieted both, turned for her bedroom—and a rest that would elude her, she knew. Because tonight she would not be able to shake her worry over Amanda—or her anxiety that she desired Rand Templeton in ways friendship never encompassed.

Chapter Four

DESIRE DROVE HIM HOME AT BREAKNECK SPEED. HE'D find Amanda. He would! He had to. Then he would tutor her, talk to her, do whatever it took to help her. And as he did, he hoped he might also become a friend—a very close friend—to Jessica Curtis.

Inside his stable, he handed over the reins to his young groom. "Gather up any boots and heavy riding coats in the tack room, will you, please, John? The search party will meet here in less than thirty minutes, and I want us ready to supply any of them who need extra protection from this rain."

"Yes, sir. The staff came back a while ago and went right up to the house to change their clothes to go out again. To a man and woman, they're coming with you. Me too."

Rand gave the boy his great thanks and left him.

Rather than go the long way around in the pouring rain, he let himself into the house through the garden doors to the drawing room. He discarded his hat and gloves, his mind questioning where Amanda would have gone.

In the ebon silence of the night, he stood there listening to the Meissen clock tick in counterpoint to the torrent that thrummed against the windowpanes. He recalled sequestered nooks along the shore, which he himself had explored as a child. He hoped to God Amanda had not fled toward the coast, especially with this storm upon them. The waves could come into shore quickly, flooding coves that looked safe to a child's eye.

Fearing that he might be too late to save her, he cursed beneath his breath and headed for the door to the hall. But a gasp made him freeze in his tracks . . . and turn.

Bathed in the shadows of the tempest outside, the room took on tones of silver. A petite form of dappled grays rose from the Empire divan. She rubbed her eyes with the backs of her hands and stared at him.

"Amanda?" He couldn't believe his good fortune.

Eyes as big as apples, she moved not one muscle.

A gust of fury rattled the glass-paned doors. Lightning zagged, soundless, illuminating her thin form, hands folded in her lap now that she sat upright.

"Yes, sir," she said without inflection, though her voice was rough with sleep.

He walked forward, purposely, slowly. He didn't want to frighten her and send her to the four winds. He had to hold her, keep her, help her. Leaving his coat in a chair, he went down on one knee before her. "Are you all right?"

She nodded, her dark hair falling forward about her face as she considered her hands.

She wasn't wet. Not tattered or dirty. Where had she been the whole day? "How long have you been here?"

She lifted one shoulder. The shrug reminded him of Jess. "A long time."

Exultation ran through him like electricity. Impulse said to touch her, confirm her presence and her health. Reason warned against it. "Since before the storm began?"

She nodded once. "I came here after the sun went down."

He let out the breath he'd been holding. "Thank God. How did you get in?"

Her eyes went wide, as if he'd asked if she had broken in like a London urchin bent on thievery. "The doors were not locked. No one was here."

"Everyone was out with the search party."

She examined him. "I did not think you would be with them."

"Why wouldn't I be?" he urged in amazement.

She frowned as she searched for an answer. "I don't know. . . . That makes another thing I don't know." She lowered her eyes, ashamed of herself for asking something that did not make sense to him. "I will go."

Rand saw the mental confusion Jess had described and how Amanda noted it, hated it, and had no way to deal with it. But he wouldn't be deterred. He had to explore what paths did lie open to them. "Please stay. You must be starving."

"I ate this afternoon. I had two pasties from Mrs. Pettibone."

Rand was taken aback. Liz Pettibone was the carpenter's wife. At midday she'd joined the search party but never said a word about having seen Amanda or offered her food. Moreover, Liz was a God-fearing woman who didn't lie. "How could that be?"

"I took them from her window ledge."

"I see," he said with appreciation and let a twinkle into his eyes. "I understand the lady is a good cook."

"The best, sir."

"But that feast of meat and potatoes must have been hours ago. Mrs. Pettibone went home to serve her children supper before dusk. Will you come with me to see if my cook's talents rival hers?"

As if he'd waved a wand and banished the night, dawn broke on her features. "I would like that."

He beamed. Was it so easy to draw feeling from her? Jess had said Amanda showed little emotion until this morning. Why did he see this from her now? Here with him? But that was a question to which he would gain no answer from her. He had to act on the issue at hand. And he had to see if he could make her grin again.

"What do you crave? Yesterday we had roast chicken for supper, and there must be some left. If not, we always have scones or gingerbread. Cake, perhaps? Or . . . how about plum pudding?"

She snorted in humor. "You don't have plum pudding."

"How do you know I don't?" He could play, too.

"It's not Christmas."

"I don't care. If you want it, I'll order my cook from her bed to make it."

"Oh, sir," she was speaking in her even pace while her eyes told of her delight. "Plum puddings take *hours . . .*" She stopped to cock her head, remembering. "No, *days* to make."

He wanted to shout with joy at the tiny inflection in her voice. "Only the kind that sit in a bath of whiskey."

"But they *are* the best."

His features fell as his heart took flight. "Whatever you want is yours." He extended his hand, palm up. "Come to the kitchen?"

If he worried that she would jump from her nest and fly from him, he needn't have wasted his energy. She simply took his hand and walked beside him.

He led her along the corridors quickly, while his mind asked why she was here and how soon he could take her home to Jess, safe and sound.

They'd traversed the east wing and headed past the dining room and the butler's pantry, when Amanda stopped in front of the kitchen door. "About this morning . . ."

"Yes?"

"I was rude to you. I am sorry. I came here to see you and say that."

"Thank you. I accept your apology." He smiled at her, restraining the urge to pick her up and hug her. Not only was she unscathed and here, but she had come to him to act in a socially correct manner.

He thrust open the heavy oak door and let her precede him inside. Clean as a whistle for the night, the kitchen gleamed in welcome. He gestured to the giant oak table before them, and she sat down in one of the huge armchairs. He turned up the gas in two wall sconces and went for the cupboard.

He set a plate, goblet, and utensils before her.

"When you ran away this morning, you frightened us to death. We've been out looking for you ever since then."

She bit her lower lip. "I know."

In the brighter light, he could see things now that he'd not been able to before. Amanda was tired. With a few bits of straw stuck into the fabric of her pinafore and dress and small cuts on her hands, she gave evidence of her day in hiding. Now that he had reprimanded her, she retreated to a private sanctuary. He ridiculed himself for acting like a frustrated parent. He had acted spontaneously and had driven her away.

He swallowed remorse and sank down before her. "It is now my turn to say I'm sorry. I didn't mean just now to make you feel bad. You did what you had to do. We do things sometimes"—he recalled his behavior toward Jess during three years of grief—"that others cannot understand. That we ourselves cannot define."

She looked at him so blankly that he wondered if she had absorbed any of his words, until she said, "I know why I left." He wanted to ask her to tell him, but good manners kept him silent. "That's the reason I stayed away so long. I was thinking about why I ran out. I . . . decided that I liked thinking, even if . . . even if I didn't like what came into my head."

"And so now that you see some things more clearly, you decided you are ready to rejoin us. Is that it, Amanda?"

"Yes, sir. I came to you first because I needed to apologize"—she smiled a little sheepishly—"and because I thought no one would look for me here."

He laughed lightly. "Your logic was wonderful."

She appeared pleased with herself. "I thought so too."

"Well, then, it's time to eat."

He opened the door to the cold pantry and stepped down. Scanning the shelves, he saw a pie and a bowl of oranges. He took both, eager to sate Amanda's hunger for food—and his own for information.

"This should do for a start," he offered as he put them down before her and grabbed a kitchen towel for her to use as a napkin. As he returned to get a pitcher of milk, she smoothed the towel in her lap.

But she simply gazed at the items he continued to produce and shook her head. No milk or bread or lamb took her fancy.

Dejected, he watched her as her mind wandered away from him. He thought he understood children, but here with her, he dealt with someone very different from those who lived in his orphanages. True, Jess had told him some facts about the behavior of a person with such an injury, but he knew only minutes' worth, not nearly enough to cope with a situation like this. But he must, mustn't he?

Taking a chair, he faced her. "The pie is mincemeat. Don't you care for it?"

She did not respond.

"I'll look for more. There's no chicken as I thought." When she didn't comment, he grew frantic. "If you're still upset with me about my reprimand, I am sorry, Amanda. I didn't mean to sound like an old sod. I was worried. So were we all. If you think I'm not grateful you came to me, let me disabuse you of that idea. I am!"

He broke off, uncertain if he made sense. The child had suffered a brain injury. Were polysyllabic words too cumbersome for her? He could not assume that, because she recalled some things, like social graces, she now remembered everything prior to her accident or that she could concentrate on one topic entirely. His insecurity had him groping, pausing.

In the abyss, Amanda finally replied, "I understand. You see"—her eyes fastened to his—"I came here to explain why I ran away today."

Few thrills of his life matched this one. That she would come to him of her own accord to make amends was one thing. But that she would come so purposely, single-mindedly, *bravely,* to a house she'd never visited—ah, yes, that overjoyed him. She had conquered whatever emotion had driven her from the music room to seek him out. That meant what had happened there in those few minutes not only had struck a chord in her consciousness but also had inspired in her the courage to examine it . . . and now to discuss it.

He sat back and smiled at her. "Please do tell me. I am eager to know why you left."

She fingered her fork. "I hate that music."

He waited.

"My mother played it. She liked . . . sad pieces."

There was much more to the emotive power of the waltz than sadness. But that was irrelevant and he would not debate it with her. If Amanda wished to share her thoughts on this, he would listen. He desperately wanted to know why she would run from a room at the sound of a song . . . and he wondered why another piece would make a grown woman rake her hair and blanch as if the hounds of hell pursued her. But he'd discover that from Jess another day. Now it was Amanda he had to help. "Do you think many people consider that waltz sad?"

Amanda lifted sorrowful eyes to him. "My mother did. Or . . . at least the way she played it made it seem gloomy. I miss her. She was a very good musician. Better than I. My father says I imagine that. But I don't."

This was a subject that Rand had experience exploring. "Sometimes we can tell instantly just by listening to someone if they have special talent."

"She felt the music. With her hands. In her whole body." Amanda closed her eyes, and he thought she heard renditions he never could. "She was *absorbed* by it. Or it took her. I'm not sure which." Her gaze shot to his. "Do you know what I mean?"

"I do." *I marvel at your ability to understand your mother's absorption and your ability to convey it in words and rhythm—and emotion.* "What is music if one plays impassively? Merely a physical exercise for the fingers."

"I heard talent when you played. It made me remember my mother. She liked to play. She did it morning, noon, and night. One time she woke me up. She was banging on the keys. Laughing. My father ordered her to bed. He told her he didn't want her to play anymore . . . though I don't recall why." That wrinkled Amanda's brow. Suddenly Rand could see she grew angry with herself for her inability to recollect the reason for her father's actions. "I wish I could."

"You need not remember it right now." He inclined

his head toward her supper. "I'd say you could do with food more than anything. Wait until tomorrow or the next day for more memories."

"Do you think they'll come?"

"I'm not a doctor and can't say for certain." He wondered if her memory could be tapped with the same piece of music. Or another one. Whenever Amanda—or the rest of them—least expected it.

She shook her head as if she wanted to erase something awful from her mind. "I was surprised today. I didn't like being surprised. I was frightened that it happened so quickly. That's why I ran."

"I know. But you must not fear. Lady Curtis and I are here to help you. We won't see you suffer."

"I had a feeling you played especially for me. Was I right?" When Rand nodded, she said, "My father must have told Lady Curtis I like that waltz. But I don't. I learned that when you played."

"You used to like it. Lady Curtis asked me to play it because she remembered from your first interview with her before your accident that you enjoyed it."

"That would explain it, yes. I didn't think you performed it to hurt me. You don't harm people."

Such honesty—and insight—from her warmed him immensely. "Thank you. I shall tell my business rivals to take a gander at me and see if they can lay down their swords as quickly."

"Miss Curtis likes you, too."

Well, well. From the mouths of babes. "The feeling is mutual."

"Yes. I see it. In your eyes. You've never had a wife, and if you ever had a mistress, you don't now. That's what the villagers say. Is it true?"

"Completely."

"I would guess lots of ladies like you."

"Some find me interesting. But I have not found anyone I care for enough to propose we spend our lives together."

Amanda finally decided to tuck into the pie. As she chewed, she examined him. "The girls say you seem to be a good catch. But you're very old."

He chuckled. "My dear, thirty-eight is not ancient."

"No. But most men with a title and money get married at an early age," she said around another mouthful of pie. "Don't you want a son?"

He stilled, his heartache at the loss of his only child a raw wound he thought might never heal. "Yes," he managed, while he wrestled with his old fury at Susannah for aborting the baby. "Sons and daughters." With a woman he could love. One who took him at his word and who kept hers when she declared she cared for him and would marry him.

"My father wanted a son . . ." She tilted her head as she considered middle space. "Or did he? He wasn't happy when my brother was born . . ." She blinked, her attention back on Rand. "It must mean you're waiting for Miss Curtis. Meant to be, and so on." She swallowed, rather as an afterthought, while she paused once more to scowl.

When she didn't move for the longest time, he became concerned. "What's the matter? Are you ill or—"

"No. I . . . Suddenly I could hear my mother yelling at my father that he hated my brother. I could see her face. It was ugly. She was very pretty . . . but not that night. She threw the fern at him. Broke the china pot. He—" Amanda fell back in her chair. "He grabbed her and tried to carry her upstairs. She kicked him and bit his hand. That's when he saw me in the doorway and stopped. She turned to me then and ran out . . . to her room . . . or to the stables . . . I can't remember. None of us ever talked about it. Papa wouldn't, of course. Neither would my mother. She hardly spoke to anyone after that. Not even to me."

Her voice died, her head bowed. She folded her hands in her lap again while her complexion turned a ghastly white. He could have sworn she meant to cry, and he struggled between elation and despair that she could feel pain so deeply.

But as if a magician had snapped his fingers, she raised her face and smiled sweetly at him, all traces of her sorrow vanished. "Did you know that Miss Curtis doesn't have a beau?"

This constant flux from one subject to another unnerved him so that he could only shake his head.

"The other girls say she never did. But we don't know why. She isn't a harpy. Not like other governesses and headmistresses. She is beautiful and young and very kind. You're right to like her."

He relished the joy that lined Amanda's features, but became even more eager to know if she changed topics deliberately or simply because she couldn't focus well on one subject. He needed to ask Jess. He also had to tell her the disturbing revelations Amanda had seen here. For now, though, he took the only course open to him and responded to the issue she wanted to discuss. "Are you matchmaking?" he teased.

"I would say so, yes," she offered with a smile.

"Well, then, you had better clean your plate, hadn't you, so that we can get on with it?"

Within minutes he had called his staff together and canceled the search party. Then he ordered around his brougham, climbed in beside Amanda, and had his coachman head for Farrell Hall. The short ride took longer than usual as the rain poured down in sheets, deterring his horses from their duty. Wrapped in a blanket, Amanda fidgeted as she gazed out the window at the front of the mansion.

"A light is still on in Miss Curtis's bedroom."

Rand confirmed it with a glance above the main entrance. "She's very worried."

"Do you think she'll punish me?"

"She'll be so ecstatic to bundle you off to your bed, she'll probably burst into song."

Amanda smiled. He understood enough about her now to conclude that she might not dwell on any subject for long, but she did follow joy wherever it led. "It's a treat when she does sing. Have you ever heard her?" When he shook his head, she urged, "You must ask her sometime. She doesn't do it often. Do you sing?"

"I don't have occasion to do it much."

"Can you carry a tune?"

"Simple ones, yes."

The coach came to a swaying halt.

Amanda shrank into the squabs. "I'm afraid."

Something about her told him she was not so much terrified of what Jess might do as of some other element, perhaps even another unbidden memory. These could come to her any place, any time. She had to go on, no matter what she might recall.

He put out his hand. "Don't be frightened. I doubt heartily that Miss Curtis is the type of person to heap coals on an already blazing fire."

Amanda cocked her head.

He'd spoken too metaphorically for her. "It is not in her nature to hurt you or anyone. Let's go and make her feel better, shall we?"

His coachman opened the door, and Rand stepped down to the drive. The rain pounded on his shoulders, but the sound of his name shouted down to him made him look up.

Jess—who must have heard the clatter of the horses—was bent over the balcony, astonished. "Rand?"

He put a hand to his brow for all the good it did to shield him from the rain. "I've got Amanda!" he yelled up.

He helped her out, and they both scurried to the door just as Jess flung it open.

Drenched from the rain on her balcony, Jess stood like an alabaster statue. Eyes wide, mouth open, panting. The white cambric nightgown clung to her body like a second ethereal skin. Translucent as it was, it revealed in sculptured shadows what no lady would ever display in the light to a man she barely knew. With a hunger turned ravenous by the delicacies before him, Rand noted a cloud of wild hair, lavish breasts, large nipples, small waist, good hips, and never-ending legs which his connoisseur's eye told him he needed to trace with his hands and adore with his mouth.

"Oh, God," she was babbling as she drew them both inside with trembling hands and he shut the door. "You found her." She grasped Amanda by the arms and hugged her, while her eyes sought his. "Thank you, thank you." She was kissing Amanda's hair, discarding the blanket, running her hands down the girl's body.

Barely recovered from his visual feast, Rand stared at Jess until he had schooled himself enough to sound rational. "I found her in my drawing room, napping. Jess, she's fine and healthy. She just had something to eat, and she's dead tired." Meanwhile he was having the damnedest struggle to keep his eyes from admiring the sway of Jess's breasts as she moved forward to embrace the child and knelt so that the hem of her gown bunched up to reveal slim feet, trim ankles, and calves.

He cleared his throat. Looked up at the vaulted ceiling. Listened to Jess ooh and ahh over the student she thought she'd lost. While he wondered what he was supposed to do with his body's rigid declaration of appreciation for Jess's finer assets. Before she noticed, he had to get out of here. "Jess, I must go."

But she surprised the hell out of him when she rose and sailed straight into his arms. What he had sampled with his eyes, he could now savor with his body. He stifled a groan as she wrapped her arms around him. Her fingers in the hair at the nape of his neck, she held his head, and damn if she didn't kiss him!

It was a hearty smack. One of delight. Friendship.

He drank every drop of her gratitude—and thirsted for a deeper companionship.

"You're wonderful," she breathed.

He wanted to murmur other adjectives, like "tempting" for her firm breasts and "enticing" for the hollow of her spine, "fitting" for the way her hips matched his. But lest she perceive how intimately they merged together—and how dearly he desired more—he pulled away.

She didn't notice but framed his face and declared over again how much she valued his assistance.

At the other end of the hall, Jess's housekeeper appeared. "Excuse me, madam," she said in a cool voice. "You rang?"

"I told you she did," Pool said appearing behind the vexed woman. He had on his coat, hat, and boots, prepared to join the search team. "Milady, what is it?" he asked before his gaze found Rand. "Lord Templeton? You're here? My God! With Amanda. You found her," he said reverently.

Before the butler took note of Jess's scandalous state of undress, Rand shrugged out of his Inverness, sending raindrops to the floor, and swirled it about her shoulders. Shocked, Jess came to the realization of what he'd done for her—and why. She brought the lapels of his coat over her chest and faced her servants.

"Lord Templeton has brought Amanda home," she said, as each man's eyes locked on the other's.

"I told those who had arrived at my stables to go home," Rand informed Pool.

The butler inhaled, but directed his attention to Amanda. While the housekeeper stood eyeing her mistress, Pool went to the child, grinned at her, and offered the benefits of the kitchen or a bath. When Amanda refused the first and accepted the second, Pool exclaimed over how wondrous it was that Amanda was safe. Not to be outdone, the housekeeper ambled forward to shepherd Amanda to her bath. The three of them bade Jess and Rand good night and took the stairs.

Meanwhile, Pool's presence had inspired a self-consciousness in Jess. Rand could see it in the taut line of her mouth as she turned to him. "I can't tell you what it means to me that you brought her home safe and sound and so quickly."

"That she's in good health is her doing, Jess, not mine. I merely found her in my drawing room; then I fed her and talked to her a little before bringing her home to you."

"What did she say? Why did she go to you?"

"She wanted to apologize. She thought she'd been rude to run out this morning."

"Oh, Rand. That marks the return of her social conscience." Joy spread over her fine features with a rapture that banished her self-consciousness. "She is getting better. You're helping her. I knew you would."

"I think anyone could have played Chopin's Minute Waltz and evoked the same response. The music has significance for her. Her mother played it very often."

Jess looked stunned. "Really? She told you this?"

"Yes, she remembered some of her past tonight. Things she'd forgotten because of her injury."

Her brow wrinkled. She crossed her arms. "What things?"

Rand narrowed his gaze on Jess, detecting desperation. "I suspect Amanda's mother was unhappy in her marriage. She and her husband fought. The woman played the piano to escape—or meditate on her woes. Who knows for certain?"

Jess's fingers dug like talons into his coat. "I never knew . . ."

"No, of course not. How could you? Her father wouldn't tell you. People don't discuss such things."

"It's too disturbing."

Rand stepped nearer, his hands going to Jess's elbows. With her mind so absorbed with Amanda, she didn't object when his hands circled her back. But neither did she welcome the embrace. She stood, quite frankly, like a block of ice.

Her chill terrified him so, he brought her more securely to his chest. The minute he had her flush against him, he knew that the empathy Jess felt for Amanda struck some discord in this woman's soul. "What's the matter?" he urged against her temple. "Jess, tell me what's wrong. I've brought her home. She's well and happy to be here. I've talked with her as she remembered her past and nothing upset her. Things she recalled did puzzle her, but"—he pulled away a bit to scan Jess's rigid features and lifted her chin with a finger—"if she's not frightened by her memories, why are you?"

"Sometimes"—she licked her lips, squinting at his cravat—"when the memories come, they arrive in clumps. They're not in order. Pieces are missing. That can confuse a person and cause odd behavior."

"Rest easy, Jess. I told you she didn't have any tantrums."

"But as a result, she could experience the opposite,

too. Quiet periods that can last minutes or days. Weeks, even. Along with that, she might be unable to do or think of ordinary events or tasks in order. You can't take the next step because you can't see it. You wonder if you will ever be able to think in a straight line again. I don't—" Her gorgeous aqua eyes swam with desolation as one of her hands gathered a fistful of his shirt. "I don't want to see Amanda endure this anguish."

He tugged her fingers free and brought them—open, needy, and trusting—to his mouth to press a kiss against them. "I don't want to see you endure it, either."

She curled her fingers to her palm as if to trap his endearment there. He'd give more to her keeping.

He brushed his lips across her cheek. "Don't look for trouble where there is none. Live for each minute. Please don't become overwhelmed by what you think might happen. You'll not be able to enjoy the successes when they come. And they will come."

"So will the failures. The terrors."

"You cannot predict that." Adamant, he held her gaze. "Because your accident and hers seem similar does not mean your injuries were, nor your recovery."

She swallowed and glanced down. "You're right. I have told myself the same thing, over and over."

"We will work with her. Both of us."

She raised her face, her expression more serene—and appreciative of his efforts.

Before she had a chance to speak, he placed a gentle finger across her lips. "Don't you dare tell me how grateful you are." He outlined her lush mouth, and the desire to feel her flesh against his flared to full blaze. "Show me instead."

She gave a little shake of her head. "How do I do that?" she whispered.

He caught her mouth between his fingers and thumb so that he plumped her lower lip. "I think you know," he rasped.

"I don't. I've never kissed a man."

He grinned. "*I* am infinitely thankful for that. I get to teach you. And I'll need to call on all my skills"—he crushed her closer—"because I've never seen such a willful pupil."

She tried to push away, but he tugged her back. "Look at me, Jess. I'm not going to eat you up, just put my mouth here . . . on yours. You might like it."

She moaned. "I might want more."

Her bluntness urged him on. "Let's try one . . . and find out how many we need." When she gasped, he murmured, "Don't worry. If you want to do this often, there is no ration I'd ever impose."

Shock, then humor sparkled in her eyes, and he knew then that he had to first taste her in joy.

At the instant their mouths met, he went blind, deaf, dumb to everything except the erotic delight of caressing her so completely. His fantasies of how her mouth would feel had not included this hunger to never let her go.

"Oh, sweetheart . . ." He satisfied himself by capturing handfuls of her hair to hold her securely while he gave them both the pleasures of a longer, fuller sample of delight. Her lips were sheer silk, finer than any he'd ever felt. "Tell me I don't have to count."

"No." She ran her hands over him like a starving woman. "I am counting. That was only two."

He would have barked in laughter if he hadn't wanted to kiss her so often. "Here's the third, then. Open your mouth. *Yes . . .*" She let him nibble her lower lip. She sighed, and he took it as permission to slant his mouth over hers and dip his tongue inside. He felt her surrender completely . . . unconsciously.

That had him pulling away to view her reaction to him. Her eyes remained closed, while she drifted in the ardor they'd created in mere seconds. If he'd been a poet, he would have said she looked as if she were in paradise.

Dying for more, he scooped her up, found the huge porter's chair, and took her to it, where he sat with her in his lap, giving her no time, no space to refuse him before he bent her over his arm. Pirate, she might think he was tomorrow when she remembered this embrace. But he'd go to his bed tonight content that he had enjoyed the bounties she had placed within his grasp.

"Darling, feel how good this kiss can be." He placed a sweet one on her cheek and throat, trailing the contours exposed to him and offered him with such abandon. His hand lifted one breast. Her round nipple had risen for him long before. He had only to satisfy its begging crest with the admiration of his mouth and tongue as he claimed it and laved it, urging it to a point with his torrid words. "You taste willing, my Jess."

She whimpered in delight.

He shifted, dropping kisses across the swell of one breast into the valley and onto the other. The wet nightgown complied. His coat fell from her shoulders while his lips praised the flawless beauty in his arms. His mouth found hers.

She grasped his hair. "We've got to stop."

"I know. I don't want to." His thumb grazed the diamond peak of one nipple as he smiled down at her. "Neither do you."

Her eyes opened languidly. "I have to. I've lost count."

He burst into laughter and hugged her. "I'm going home."

"Now?"

He pulled away to examine the sorrow in her expression. "I'm coming back tomorrow, Jess."

Her sadness gave way to modesty—and fear. "For Amanda."

He chastised her with his eyes. "For you, too."

This time when she pushed away, he let her go.

She went to the front door and opened it.

He picked up his coat from the floor where it had fallen and put it on quickly. He went to stand behind her, as close as he could bear without giving in to the impulse to reach for her. "Jess, we are going on from here. Slowly. Deliberately. As befits two people who cannot seem to get enough of each other, and who must remain creatures of reason."

He trailed his fingers into the wealth of strawberry-blond hair that fell down her back to her waist. He vowed that one day soon he'd comb his fingers through every curl of that bright cloud. For now he'd keep his hands—and his ambitions for them—to himself.

"I'm leaving, Jess. But I'm coming back tomorrow

and the day after that as well. I'll be here for Amanda, but know I am here for you and me."

When he took a step around her and looked down, tears lined her lower lashes. He felt such compassion for her that his heart twisted. "Am I so frightening?"

"No. Not you."

If Amanda was right, Jess Curtis had never had a beau—and he dearly wanted to give her one. He took her wrist, and this time when he raised her hand to his lips, she opened her palm to his kiss. "We'll find a way together to rid you of your fear of friendship."

Her tongue glided along her lower lip. "Your kisses taste stronger than any friendship I've ever known."

"I thank God for that," he said beneath his breath. "Dream, will you, darling? Tomorrow will be a new day for both of us."

Chapter Five

DREAM?

Fiddlesticks!

She didn't have to dream to see him. Want him. His conversation, his laughter. His eyes on her.

But here he was again!

Rand emerged from the copse that separated the Farrell School grounds from his own Temple manor lands. He strolled toward the group, his deeply muscled thighs drawing her gaze to his fitted chamois pants. She forced her gaze up to his forest-green riding jacket, which he slung over his shoulder, his other hand trailing the reins of his huge stallion, who trudged quietly behind.

She lowered her bow, listening to Amanda and the other girls in the archery class greet him as he came across the field. His dark blue gaze held hers with a light of satisfaction.

He'd finally found her—and she couldn't come up

with a quick excuse to leave, because she had just begun this lesson.

She'd spent the last three days avoiding him. His brand of friendship. Her desire for the fire of more. And her fear—her *knowledge*—that if she liked him too well as a companion, she'd crave him as a constant one.

Her life was too hectic to nurture such a relationship! She had a school to run. Classes to teach. A quiet, fulfilling life to protect from disruption.

But her routine seemed just that since he kissed her, awakening a longing for a husband to adore in a home with children of her own. Oh, she saw how blissful Cat and Spence were and knew how happy Cat's parents had been together. But her own mother and father set the most influential example before her that love did not necessarily bring happiness—and that passion could kill.

"Good morning," Rand offered to all of them.

"Hello, sir." Amanda stepped forward and smiled. He was to tutor her today at eleven, after this lesson. Each of his lessons this week was at a different time because of business appointments he'd scheduled before Jess's request of him. This morning marked the first time Amanda had joined this group and Jess thought that might have been a result of Rand's encouragement.

He responded to her as several older girls sprang forth to gush over the dashing marquess of Ashford.

"Oh, Lord Templeton, we're so pleased you've come!"

So am I, Jess wanted to let him know, but repressed it. Instead she greeted him with a pleasant look of a spinster schoolmistress. Decorum might be the best tactic to block his advances.

"Practicing your aim?" he asked her, his voice carrying a resonant nonchalance that belied the ardor of his gaze.

"Perfecting it," she told him, wishing she had the privacy to express her delight in Amanda. The girl had not only come out today but also held the bow, nocked arrows, and drew back the string with more power in her hands than Jess had noted before Amanda's three days of practice with Rand. He eschewed scales for duets and rounds of whatever Amanda wanted to play. Rand had encouraged her to come here.

The girls rushed about him like goslings.

"Do you like this sport, sir?"

"I'll bet you're very good."

"Can you stay awhile, my lord?"

Rand demurred, but looked at Jess.

"Would you like to join us?" she had to ask to be polite, praying the older girls would detect no flushing of her skin.

"Of course," he replied as he handed Amanda his jacket and took Jess's bow from her fingers—after brushing them with his quite unnecessarily.

"Would you show us your stance, sir?" asked one smitten sixteen-year-old, pouting at him prettily. "We're not doing it correctly."

"Yes! Teach us!" said her best friend.

He tested the resilience of the bow and string. "I have watched Lady Curtis, girls. She is very adept. I don't think I can improve upon her form."

Jess was inclined to have him demonstrate his anyway. "We learn in many different ways, from many people. We need others' perspectives. If you will do this, Lord Templeton, we'll be very grateful."

Gratitude was pitiful compensation for what he gave her.

Oh, Lord, Lord. In front of all those girls, he drew her about, put his hands on her shoulders, down her spine, around her waist, at the arc of her hips. She swallowed while he positioned her.

Was it her imagination—or her desire—that screamed at her how tender he was, how precise, how restrained?

It really didn't matter.

She really didn't care.

Answers, analysis, seemed irrelevant compared to the glorious heat of him so near.

And then, after he handled almost every part of her, he placed himself behind her, swung the bow before her—and pressed every inch of that rock-hard body of his against hers.

In the interest of higher learning, she could not move.

"Now place your legs like this, sufficient to become your brace," he instructed the girls, while his lips came so close to her temple that his hot breath warmed her mind. "Hoist her hem a bit will you, Ann, so that the girls can see how Miss Curtis's legs are positioned. . . . Thank you. Now, in this way you have anchored yourself to put your power into the tug of the string." He had his hands over hers. On the wood of the bow. On the pull of the string. On the thump of her heart.

She could not draw air, let alone the damned silk string.

She could have sworn she felt him quiver. Against her back, it was like feeling a volcano rumble.

"The resistance of the bow"—he cleared his throat and shifted mightily against her derriere—"stores energy. Compelling you to snap away. But you must not. You must instead learn to use it to your own purpose. Release it for your good. Like so much else in life," he crooned into Jess's ear in a caress of sound.

"The tension that exists," he went on, while she sensed that her body betrayed her and fused to his, "is the means by which you put force into the arrow. Perhaps you need to build strength in your hands and arms to handle the weight of it. Do what you must. The rewards will be infinite. You'll feel in command. You need then only focus your sight to hit your target. Nothing is so rewarding as working for success in a measured way. Don't you think so, Miss Curtis?" He had turned his lips for the briefest of seconds to her skin.

"Yes," she thought she said. "Oh, definitely."

"And so let's try an arrow to the mark, shall we?"

Again she'd felt the massive persuasion of his body. He accepted an arrow, nocked it against the pass, teased her fingers and her arms and her backbone with his lure and his strength. He extended his left arm, drew her right arm back to the comfortable limit, and whispered for her alone, "Let's aim for the heart of it, darling. *Now!*"

In synchrony, their bodies did their will. Loosed, the arrow arced in a clean, smooth trajectory. Watching, she and Rand stood like a duo done in stone.

As the arrow thunked into the hay at the very center of the cloth target, Rand moved against her. "Didn't you believe we'd hit it right?" he asked, his voice a rasp.

"Oh, I wanted to."

The girls danced about, ecstatic and eager to try it. Though a few of the older students asked enough questions to show that they may have wished Lord Templeton would demonstrate his skills as closely with them, he did not.

Perfect gentleman that he was, he kept his distance while he used words to instruct them—and his gaze ate up Jess's every movement.

She scolded him with eyes alone, but when she had the chance to step aside, she said, "You're very good."

"My pleasure to assist you, my lady."

His implications had her perspiring.

He turned to Amanda. The fact that she drew Lord Templeton's attention meant that the other girls, to interest him, had to humor her.

Jess frowned. It might not have been the best means to get the other students to include Amanda in their camaraderie, but Jess would take what she could and build on it, however possible.

By the time they had finished their hour's lesson, Amanda had gained a few more friends than she'd had when they started.

Jess breathed a sigh of relief as they gathered up their bows and quivers, then headed for Farrell Hall.

Rand strode with her. "That little lesson helped move affairs in the right direction."

"Rand—" She meant to warn him away from any closer relationship. But how to do it with these students around? "I appreciate your taking time to instruct the girls in archery and Amanda in piano, but—"

"You're not going to admit you liked what we did. We'll have to try another sport." He chuckled at her shocked eyes, and clarified, "Tsk, tsk. I *meant* you need instruction in other games. Perhaps . . . fencing?"

"Yes! But not with you, sir."

"Why not? Your guard is already up."

"But you parry too well"—she glanced about at the students—"for me to engage you."

"You are now, and you're grinning at me in the bargain."

She shook back her hair and looked at the blue sky. "Why can't I resist your banter?"

"Because you've never laughed with a man."

She gazed at him.

"As I thought. And you never wanted to kiss one—again."

"Rand." It was a plea to stop teasing her.

"Very well. I've often admired Black Jack Farrell's famous gun collection in the front hall. I itch to take those pistols out for a trial. I'll bet they haven't been fired in years. They should be used to keep them at top performance. In addition, something tells me you'd love to practice aiming."

"At your heart?" she countered, too fast.

"You already have, darling. You blasted a hole in me before I knew what hit me."

She gloried, she despaired. She fell back on some middling comment. "You don't seem disabled."

"That totally depends on what you're viewing," he added with ardor. "So what do you say? Can we take down that brace of Beretta flintlocks from the gun case? I need to feel my hands around something strong and purposeful when I'm with you. If it can't be you, then—"

"No, it can't." She thought she sounded odd. Rather like a forest animal in a trap. She knew she had to end this with some severe remark. She found it, God help her, and it was not difficult to be honest about it, either. The truth was as appalling as her memory of the one time she had used a pistol. "I am a terrible shot."

"Good. I'll take joy in teaching you how to improve."

"I cannot bear to pick one up. I don't hunt for sport or play with guns."

"Jess, sweetheart." He frowned. "I didn't mean I would use them for anything other than target practice. I don't hunt, either. Nor do I ride to hounds. Such pastimes are violent, and I'm not."

"Believe me, Rand, *that* I know. But I don't take down those pistols, or even Black Jack's field rifles. No firearms. Ever."

She walked ahead of him then, with fear nipping at her heels. Fear of discovery of her secrets about a mother who loved too much too late, and a father who loved his wife too little—and killed her.

"Pruning roses is more than an art." Jess smiled down at her two rapt pupils holding their small shears. "It's a necessity. A bush untamed, like this one, grows in all directions, flowering often but with small buds for its efforts."

She cupped two tiny examples in her fingers to show them while strains of Mozart floated out to the garden from the music room.

This morning—the fifth Rand had come here since the night he brought Amanda home—Jess noted with bristling pleasure that the child's playing flowed a little more smoothly than it had yesterday or the day before. In fact, each morning confirmed what she had hoped—that Rand Templeton knew the way to open Amanda Emory's mind to the music that once had brought her so much fulfillment.

Together, they played duets in ways that struck their fancy—two-fingered children's ditties, an irreverent rendition of "God Save the Queen," or a polka that Rand turned into a hand-clapping game.

Jess heard the best results, though, in the sound of Amanda's laughter as it trilled upon the morning breeze. She recognized it in the more frequent lilt of the child's voice as it mixed with the deeper bass of the man's. She'd noted it—and admired their mutual gaiety.

Or to be precise, she envied Amanda her company.

Rand brought the child companionship, arriving each morning as promised. Since Amanda had not at first committed herself solely to playing the piano with him, Rand would come dressed casually in some outfit appropriate to the pursuit Amanda had named the day before. Riding, playing croquet, even fishing in the river, he amused Amanda and her friends. For propriety's sake, Jess always sent along a female instructor or two; they always returned from the day's outings agog over the marquess of Ashford.

And Jess grew hungry to go on the excursions, and admitted to herself she wanted to share them with no one but Rand.

In less than a week he became stuck in her mind like a note she could not forget. Whether he was chuckling in her music room or persuading Dahlia to walk a little faster along the pony track for Amanda or appearing on the archery range, he fascinated Jess. And she knew she was right to evade him.

She dropped her flower and squeezed her eyes shut. *As for you, old girl, you'll busy yourself with other occupations. You'll teach this little botany lesson and archery and music, but you will not—you* must *not—even think of going near Rand Templeton.*

Her fingers took up another rose and brushed the petals. Satin velvet that they were, they reminded her of Rand's lips.

She snatched her hand away and swallowed the lump in her throat. She gazed at her students and spoke of horticulture.

"Flowers that enjoy adequate sun and nutritious soil can flourish beautifully, as you see here. But, like humans"—Jess nodded at her two pupils—"they need direction, shaping, help defining their urges and identifying their talents."

"So that's why children must go to school," offered Belle, one of her precocious charges. Grinning, minus a front tooth, she elbowed her friend. "We know that, Miss Curtis."

"That's a very good insight, Belle."

"Like Bones's urge to point." The second child, Ann, giggled and inclined her head in the direction of the aged black canine. As if on cue, he rose from his crouch to balance, lift a foreleg, and extend his nose toward a courageous robin who perched on the back of a garden bench.

"Bones's urge is what we call instinct."

"How is an instinct different from an urge?" chirped Belle.

"Instinct is behavior that . . . animals can't control." *Like the way I reacted to Rand's comfort . . . and kisses.* "There are things we do, actions we take, which we don't think about." *Which we feel compelled to do. Like hug a man in thanks. Or kiss him beyond propriety.*

"That sounds scary," said Belle as she made wide ghastly eyes and curved her fingers like talons at her classmate. "I could do mad things, like Frankenstein's monster, and blame it on instinct."

Ann chuckled. "Not *you!* You're too scared of what your mother would say."

Belle sniffed, indignant. "I just might." She crossed her arms. "I could surprise you. Every one of you."

Jess smiled compassionately at Belle and wiser Ann. "Instincts often startle us." Wasn't that the God's truth?

"How?" pressed Ann.

"They come upon us without thinking. They simply . . . exist. Sometimes we never see them, don't have any way to know they're there until the right circumstances come along and then . . ." *You're in a certain man's arms and the solidity of his chest feels like rock-hard shelter and the words he utters taste like strong Burgundy. He's crooning to you and you're lost in the mist of his voice and the fog in your brain can't match the storm in your body. He's caressing you, and you've forgotten time, place, decorum. You know only that you can't stop kissing him because, somehow, this feels so right.*

"Miss Curtis?" Ann was tugging her sleeve.

"Hmm? What, dear?"

Ann's hazel eyes twinkled. "You've gone off again, Miss Curtis." She squinted at Jess. "Are you certain you're well? You've been doing this for days."

"Have I?"

Ann frowned as ten-year-olds were wont to do when adults seemed blockheaded. "Ever since Amanda came back, but especially today."

"Really?" That noticeable, was it?

Two pairs of youthful brows rose in unison.

"Yes, ma'am," murmured Belle.

"Are you worried about her?" asked Ann with a sidelong glance across the garden to the music room doors and back, which told Jess that this child was too shrewd for her years.

"Not as much as I was. She seems to be recovering more quickly now."

"You mean she's happier since Lord Templeton began coming every morning to tutor her on the piano, and in all those other activities."

"I'm very pleased with Amanda's progress. She's smiling. She's even giggling, like you two."

"She plays better," said Belle in a grudging tone. "I wish *I* could. My father would let me come home more often." She hung her head, but not before Jess noted a twitch of her nose, which meant tears were in her eyes.

"Perhaps, then," came a decidedly bass voice from the music room doors, "I can bring you inside for a few minutes of practice each morning after I finish with Amanda."

Jess looked up into the kind expression of Rand Templeton. How long had it been since she'd had the elixir of his company? A day? Eternity?

Ann smiled.

Belle squealed and jumped up. "Would you?"

He nodded and then turned his gaze on Jess. He resurrected memories of bows and arrows, sweet embraces, and hot kisses to her hands, her lips, her breasts. Though she had spent hours each night since then scolding herself and schooling herself to behave nonchalantly when next they met, she failed to follow her own instructions.

Her heart slammed about in her chest.

"I'll do it if Miss Curtis approves." Jess focused on the way his mouth formed words and the way they scattered her resolution to stay away from him. As if he knew the power of his enchantment, his mouth curved up in satisfaction. "She's thinking," he told the girls softly, his blue eyes never straying.

"Miss Curtis?" Belle pressed. "May I? I might never be as good as Amanda, but my father wouldn't care to have a famous pianist or a composer in the family. He'd just know I was better than before. Good enough to play in the drawing room for company. May I? *Please?*"

Amanda, who had stood beyond Rand, out of Jess's range of vision, stepped forward. "We could go and let Miss Curtis decide." She held out her hands to the two younger girls and grinned at Jess.

Jess could only gape at Amanda leading the others away.

"Surprised?" Rand strolled forward and sat on the garden bench. With the sun behind him, Jess viewed his silhouette, the gloss to his black hair and the noble shape of his head. This way it was so much easier to face him, possible to continue the convenient pretense that nothing had happened between them. But he turned and slid an arm along the back of the bench as if he expected her to sit next to him.

In this light, she could see every reason why he made her body ache at his sight, with his touch. She let her eyes do what she dared not allow her hands: she admired his bronzed face, with those perfect white teeth between firm lips.

She licked her own. "Yes. Astounded."

His mouth spread in mirth, which she could bet had nothing to do with the child they supposedly discussed.

"I'm amazed at Amanda," Jess rushed in with an explanation before he could deduce otherwise. "She not only plays the piano but she takes the initiative as well."

He hummed in agreement. "Perceptive of her, wasn't it, to take the girls off while we talked?" Before Jess had a chance to answer, he added, "She knows we have other things to discuss besides Belle's music lessons."

"How could she know that?" Jess blurted before she realized she'd tacitly agreed with him.

"She told me."

Confused, Jess shook her head. "What could she say?"

"What she feels. She has seen us together—and

apart. She says you watch for me at the window in the mornings, but when I arrive, you tell Pool to inform me you are not available. *Again.*"

She sank to her knees, dropped her pruning shears into her garden basket, and began gathering her thoughts to respond to him.

He moved forward, his elbows on his thighs, and confronted her with a knowing look. "I suspected you were avoiding me. That's why sometimes I arrive when you least expect me—like the other day during the archery lesson."

Even at this distance, her head swam with the smell of his light cologne. To break the magnetic power of his eyes, she whisked off her gardener's gloves. "I apologize if I seem rude, but I have so much to do that—"

"You have nothing to fear from me." It was a whisper.

"No?" She dragged a hand through her hair.

He captured it. "Jess, I'm afraid, too. Developing a relationship can be as exhilarating as it is detrimental to one's routine—and destructive to one's defenses to intimacy."

His confession flushed her skin, jolted her nerves. She scowled at their entwined fingers, hers white-knuckled and his as beseeching as his words.

"But, Jess, I am less frightened when I'm with you. The pleasure of your company overwhelms any objection."

She tried to tug her hand away. "How can you say that when what we've done is . . ." She almost said the one word that expressed it best: "sexual."

"Hold hands? Embrace? Kiss."

"Oh, Rand, what happened the other night in the hall and that day on the archery field occurred when I wasn't thinking."

"That day, I planned. The other night your defenses were down. You acted on instinct." He smiled sadly. "You're embarrassed again. I thought we had dealt with that. But it's back, which means it's much more important than I assumed."

"Don't assume its embarrassment. I'm not an ordinary woman. Not interested in beaux and cotillions and kisses."

"No," he said as if he'd just discovered she was right. "But you should be."

"I'm not *made* like other women."

He crossed his arms and sat back to send his eyes down her form in a journey that told her he was searching familiar territory for hidden secrets. "I agree," he finally said, then reached out to draw her up, but she would not move. "Come sit with me. We need to talk about why you're not like others—and why you are so extraordinary to me."

"I am *not* extraordinary! I'm *different*. I'm twenty-four years old. A spinster. An old maid." She watched his brows shoot up. "I *am!* I am in charge of this school, these girls. I have responsibilities to them and their parents, to Cat and Spence. To the board of directors. I don't have *time* for a love affair!"

Horrified, she worked at words. Only the two that astounded her made her gulp: "love affair." *My God, what a thing to say. She could never have an affair. If she did, she'd be acting like her mother.*

"I'll adapt to your constraints." He examined her

briefly but thoroughly. "We'll not talk about our friendship directly. We'll focus on Amanda, for one thing. Belle, for another."

He was rushing ahead, confusing her. Mixing what she wanted from him—tutoring of her students—with what she shouldn't want. Courting her. Her brain hadn't been so scrambled by anything or anyone in years. "Amanda's doing better than I ever expected. Belle can take lessons with you, if you feel you have the time, but—"

"I'll make time."

"I don't want you to neglect your own work."

"Who says I am?"

"You are a busy man. Tutoring must take an enormous chunk out of your day, since you come here when you can't expect any reward."

"I have my reward." He finally succeeded in tugging her to her feet, and she landed on the bench beside him. Either that or fall flat on her face like a floundering fish. "I come here hoping to see you each day."

He held both her wrists, but she could only blink back frustration as she gazed at them. "Rand, don't do this."

"Don't do what? Be honest with you?"

"Yes, do be honest, but there is no need to be . . . kind."

"You don't merit compliments? Interesting."

"You know what I mean!"

"Explain it to me."

"Teach the girls, but don't expect to see me when you come here. I won't be available."

He clamped both of her wrists in one viselike hand and lifted her chin with the other. The act brought her gaze to his, the very contact she had feared.

Rightly so, too. His eyes and his mouth were far richer than her pallid recollections of him. "Afraid that you'll forget yourself again? Touch me, crave me, find yourself embracing me with your body and your hope? Yes, it's as I thought. But you needn't worry, Jess. I don't force myself on unwilling women."

Though she suspected some subtlety in his words, she saw truth in his expression. "Good. That's settled." She stood.

He let her go easily. Too easily. It niggled at her as she faced him with a look she tried to make purely friendly. "Return any time."

"Never doubt it. Each morning, till you see what I see."

Warning bells rang in her ears. "What do you mean?"

"You're not unwilling, darling Jess. You just think you are." She gasped, but he held up a palm. "I'm not going to deny this attraction, and I won't let you deny it, either. You're an intelligent woman and old enough, despite the fact that you are innocent of men—"

"Rand!" She would end his interest once and for all. *"I am* not *innocent!"*

His chiseled features turned to marble. The minute became an eternity during which she wondered how she could have been so unthinking as to reveal this crucial evidence of her singularity.

Meanwhile, Rand dealt with the blow—first as shock, then as outrage, and finally as protectiveness, as he concluded, "The experience made you fear a man's touch."

"I *do,* but not because I've been to bed and hated it!"

Relief diluted his horror to grimness. "But whatever happened with that man prejudices you against any relationship with another."

"Yes, but not like you think. It was my father who hurt my mother and who tried to— Oh, God," she groaned and clamped a hand over her mouth. "I *do not* talk about this."

"I am not asking you to. You'll tell me when you're ready."

"No, *never,"* she groaned, like an animal writhing in a trap. "If I speak of this, I defy every rule I've ever made for myself, revealing facts—" Things no one knew about how her mother died and how her father killed her. Arguments she had instructed herself she'd never think of again. Brutalities she'd never described to Cat or to her sweet aunt Mary, who'd nurtured her and brought her up from the abyss of her sorrows. "Reasons too terrible to utter. Painful issues from the past which you cannot change and I cannot forget."

"I repeat: I won't ask. I see what you are, Jessica Curtis. I know inside who you are, sweetheart. A knowledge like that comes along once in a lifetime, if a person is very fortunate. I am—and I am not going to disappear."

"I wish you would."

"You might gain relief but no peace. Not now. We've gone too far. We have shared caresses and wonderful kisses."

She pressed his hand to her heart. "As a suitor, you

stir too many fantasies from their hiding places. You are very dangerous to me, Rand Templeton. I want no man to lure me from my safe existence. No man to charm me into another one."

There she might lose herself in passions, as her mother had. Elise had lost her sanity and, finally, her life for her folly. Jess had learned the bitter lesson early not to emulate her. She wasn't going to change now simply because a debonair man had turned his attention to her. How long could his interest last?

Not forever.

How long would she want it to?

For all her days.

How easy would it be to continue?

With Rand, she needed only to lean closer now to touch his cheek, taste his darling mouth and she would allow herself to savor the flavors and textures of desire.

Then, like her mother, she would know bliss, its fire and glory. Her mother had spent her good reputation and squandered her self-respect to purchase passion. Her life had become consumed by frustration, sadness, the loss of her self.

Jess would not do that! She would only find herself still alone, but floating in a spiritual vacuum, minus her self-respect and her integrity.

"Jess, I see what I do to you." He pressed one hand more firmly to her pounding heart and circled the other around her waist. "I call your name and you shiver, but you hunger. I look into your eyes and you tremble, but you admire me. I touch you and you quake, but you want me even more. And you can't help yourself."

She wanted to cry like a schoolgirl, run away, kiss him.

"But, Jess, do you know what else is happening?"

Bereft of words, she shook her head as tears gathered.

"You do the same thing to me, sweetheart."

That speared her, and she tore herself up and away.

She'd taken only two steps when he rose and caught her so easily she wondered why she'd even tried to escape him. He pressed her back along his torso and his long legs. His hands spanned her ribs while his voice strummed her heartstrings.

"You're looking at your reasons to flee from me, from us. Fix your sight instead on those joys your soul desires. You'll soon find that the delights surpass the need for comfort. I shall come back each morning to watch you marvel at how this is happening to you. At how you accept me in spite of whatever your father did to make you reject a relationship with a man. Whatever lesson he taught you about how men treat women is not one I've learned. My father worshiped my mother. She loved him without reservation. I've always wanted the same kind of lasting relationship. I have desired a woman I could admire and adore. I never found such a person. Until a week ago." Gently, he nuzzled her hair.

"Sweet Jessie, delicate as jessamine, fragile as a flower. Your instinct shows you care for me." His fingers stroked circles beneath her breasts as his voice dived lower. "You cannot ignore it or stop it. Can't change it or reason it away. It's fruitless to try. Give yourself over and treasure what follows." She could feel him smile as he whispered, "God knows, I am."

He brushed his nose along the tendrils at the side of her face while nestling his body along the contours of her back from shoulders to hips to thighs. Moving one leg forward, he forced her body to curve backward. She felt his rigid male reaction to her, and instead of being startled, she bowed her head in anguish while she reveled in his declaration of how much he cared for her. Dropping his hands, he stood there for an eternal second as she braced his hips. Decadent and delicious as the pose was, she took what pleasure she was offered: she undulated against every masculine muscle.

"Good-bye," he said with sorrow. "I'll see Amanda tomorrow at nine and Belle at ten. But I want to take tea with you at eleven every day. Offer it to me, Jess, to be polite because you owe me a favor for helping Amanda and Belle. Serve tea because it will grant you time to satisfy your curiosity about this desire that scares you half to death but feels so damn right."

He turned her to face him and brushed her mouth with three fingers. "Give it to me, Jess, because you want to. Because I am safe to enjoy."

Chapter Six

THE MONKEY IN SHORT PANTS LEFT THE ARM OF THE settee to climb upon Rand's broad shoulder. The cat, Precious, who had only this morning introduced herself to Rand, draped herself along the back of the settee and hissed at the monkey. The simian bared his teeth in a grin, then chose another route across the man's lap to his other shoulder. There Darwin settled down to run his bony fingers through the man's hair.

Jess coughed to suppress her laughter.

Rand reprimanded her with his dashing smile.

"More tea, my lord?" Amanda offered, pot raised, as they sat in the music room.

"No, thank you, my dear. I've had quite enough." He set his cup and saucer on the table before him as Belle plunked herself down next to him.

"Do you like animals, sir?"

"Of course. Why would you wonder?" Rand rolled his eyes at her playfully. Meanwhile, the cat rubbed her head against one side of his neck as the curious macaque talked to himself about the shape of a human ear and the loop of the odd creature's cravat, both of which he manipulated without delicacy.

"Pardon me, sir, but you seem to grimace often with these three about."

"We must face the facts of life, Belle. Bones is no trouble because he is so old and must have his sleep. His only activity is to point too often at nothing or graze an ankle or two for no reason." He wiggled his left foot, on which Bones dozed and which the canine occasionally liked to nip in morning greeting. "Precious," he glanced sideways at the white angora who lounged like a princess over his body, "does precious little."

"Except shed white hairs on your coat and trousers." The child snickered. She and Amanda cast meaningful glances at his coat, which he had removed after their piano lessons—and before the cat could do worse damage than she had.

"Darwin, however"—Rand made a face at the animal, who was now picking through his waistcoat pockets—"is a little monkey, all right. He's inquisitive—and he tickles."

Jess stifled a snort. "He finds you fascinating." *Smart monkey.* "But he likes timepieces, especially softly ticking ones like yours."

"He thinks the gold is pretty, and he likes to wind the stem." Rand extracted the piece from the monkey's eager grasp. "Too much." He put the watch to his ear to listen and shook his head as he returned it to his pocket. "Darwin can't tell time."

"How do you know?" Jess loved teasing him during

morning tea, which in the past week had become a habit. "He may have a way of understanding it from how the sun moves across the sky, or how it enters this room."

"He's aptly named if he understands progress. I wonder if he sees it in any of us?" He smiled at Amanda and Belle, who hastened to say they hoped so.

Jess glanced at the teapot, aware of Rand's double meaning. He meant the journey of their own relationship, which after two weeks, had traveled like lightning past acquaintance to camaraderie—and enchantment. The banter of the students plus the antics of the animals gave these morning visits a carefree gaiety, sweetened often by Rand's implications about their relationship. Their discussions also heightened her desire for more substantive talks, and her curiosity about his past mounted. In particular, Jess wished to learn how a man could care for a woman deeply, mourn her death for three long years, and yet not admire her. But no opportunity for such an intimate conversation had presented itself in the past few days. Instead, she gave herself to enjoying their tea. "Darwin likes the company, too."

"He's not alone." Rand spoke to Amanda and Belle, but Jess thrilled at his words and beamed at him.

Amanda glanced from one adult to the other. "Well, I must be off to the stables to check on Dahlia before my afternoon classes. She has not been eating much lately. Will we expect you tomorrow, my lord?"

"Yes." Rand shifted his attention to Jess. "At nine o'clock."

Belle stood, too. "I guess I'll go. For my French class, you know. Mademoiselle Dumont likes us to be prompt. Good day, sir. Miss Curtis."

The two girls backed out the door.

Bones groaned loudly as he got to his feet and stretched all fours.

Jess hated to see Rand go and tried not to show it by acting as if this were simply a neighborly visit. "I know you must have work to do."

"Some, yes. I'll catch up later in the day. The country fair opens on Friday in Ashford. Have you thought of taking the students—say, on Saturday afternoon after their riding classes? It would be fun and something different for them. I'd be happy to escort you and any of the girls who'd care to go."

A smile broke over her face. "It sounds—"

"Delightful!" He hit his knees with both hands and rose in the same motion, sending the monkey into chatters and the cat into a sniff. "I'll bring around my carriage and two wagons at ten o'clock. With my vehicles plus yours, we should be able to transport quite a few girls, don't you think?"

Darwin muttered his disapproval that the man he'd been inspecting was departing long before he'd finished with him.

Jess chuckled at the animal. "He's never satisfied."

"He's not the only one," Rand grumbled as he made for the side chair where he'd left his jacket.

"If you're hungry, I can have Cook make other things for tomorrow morning's tea. Perhaps more of those currant scones you like or a jam tart, hmmm?"

Rand grimaced. "Cook can't serve what I want, and

well you know it. On Friday I thought we'd go to the fair, then perhaps you'd attend a charity function at the guildhall with me next week. What do you say?"

With his invitation, Jess knew Rand was trying to convert their friendship into a courtship that others would witness. Social rules permitted an unmarried man and woman who were neighbors and friends to take tea each morning together in the presence of others. That their witnesses were students and animals made the meetings seem innocent to her. But she wondered what others might think and say. She abhorred the idea that rumors might begin about her, as they had about her mother when she engaged in affairs.

"Why are you frowning?" Rand drew near but went very still. "It's perfectly acceptable for us to go to the fair together and take the girls."

"I was thinking of my mother."

He trailed a finger down her cheek. "Why is that? Did she like fairs . . . or do you still miss her?"

"Yes, she did like to go to plays and fairs, and to the symphony, too. But grieve for her? No. I have come to terms with her death." *If not the way she died.*

"I want to see you laugh, Jess, and I want you to do it with me."

"That happens more often whenever I'm with you."

"Jess," he whispered and stepped near, she was certain, to kiss her.

The hall door flew open and banged against the wall.

"*There* you are!" yelled a huge man, his meaty face

mottled, his top hat wobbling precariously. He brandished a dark walking stick like a spear as he stalked toward Jess.

Jess's vision went to red as she stood rooted to the spot.

In a crimson haze, she raised her sight to the long black cane, which looked so like one her father had used to beat her mother.

The room blurred with motion. Bones scrambled on the carpet to get a hold on the man's leg. Darwin screeched and sprang for the giant. Rand had the interloper by both arms. The man's cane clattered to the floor, as he wheezed, "Turn me loose!"

Big as the intruder was, Rand matched him. Stronger, more muscular than his fleshy opponent, Randall Templeton halted his advance, though the man struggled desperately to get free.

Jess's eyes glazed over as she looked past the man to the hallway, and the guns she hated—and avoided.

You could use one. To defend yourself. You could load it. Lock it. Point it . . . like that other time, when you aimed it at Papa.

No, came the other part of her. *Never again will you take up a pistol.*

She stepped forward. "Rand, this is Lord Harrison Emory, Amanda's father. You may let him go."

Pool, who stood behind Rand with an umbrella hoisted like a club, yelled loud enough to be heard in Drury Lane. "My lady, I don't think that would be wise! He was cursing when I opened the door! Amanda couldn't stop him. Why do you think *you* can?"

Amanda slowly came around the butler. "Please let

him go, Lord Templeton. My father's not a bad man. I've never seen him act like this. Honestly, Miss Curtis."

Jess swung her attention to Amanda. Tears dribbled down her cheeks while her tone and cadence expressed her fright as she pleaded for leniency for her father. Jess rejoiced at these additional indications of Amanda's recovery.

Meanwhile, Rand waited for Emory to stop fuming.

"It's all right, Rand," Jess reassured him. "Lord Emory and I can have a civilized discussion. We have done so before."

Rand's stormy blue eyes narrowed on hers as if to ask if she was certain.

She nodded.

"I'm not leaving," Rand bit off and slowly, reluctantly, released Emory.

The animals took their cue from Rand and, one by one, disengaged. The cat resumed her nap on the settee. The monkey retrieved the man's hat and escaped to the piano bench with it, turning it around and around like a worried little man. Bones, who had managed to get a mouthful of ankle in black serge, smacked his jaws together in testament to his distaste for Emory's choice of fabric. But he did not leave Jess, only sat down, a sentry frowning at the man who'd trespassed into his mistress's territory.

Pool was an entirely different matter. Crossing his arms, he guarded the exit. Yet Jess knew that someone of Harrison Emory's sensitivities would prefer not to have a servant present during a personal discussion. She caught her butler's eye. Pool relented, muttering his displeasure as he left.

Emory rubbed his injured leg and shifted inside his collar. He reclaimed the rest of his dignity by straightening his waistcoat and yanking at his shirt cuffs. Avoiding the others, he went to the garden doors, contemplated the scenery for a minute, and then turned. His face was florid, but his expression was devoid of emotion as he considered Rand, Amanda, and finally Jess.

"Lord Emory." Jess heard the solemnity of her own voice and realized how forceful she sounded. To her amazement, she *felt* strong, which was surprising, given the way the man had entered the room. "I resent the intrusion and in such a manner. Had you asked, sir, I would gladly have seen you."

"Lady Curtis, I am not ill-mannered . . . usually. I . . . I was undone when I read your letter to me about Amanda's disappearance."

"But I wrote to you days ago." Jess wondered why he had become so irate more than a week after the event. "I followed the first letter with a second to tell you she was safe. Did you read that one, too?"

"Yes," he said quietly.

She walked closer and caught the smell of cigars and liquor on his rumpled clothes. "I assumed you had simply read them ages ago and understood that we had found her well."

"I was still taken aback when I learned of her escapade. Imagine my surprise when I returned to London from my lodge in Berwick to learn that Amanda had acted so foolishly."

"If you had informed me of where you were, Lord Emory, I would have written you there."

"I don't always know where I'm going or when. The moods come upon me because I am . . . lost without my wife. I go to Berwick often without planning or giving notice to anyone. It's a place I seek out frequently, especially since . . . last June." His pale eyes drifted to his daughter. "I am sorry, sweetheart." He opened his arms to her.

Amanda went into them in a rush. He scooped her up and clasped her close, his eyes squeezed tightly shut. Then he lowered her to her feet and took her face between his big hands. "You were bad to leave here. I suppose most of Kent knows by now, and you and I are a laughingstock. You must not do such things. You make us appear an odd sort of family, and I am certain you had Miss Curtis worried. I hope you've been properly punished."

Jess winced. "Lord Emory, I didn't think any discipline—"

"What? She ran away, madam! She was *irresponsible.* Just like her mother, who took it into her head to leave anytime she fancied . . ." He realized what he'd said too late and tried to cover his traces. "I *mean* Amanda is a child who must be shown the correct way to comport herself. That's one reason why I brought her here to you. The second reason is that you said you had suffered a head injury yourself and you could help her, understand her! I had other solutions available to me—"

Oh, yes. An asylum for the insane. Of which Amanda knew nothing because Jess herself had begged Emory not to commit her there, but to give the child an opportunity to recover with her at Farrell

Hall. "Such an institution as you described to me would not have helped Amanda recover her intellectual, emotional, or physical well-being."

"Well, I don't think this little jaunt of hers means that *you* know how to aid her. She's worse than before!"

Jess had no idea what Emory's problem was with his wife, but some of Amanda's physical and emotional challenges she did understand. "I assure you Amanda did not run from us voluntarily!"

"She was not forced. She was impetuous. Failing to discipline herself!"

"She couldn't!"

"Then she must learn, Miss Curtis."

"She will. Give her time to heal."

"It's been almost ten months since her accident. I despair that she is capable of acting normally. From what we have seen, she can tie her shoes, read, write, but she cannot control her actions. What kind of recovery is that? She still does not even remember how her mother died!"

Jess began to see red again. That he would speak like this in front of his daughter fired Jess's protective nature. But she spoke more calmly than she felt.

"Sir, she may never do that. I told you before that recollection of her fall and her mother's death is not necessary to her coming to terms with her mother's passing. Look at her now. She's crying. She feels bad for you. She has recuperated so well, gaining many of her physical abilities and her intellectual ones."

"Those things are important," Emory hurled back at her, "but I am outraged that I have not heard

Amanda say she misses her mother nor have I seen her cry over her loss."

"Amanda will mourn her mother, Lord Emory,' Jess stated, wondering if the man wanted his daughter to grieve for her own catharsis or his. Evidently the Emorys' marriage had problems to which Amanda's father had not yet reconciled himself. "This constant harping on it won't make it happen any sooner. In her own time and place, Amanda will cry."

"Wonderful to hear you predict that," he told her sarcastically. "While we await the day, I repeat that Amanda must take responsibility for her disappearance. She ran away. Wayward souls must pay for their transgressions!"

"She *has* paid."

"How? Did you send her to her room? Put her on bread and water? I want to know!"

His tirade made Jess even more calm. "She has had correction."

"Oh, I know," he said dryly, "you both *talked.*"

"No. Amanda did. About her life with you and her mother before her accident."

Fear flashed across Emory's features, but Jess gave him no time to recover, nor did she allow herself a second to ponder the cause of his fear. "Discipline is what any person imposes on him- or herself. Amanda understands that and will attempt to control her actions when next she meets the same set of circumstances. Even if I believed in corporal punishment, which I don't, it would do Amanda no good. Her condition, my lord, requires tolerance and circumspection on our part. Remember what I wrote to you in my letter, sir: Amanda did not run from us *willingly.*"

"I care little for analysis and doctors' prattle! What good did they do for my wife, eh? She was very ill. Extremely so. The quacks could only hang about, pontificate to me, and shake their heads. They could not help her. Now you stand there and tell me that this child of mine acts in the same irresponsible manner? Without will?" he asked, incredulous. "How *does* one act, then? Totally at the request of some puppetmaster?"

Rand was seething, but Jess was quicker to respond with the answers because she had lived them. "The strings of our mind are many and interconnected, Lord Emory. Your daughter has had a head injury, not a moral crisis. The threads of her conscious and unconscious mind have been frayed, cut, and perhaps snarled in new ways that none of us understand—*yet.* Amanda ran from us because she felt compelled to flee an uncomfortable set of circumstances—a memory, sir. Of her mother. Long before that lady's accident."

Emory's blotchy complexion blanched. He flinched. To be reprimanded by a woman in front of his daughter and another man who was his superior in nobility brought embarrassment. But Jess didn't care about his dignity. Emory had already sacrificed that.

He thought he could recapture it, and so he puffed himself up, then speared his daughter with his bright scrutiny. "Is this true? What kind of memory?"

"Well, Papa, I . . ." Amanda didn't shrink from her father, but neither did she have an explanation that alleviated any of her confusion. "I recall little, only Lord Templeton playing the piano and—"

"Templeton!" Emory pinned his attention on the man who stood so solidly beside Jess. She sensed Emory's coming attack, if not its nature or cause. "*Why,* sir, are you here at a girls' school playing the piano?"

Rand set his jaw so hard that Jess could see his muscles flex at the implication in the man's words.

Jess put a hand on Rand's arm before he could utter words that might end this interview on some dueling field.

She swung her gaze to Emory, hardly concealing her outrage at Emory's scandalous suggestion. "I asked the marquess of Ashford to come here. His talent at the piano is renowned. I thought his expertise might benefit your daughter, and I am pleased to report that after nine days of his lessons, Amanda is more physically agile at the keyboard and more emotionally facile as well. Her tears and her happiness during this audience with you this morning illustrate that admirably."

Emory mulled that over and shot an inquisitive glance at Rand. "I see. I must thank you, then, if this is true. Forgive me, my lord," he said flatly. "I am concerned about my daughter."

Rand had not moved, but his eyes became shards of blue glass. "Love does not justify your behavior, Emory. You may explain it away, but the act stands as an example for your daughter."

Jess felt her heart pause. No child of Rand's would ever see him as Amanda had seen her parent. Nor would Rand's offspring ever have occasion to question his honor. Further, no wife of his would ever have cause to question his veracity—nor would she witness his loss of integrity.

Rand cocked his head, examining her serene expression in the midst of this confrontation.

Emory had other priorities. "I can make amends to Amanda, can't I, my pet?" he was asking his child, with a silkiness to his voice that made Jess's skin crawl.

The girl nodded as she threw her arms about his neck and planted a huge kiss on his cheek. "Oh, of course, Papa." She faced Jess, her eyes bright with expectation. "Do you think I should show him?"

"Certainly."

Jess watched the girl take her father by the hand and lead him to a Chippendale chair near the piano. With a smile wreathing her face and growing more glorious with expectation, she patted his knee and left him. She arranged the bench, sat down, adjusted her arms and shoulders, then positioned her hands.

She paused, her eyes closed.

When she opened them again she was playing.

She took Jess's breath away. With great dexterity, with honest passion, with sublime delight, she played the Moonlight Sonata, the very piece that had caused Jess to remember too much of her own girlhood that morning nine days ago.

Perspiration formed on Jess's brow. Her corset cut off her air. The music floated about the room like old ghosts swaying to the rhythm, chanting a dirge to their buried past.

She bit her lip. Jammed her hand in her pocket for her handkerchief, which she pressed to her forehead.

Amanda played on, her rendition making Jess's stomach fluids turn to bile, her vision dwindle.

Amanda was smiling, reminding Jess of . . .

Her mother. Delicate, exotic Elise Curtis, who had curved like that over the keys. Arched like that to the drama, the tempo of the notes. She had moved effortlessly as if God designed her fingers to span the keyboard and do only that till kingdom come. Her mother would shut her eyes, throw her head back, and punctuate every stroke, every crescendo, each pianissimo, as if she were undulating with her lover. . . .

Jess swallowed. Reeled.

Rand was bending over her, calling her name. She stared at him, sweet man.

The sonata ended.

But she could hear her mother, see her, *touch* her ecstasy in the music and her wildness at the loss of her hope. "Everything I have is gone!" she had shouted at Jess that morning when she announced she was leaving. "My good name, my talent, even my hope. Do you think you can come with me?" Elise had gripped her arms so viciously that Jess could feel her nails cutting her flesh as her mother shook her. "You'd be branded the same way if you followed me. I won't let you be ruined, the way they ruined me. Do you hear me?"

"Jess, do you hear me?" a thundering bass voice echoed her mother's.

"Miss Curtis looks sick," said a girl.

"Green," declared the other man.

Jess clamped her handkerchief over her mouth.

"Amanda," rasped the desperate man before her, "run and fetch Pool."

In a crush, Jess was swept up, bound by strong arms in an iron embrace, and rushed up the stairs of Farrell Hall into the room that was hers. Gentle hands propped her against her pillows, unfastened her collar and her bodice, while the rough voice murmured profanities about his fumblings with the tiny buttons.

She knew what her horror came from, why, and how. The damned sonata. She flailed on the pillow. Rand plunged his hands into her hair, in one move halting her, removing hairpins, scattering and brushing them to the floor, freeing her from any possible injury from them as she thrashed. He grasped her by the shoulders and pinned her to the sheets. Her teeth were chattering so badly that her limbs jerked.

"God above, what's wrong with you, darling?" he was exclaiming as he plucked off her shoes, felt her forehead, and spun away.

She curled up on her side, rocking.

He returned, hoisted her up, and held a glass to her mouth. "Sip this. Can you? Slowly. That's good."

He let her sink to the bedding.

But he was so far away.

"Hold me," she whispered, and without hesitation he did so. She clutched at him, pressing him closer, wanting to absorb him into her so that his goodness might fill her and drive away her fear of Elise's ghost and that of her father.

Rand reclined and molded her to him. She buried her face in his massive chest while his arms clasped her to him and one muscular leg hooked over her skirts.

Nonetheless she shuddered. "I'm cold. So cold."

"My lord?" Pool hovered over the four-poster.

"Get me tea. A warming pan. Stoke the fire. *Fast.*"

The butler dropped an afghan over them both—and then disappeared.

Rand's lips moved against her forehead, his arms stroked her back. "I'll get you better, sweetheart. I'll take care of you, trust me. Talk to me, Jess."

What was there to say? He had lived a normal life, not one impeded by a faulty brain or scandalized by a murderous father and an adulterous mother. Rand had fond memories of his parents. Such a fine man sprang from honest people, ethical human beings. He was a good man, the best man she had ever met.

Rand Templeton gave affection with both hands, hoping for, but not demanding, love in return.

Jess pulled back from his arms to consider his well-hewn face. At once she realized another truth: she was nothing like her mother!

She was stronger, with meaningful work and goals of her own. She had never sought to attract men, as Elise had sought to fill her empty days and nights with numerous affairs. Jess desired the attention of only this one man who merited her admiration.

Rand peered into her eyes. "You're coming around, thank heavens, although you're not warm enough to convince me you've recovered completely. How do I help?"

"Keep doing that," she urged him to continue his massage of her neck and back. Lassitude crept into her veins, and she moved against him, seeking more solace.

He arched away. "You look like hell. You almost fainted, and now you have recovered so quickly my head spins. Do you think you're taking a spring chill?"

"No."

"But you were sneezing the night Amanda disappeared."

"I'm over that."

"Perhaps it's back."

"It's not."

"Do you have these attacks often?"

Only when I hear that sonata. "I haven't had one in years."

"Jess, you looked the same way the other day when I played the Moonlight Sonata. If I hadn't switched to Chopin, would you have fallen apart like this? Answer me. What happened downstairs just now?"

For what he had given her, she owed him as much truth as she could bear to speak. "I hate the Moonlight Sonata."

"I know that!" he replied wryly. "What I don't know is why you are as chilled as a corpse." He pressed his lips to her temple, more in benediction than in ardor.

"Pool understands what it is. He'll be back with all manner of assistance, but the chills pass quickly." She shot Rand a look of wonder. "Never as fast as now, though."

His lips smiled, but his eyes didn't. "Then I think you must make sure to have the cure with you at all times so that when the malady strikes, you can recover." He combed hair from her cheeks. "I'm confused now. Is this affliction a result of your head injury?"

"Not directly. I . . . remember things that I have no way to deal with, because I get so frightened that my mind . . . can't dismiss them as old woes or unimportant ones. Do you understand what I mean?"

She would give him the truth in little portions, none of them palatable, but at least that way she could see if he was appalled. If he was, she could cease her tale of misery before he left her, as so many had when she was younger. When they heard whispers of her mother's behavior and her father's insane attempts to end his wife's ruinous liaisons, those who Jess had thought might be her friends had deserted her, leaving her alone. Again.

"Jess, I'm not leaving you alone until you tell me the source of this terrible chill. What kinds of things frighten you?"

"I hate the sonata because my mother adored it, abandoned herself to it and"—*the euphoria of sexual surrender*—"its power."

"Why did she do that?"

"She was very proficient at the keyboard. She might have been a concert pianist if she had been a man. But she married instead, and she played the Moonlight Sonata . . . as a kind of punishment for those of us who kept her, as she called it, 'in bondage.'"

Rand was startled. "Who was that?"

"Her father, mine . . . and me."

"She didn't like being married? Being a mother?"

"She loved me, in her way. I could ride so well and play the piano as if I were her shadow, so I was worthy of her attention. She enjoyed, I think, the leisure of being married to a man with some small measure of wealth. She reveled in giving parties, buying new clothes, and acquiring new livery for the staff, but she . . ." Jess turned her face to Rand's chest and inhaled his comforting scent.

"She what, Jess?"

"She hated 'carrying.' "

He turned to stone. "Being pregnant?"

"Yes. She was with child four or five times; I can't remember exactly how many. She wouldn't carry them to term, and she'd be very happy when it was over. She said nine months would destroy her figure. She told me so often how I had ruined her appearance that I felt guilty. As if I had planned to hurt her."

"What a thing to do to a child! And what did you do?"

"I tried to make it up to her. Please her, as children do who want to curry the favor of their mothers. I listened to her play the piano whenever she required an audience. I learned to play duets with her, often as well as she. As I grew older, vanity about her age loomed and she told me to never refer to her as Mama, but to call her by name, Elise."

"Is it an old habit, then, for you to play 'Für Elise'?"

"I don't play it to remember her, not in the way you think. I play it for myself, because I want to remember how I disliked her when she was coy, performing for guests, forgetting the beauty of the music for its ability to lure." To seduce. "And yet I loved her."

Rand stared straight through her. "It's torture to discover you love someone less than you thought you did . . . less than you should." His tragic tone struck a chord in her heart. And she wondered who fit that description. Was it that woman he had mourned so deeply?

"Yes. It's as if *you* have failed *them.*"

"You become angry at yourself. Furious at them."

Her hand went to his cheek, and she smoothed it along his skin. "This happened to you?" When he shut his eyes, she tried to console him. "Don't be angry at yourself. I'm certain you did what you could. I know you. You're too persistent. You would never disappoint anyone you loved."

A long minute passed while he examined her and then whispered, "Thank you."

She smiled, the joy he had given her these past days a gift she could attempt to return in kind. "You're very welcome."

"I'll try never to disappoint you," he murmured as if it were a vow.

If she could have managed an appropriate response, it took wing when Pool pushed the door open wider and asked, "Are we warm yet?"

Chapter Seven

"A BIRD?"

"A parrot," Rand clarified, eyes twinkling, mind applauding his victory in having lured Jess close enough to the fair tent, and to him, to take a gander at the hyacinth-colored fowl. Jess surveyed the other birds—Senegal lauries, rose cockatoos, and whack-bills—but no matter what she did, she was trapped between Rand and the canvas tent, for the moment. Finally she examined the parrot he held aloft in the steel cage.

The fat creature stuck his neck out, blinked at Jess with golden-rimmed eyes, and yelled, *"Pretty lady! Pretty lady! Take me home!"*

"Wise bird," Rand chuckled.

"Trained by a shrewd old owl." She tilted her head toward the peddler.

The bird got insulted and hopped about, repeating his entreaty in a rising cadence. People turned.

"Better do as he asks," Rand admonished.

"What if I don't like birds?"

"Take me home! Take me *home!"*

"Persistent cuss, isn't he?" Rand was nigh to choking on laughter.

Jess was flushing with all the attention from the fairgoers. "Cover him up, will you?"

"Take me home! Take me home!"

The huckster ambled forward and smiled with no front teeth. "A rare one, 'e is. From the tropics o' Brazil. 'E likes ladies, too. Fancy him, do ye, mum?"

Jess eyed Rand.

"Do you?" he asked softly.

For the past several days since her attack during the Moonlight Sonata, Jess had barely looked at him, much less come within a foot of him. Hell, he could have lost his winning reputation if he had not insisted that they come to the Kent May Fair where he could at least walk with her. But this morning when she had decided to ride in her own carriage and not with him, he'd begun to panic that he couldn't gain that which was more precious to him than her companionship—Jessica Curtis's laughter.

Vowing to win that, he decided a bird might help him immensely.

"Why would I want a parrot?" she asked him, her eyes mellow in his.

"To add to your menagerie, of course."

A streak of delight lit her face, and her fragile beauty struck him once again. "I thought I had too many animals to suit your taste," she teased.

"The ones you have keep me from you." *As do other beasts about which I know too little to help you control them.* "This creature stays in his cage, where he cannot get at me."

"Why do I need him, then?"

"He possesses an attribute I wish you'd employ more often."

She crossed her arms. "What would that be?"

Rand leaned forward, so close his hair touched the wide brim of her straw hat, so near he could smell her soap, her skin—and her fear. "He *talks.*"

She spun toward the performers' tents.

He handed the bird to the tradesman and told him he would return for it. Then he caught up with her as she waved to two of her students who stood in line to see the ventriloquist.

"This is an improvement."

"What is?"

"You're angry."

"I am not mad at you."

"Good. Well, then, smile, will you, sweetheart? Here are Vicar Winslow, his wife, and the Mellwyns."

With the Tuttle village vicar and his kindly spouse stood the biggest magpie south of the Thames, Lady Mellwyn. Beside her stood her long-suffering husband. The man held the local seat in Parliament and did a damned decent job of it, but his wife did her perverse best to blot that out.

Beautiful but self-centered, she possessed some charm but failed to employ it. Though her husband had often declared how he and his wife had wished for children, Rand thought it a bit of divine justice that none had come to them. Because of Patricia's razor tongue, her husband paid a devilish price, politically and socially, to cover the diverse damage wrought by her mouth. Why the lady could not see the destruction she did was a question for which Rand had never been able to find an answer.

"Good afternoon, Lord Templeton. You remember my wife?"

Rand bowed. "How could I forget? And you know Lady Curtis, naturally."

The conversation floated around the upcoming church strawberry festival until two of Farrell Hall's girls walked by, giggling madly.

Lady Mellwyn huffed at Jess. "I am amazed you've brought your students to the fair, Lady Curtis. I was of the opinion the very reason they attended your school was because they did not do well in public."

Jess bristled. How she hated such small-minded people who mistook veneer for substance. "They are quite accomplished. It is the public who often does not do well with them."

Mellwyn inclined his head, sweat beading on his forehead as he seized his wife's arm. "Patricia, please—"

"Perhaps," the woman persisted, "you'll be interested in attending the next Women's Society lecture at the guildhall. At my suggestion, they have invited a professor of neurology, who believes that abnormal behavior is a factor in species natural selection."

An angry flush burned Jess's cheeks. "Who is it?"

"A gentleman who trained at the University of Pavia. His name is Andretti. Perhaps you have heard of him."

"No."

"You should attend," the woman insisted with the look of a cat over a tasty mouse. "He tours England

and Scotland recounting his latest scientific analysis. He has worked with another scientist whose studies show that erratic behavior in organisms is predictable. He says criminals are born, you see. They can tell by the shape and size of the head and hands, and heaven only knows what else!"

"Criminal tendencies," Jess remarked with dead calm, "are quickly identified in those who make asinine assumptions and engage in rude behavior. Excuse me, do." Jess swept up her skirts and rounded the open-mouthed couple with her head high.

When Rand caught up to her, he was still chortling. "Pouting Patricia was reaching for her smelling salts as I left."

"She'll be asking for my public execution next. And she'd better, curse her! Before I ask for *hers!* Crazed woman. Who does she think she is? She gave Cat and me a royal fit before we opened the school, saying we were bringing in children who would roam the shire and commit mayhem. What does she know? *She*'s the biggest problem in this shire." She flipped down her parasol and whirled to face Rand, a finger to his chest. "Mark my word, I'm going to this Andretti's lecture. The simpleton. I'll have his—" She halted, her eyes widening at what she had almost said.

"His what, darling? You'll have his reputation for breakfast, perhaps? Or his head on a platter?"

She snorted and snapped up her parasol, which unfortunately got stuck. She pumped the thing, failed, then ground her teeth as she whirled away.

"Just think," he speculated, following her as she blindly trudged beyond the last fair tent toward a copse. "If you have his head, you could measure it for regressive traits. You might find he is a caveman or a—"

"Charlatan." She pierced the earth with the point of her parasol as she walked.

"Undoubtedly."

"Taking people's hard-earned money for his counterfeit ideas."

"Indubitably."

"Prejudicing people against others who seem different."

"Exactly."

"Failing to find and explain the real reasons why they act the way they do."

"Certainly." Rand paused and turned her toward him, now that they were in the shelter of oaks and evergreens. "If people could explain their actions, they should."

"Absolutely."

He gently caught one tendril near her cheek and rubbed its silken strands. "So tell me why you are avoiding me—and this."

His kiss surprised him for its politeness. Her response astonished him for its fire. A clean-burning desire was ignited between them, but whether it flared because Jess was already flamed by anger, he never knew. Didn't care to. He understood only that what he gave, she took—and then, when he raised his mouth, she caught him back, a hand cupping the nape of his neck for a brief bold sample that had her moaning and sinking against the tree.

Her eyes were glazed, her lips wet, her breasts heaving. Her hat hung precariously from dangling strawberry curls as she rested her head against the tree. "I want to be with you. I think, alone in my room at night, that I even *need* you."

"Wonderful. Just tell me why, when, how."

"You've become essential to my days," she mourned. "I have to know you'll be there for me every morning. For tea and necessary laughter. For May Fairs. Parrots. For your perspective."

He placed his arms on either side of her head, towering over her. "My one kiss wins me more than one truth. I'm very pleased. To match yours, here's mine: I want you in the morning or any time of day. Any day. Anywhere. In case you haven't noticed, I'm doing my damnedest to court you, Jessica Curtis."

"I noticed. I wish you wouldn't."

"Part of you, yes." He smiled, a little consolation for what he was about to ask. "But is that maidenly fluster or something deeper?"

She only stared at him.

"You kissed me back, sweetheart. You owe me one revelation."

Her lashes fluttered as he saw her struggle in her attempt to evade him. "I wish I *could* enjoy you."

Triumphant, he licked his lower lip. "That confession tastes like more." He reached for her.

"No." Her voice became a groan as she put a palm to his chest.

He scolded her with a look, then seized her lips for a soul-devouring kiss. He whispered against her mouth, "Your body enjoys me. So does your mind, until you remember something that freezes you. Why can't you cherish this closeness between us?"

Her eyes were desperately sad. "This close to you, it's very difficult to lie."

He frowned that she would even consider it. "Have you? To me?"

"I have tried."

Grinning, he brushed his lips across hers for reward. "But you won't lie to me, ever, will you?"

She shook her head.

"So tell me your secrets, darling. I promise you they are safe with me."

"This passion . . ." The horror of her last word broke over her expression, but she accepted it and charged onward. "What I feel with you is . . . delicious. But, Rand, I am so afraid of losing myself to you. I must be in control of myself. My *own* destiny." She dug her fist into her chest.

He scowled. "You think I'd take your *self* from you?"

"No! Yes!"

"Why?"

She was swallowing, outraged at herself and him.

His nostrils flared. "Why would I do that?"

"Because you're a man," she spat back, cornered. "And men use affection to gain power."

"That's not love. It's possession!"

"Aren't they the same?"

In the heat of the afternoon, he felt as if she'd doused him in chilled waters. "Not in a million years." His shock was transformed to compassion. "Who taught you that?"

"It doesn't matter," she murmured and tried to leave him.

He held her there. "Perhaps you're right. It doesn't matter."

Her brow wrinkled.

"I have to deal with the impression, no matter who set this poor example for you." He smiled at her sadly. "And I can't become angry at you for a misconception. Even the one woman I cared for believed certain things that weren't true. She died believing them, and not trusting me to love her enough to help her overcome any obstacles to our union."

She raised a hand to his cheek. "Oh, Rand, what happened to her?"

Memories of Susannah's last few days in a dingy room flashed before him. "She died very painfully. In a tenement. Worse, because of a drug she took at her own insistence. I tell you this: I never possessed her. But I did love her. I would have married her, too, if her parents hadn't interfered."

Jess smoothed the shock of hair from his brow. "I'm so sorry."

"I've never told another living soul any of this."

"We both have secrets," she reassured him.

"Yes," he ran his fingertips over her lips, "and here are mine, Jess." He stared past her to the woods. "Her name was Susannah Gage. I met her at a ball given by some mutual friends in Calcutta. I thought I was an acceptable escort for any young woman. At least here in England I was. But this was India, the crossroads of the world, where cultures met and intertwined. I was English, titled, rich—considered a good catch for any memsahib's daughter. But I was attracted to Susannah, who was spirited, American, obedient to no one except her own desires—and the edicts of her missionary parents, who thought I had inherited too much and worked for little of it.

"I loved Susannah's vivacity. We would meet at other people's parties where I would find a dozen other men as smitten as I. She favored me, and I asked her to marry me. Her parents refused to give us their blessing. They did not even receive me, never took time to hear me out or try to know me. The tug between them and me grew unmanageable for Susannah. Suddenly I had to leave Calcutta to attend to a business venture in Annam. I promised Susannah we'd marry when I came back. But we never did.

"Two months later, when I returned to Calcutta, I learned she had fled because she learned she was pregnant with my child and ashamed of it. I tried for weeks to find her, and I finally trailed her to London. That was as far as her meager savings could take her. I found her in a slum in Whitechapel. In rags and almost penniless, she had spent her last pence to buy a drug to abort the baby. She hated being pregnant. She had been very sick with the pregnancy and couldn't work. Her money ran out. She thought the only way to survive was to"—he squeezed his eyes shut—"kill the child. She died in terrible pain because she didn't believe that I would keep my word and return to Calcutta."

"But you didn't know she was pregnant."

"I should never have made love to her without benefit of marriage. She told me before she died that she condemned herself for acting immorally. I wondered why she thought it appropriate to condemn our baby too. . . ." He straightened. "She had no experience with people loving unconditionally." He tilted his head. "Perhaps it's a situation I'm destined to relive."

"No, don't say that, Rand. You are a darling man, and God would never be so unjust as to do that to you."

"Haven't you ever thought he gives us challenges until we get the response correct?"

"That's torture. No god would be so cruel." Her hand caressed his cheek. "Not to you. You are too lovable."

He couldn't seem to breathe. "Is that so?"

Her eyes adored his. Her lips parted. Her body swayed toward him.

"Sweetheart"—he framed her heart-shaped face in his hands—"please tell me what drives you away from me"—he skimmed his lips across her willing ones—"and from this."

"I too am afraid that"—her aqua eyes filled with tears—"I'm not worthy to be cared for unconditionally."

He held her as close as he could. "Darling of mine, what could you think you are that I wouldn't want you completely? Madly?" He kissed her swiftly. "If you think I view you as handicapped because of your injury, let me assure you that has not entered my head."

"No, no." Tears rolled down her cheeks now. "It's not what happened to me so much as . . ." She trembled as she had the other day when she heard the Moonlight Sonata and had her spell. "So much as what I did."

"What could you have done that I would turn from you?"

She bit her lip to catch back a sob. "I can't tell you."

"All right. Not now. But someday very soon. After

it's clear as day that I'm not going to leave you. Not for any reason. I'm here for you. Just as you came to me for help with Amanda, you can run to me for anything. Say you will, Jess."

"Oh, Rand, I want to."

He sensed a victory, however small. "I need to give you things, Jess. Piano lessons for your girls and friendship for you. Embraces, kisses. *Me.*" He looked into her sweet eyes. "Say you'll accept all my gifts, darling. I have this insatiable need to be lavish with you, to give you affection"—he bound her even closer—"for its own sake, because I like you for your enduring hope, respect you for your devotion to your family and your students. And I want you, Jess, entirely as you are. Unconditionally."

She was crying as she put a hand on the back of his neck, drew his mouth to hers, and gave him a leisurely kiss. Dazed by her ardor, he drew away and said, "That tasted promising."

"It is," she whispered, shaken but with a serene light now shining in her eyes. "I will come to you for anything."

"Everything."

Everything, she repeated silently.

He stepped back and reveled in the serenity of her smile. "This is the way I want to see you from this day forward. No more tears. Only laughter. Straighten your hat, darling. I have to go buy that bird and then we should return—"

"Miss Curtis? *Yoo-whoooo!*" A young girl's voice called across the clearing.

Rand sighed. "I guess we should see what your students want to do."

"There you are, Miss Curtis!" Amanda, Ann, and Belle ran toward them.

Jess chuckled as she tied the ribbons of her hat. "Do I look repaired?"

"Devastating." He winked and turned to the three girls, who skidded to a halt in front of them.

"We're so glad we found you!" Belle jumped up and down.

"Oooh, do come!" Amanda cried, hands clasped beneath her chin. "The actors' troupe will do *Othello,* and Mademoiselle Dumont says we must have your approval before we take seats. It's one of my favorite plays. What do you think? May we go?"

"Of course," Jess agreed. "We're coming, too."

Rand took her arm, and they walked off to the entrance to the theater tent, where a few of the other girls had lined up for the performance. While Jess counted noses to tally the cost of tickets, Rand went in search of more Farrell students who might wish to see the bit of *Othello.*

With each step, his mood darkened.

He may have kissed Jess and won a revelation from her for it, but would she return to her protective shell, as she did time after time?

The reasons for her behavior had driven him yesterday to seek information from the only source he had: Pool.

Rand knew that the butler would consider it his duty to refrain from commenting on his mistress. But rumor had it that Jess, like Cat, was much more than an employer to the servant. The two young women were Pool's only living relatives, though he was an illegitimate Leighton. Rand was counting on the fact that his own long standing as a neighbor to the Farrells and a close friend of Spencer Lyonns would mean he could not only speak frankly with Pool but could also gain more information than just anyone in search of personal secrets.

"I haven't had a solid opportunity to thank you for your help the other day with Lady Curtis when Lord Emory was here," he'd told the butler.

Pool replied without hesitating. "I'm glad you were there, my lord. Those spells she gets can press a fresh crease in your trousers, but they're worse for her."

"I felt it. Do they happen often, then?"

"No, sir. In fact, I haven't seen her do that in years. Not since she first came here to live after her great-aunt Mary died. She took frightful chills and stared blankly at people often then."

"Music—Beethoven in particular, she says—is significant to her."

"She told you that, eh?" The man nodded his bald head repeatedly in thought. "Well, I would say, sir, you are more fortunate than most. I don't think she's ever revealed that to Lady Lyonns."

"How do you know?"

"Because, sir, Lady Lyonns would have clarified it for me if she could. She and I had long talks before she married the earl of Dartmoor. Most of those discussions were about Lady Curtis. You see, Cat—Lady Lyonns—feels responsible for her cousin. Knowing she would travel often to her husband's estates and leave Lady Curtis in charge here, Lady Lyonns wanted me to understand that, though Lady Curtis was subject to these attacks, it was her head injury that caused them."

"Are you certain of that?"

"That's what Lady Lyonns told me, sir, and I have no reason to question—"

"No, of course not," Rand had said then but wondered now who had spun the fantasy, Cat or Jess. "What else did Lady Lyonns tell you about these episodes?"

"That they were brief and in no way impeded Lady Curtis's ability to administer this school or the estate in Lady Lyonns's stead. In truth, sir, I've watched Jessica Curtis since she came here. She may shake and take a chill so deep as to freeze a mortician. She may also seem halting when performing a task that takes time and steps. But I tell you, my lord, three things: she recovers always from her chills, she cannot be pushed in any task, and—most important—she is *sane.*"

"*That* I did not doubt, Pool."

"Good, my lord. Some people think those who are different may be mentally impaired. Lady Curtis is not, either intellectually or emotionally." The butler's eyes examined his. "She has no parents, no relatives, except Lady Lyonns . . . and me. My father was their grandfather Leighton, you see, and so I feel as though my heritage gives me the right to be so bold as to say, sir, that Lady Curtis means much to us. She is no woman with whom to trifle."

"Agreed."

The butler took the reassurance and gave more in return. "These last weeks in which you have visited us, sir, I have noticed that Lady Jessica laughs more often. I have known her since she was born, and I tell you that she was born to parents who gave her little joy as a child. She is a gentle soul and deserves happiness. These last few years she has done a yeoman's job of directing this school, and she has blossomed. But that violent incident with Lord Emory set her back. I venture to say that if it had not been for that debilitating event, she would not have suffered her spell, sir." He waved a hand in dismissal. "Even if the music she heard later was some of this Beethoven."

That discussion raised the question of whether Jess would lie to him. She had just said that she tried to but hadn't.

She seemed too fine a creature to be devious.

But people had reasons to lie. Hers, evidently, was big as the ocean.

What would she gain by telling him that her chills were not a result of her accident, when her cousin Cat believed they were? Unless . . . she had lied to Cat.

To protect herself.

From criticism? From pain?

She had not lied to him; somehow he knew that to be a fact. His heart swelled with the knowledge that he was the one person to whom she had given the truth.

So the realities that challenged any relationship she might have with him were the chills, Beethoven, and . . . the anger of a man.

A vivid impression hit him of Jess's face when first Emory had burst in upon them. Her expression was . . . heroic. With her eyes fastened to the man's walking stick, Jess had appeared not so much afraid as arrested. Frozen in time.

How were her cold fright, the music, and the

violence connected? Which was cause and which effect?

He plunged a hand through his hair. God, he didn't know!

And he cared for her deeply. Cared for her enough to discover her problems and help her overcome them.

Her behavior made him want to pick her up and run away with her. Take her to the shelter of his arms where he could kiss her reticence from her until she was secure and wildly happy in his love.

He halted in his tracks.

He loved her.

As no one else ever had.

His heart swelled with all the joys he wanted to bestow upon her. Gaiety. A home. A haven. A helper. A mate.

"Lord Templeton?"

Tara Doherty and Corinne Marlow bounded up to him with two of their friends in tow. "You look odd, sir."

"Do I?"

"As if you've just seen something fantastic."

He grinned. "I certainly have."

Bewildering them entirely, he asked them if they'd care to see the play. They immediately agreed. The five of them wended their way back to the theater tent, where Rand admired Jess as they queued up and joked with the girls.

His gaze drifted over her elegant face, the fragile complexion, the full lips. Her looks had captured him from the first. But when he'd seen beyond that, he found so much more. Then as now he admired her élan and her compassion, both of which he wanted their children to inherit from her. But she wouldn't agree to that until he helped her look upon her own idiosyncrasies as interesting aspects of her character.

Suddenly he felt beset by forces he couldn't see—a unique sensation for him. A singular battle for a man who had been taught to face reality and shape it to his needs. Intuition shouted at him to scoop her up now, take her home, propose, kiss her until she agreed to make daughters and sons and mad music in his bed.

"Are you coming?" she urged gaily.

He smiled wryly as he strode forward and took her arm. "I always enjoy a good drama."

"You like tragedy?"

"I appreciate Shakespeare."

"I don't like his love stories."

"The bard approved of love."

"His couples seem either mismatched or foolish," Jess said. "Cleopatra could care for any man with a hint of authority. Juliet loved on sight, while Desdemona was worse. She was naive."

Amanda, who walked beside them, feigned a swoon. "Desdemona was so pure. She's easy to play." She flattened a palm to her chest.

Rand chuckled. "Sarah Bernhardt–style."

"Yes," she gushed. "Imagine what it must be like to have a man *die* for love of you. Or kill you because he loved you? Ooooh, that's passion!"

Rand winced at Amanda's extreme statement but faced Jess, who swallowed so loud he could hear her. She turned as white as snow. A hand on her arm told him she was cold.

Corinne Marlow tossed her cinnamon curls and

harrumphed. "I'd rather have him in the flesh and live a bit!"

Rand was mulling over Jess's response as they began to file inside. "Corinne the pragmatist."

"Don't you agree with me, sir?"

"I do. Having found the woman of my dreams, I wouldn't consider dying until I'd spent my best efforts and at least my next sixty years enjoying her." His fingers squeezed Jess's arm.

She would not look at him, but nodded at Corinne to lead them into a row of chairs and stools, collected haphazardly for the presentation. They jostled each other in the seating arrangement so that the shorter girls could sit behind suitably sized adults. This brought Corinne to the end of a row, with Rand next, followed by Amanda, Jess, one of Farrell's teachers, Ann, and Belle. Tara and the other older girls lined the walls as more than thirty Ashford villagers took their places.

The actors took their sweet time about beginning. The audience grew fidgety. Restless, a few of the Farrell students complained to each other. Ann and Belle leaned over to voice their own objections to Jess, but Rand noted that her response was one of impatience with a troupe of amateur thespians.

Corinne leaned close to him. "What scenes will they do?"

"I have no idea. Amanda, do you know what they'll perform?"

"They did not say out front, sir. Lady Curtis?" She asked Jess if she knew.

"Only two scenes," she replied. "The one in which Iago tells the lie about Desdemona being unfaithful to her husband and the last scene, where Othello kills her."

She faced the makeshift stage draped in blood-red velvet, blotted by a massive bed of black.

He crossed his arms and considered the colors of death and passion.

Passion. Earlier, backed up against a tree, Jess had said she feared passion.

An actor dressed in a motley costume sauntered onto the stage. The crowd hushed as the man cast his beady eyes about and rubbed his hands in glee. Rand shifted at the sight of this man who personified the evil of Iago so vividly. Here stood a creature who would lie solely for the pleasure of watching the results.

Iago's commander joined him at center stage. A tall, imperious man in blackface, Othello conversed with his soldier, Iago. As he did, the famous military man listened too closely to Iago's tale of Desdemona's unfaithfulness. He asked few questions and believed fabrications so flimsy that any right-minded man would have balked, particularly at accusations about a woman he professed to adore.

The sight sickened Rand.

He had always disliked this play. Now he hated it.

He could tell a lie when he heard it. By God, he knew Jess told him the truth!

He whipped around to look at her . . . and turned to stone.

Her mouth was open, her eyes blank.

His guts twisted. She wore the same look as the other day when Emory brandished his cane.

He tried to catch her eye. Distract her. Lord, he

didn't want her to collapse here. With Amanda between them, he might not grab Jess before she swooned and hit the floor.

Jess blinked, her eyes huge pools of horror.

Rand shot a glance at the stage. The scene had changed. A young woman in white with flowing hair of gold slept on the black satin bed while her husband, Othello, far gone now with his irrational jealousy, raged to himself about his wife's infidelity. About her seeming virtue, the lie that tarnished the beauty of her face and the purity of her heart.

"Yet she must die, else she'll betray more men," boomed the wretched Othello as he contemplated his wife's death and, in the same breath, kissed her.

Desdemona roused from sleep to caress her loved one. "Will you come to bed, my lord?"

"Have you prayed tonight, Desdemona?"

"Aye, my lord."

Othello told her to reconcile herself to heaven for any crimes she might have committed.

"Alas, my lord, what do you mean by that?"

Othello leaned over her, angry with himself and her as he ordered her to confess her sins to God. "Do it and be brief. . . . I would not kill thy soul."

"Talk you of killing?"

"Aye, I do."

"Then heaven have mercy on me!"

Rand scowled. Jess had been right about Desdemona. To give in so summarily, to love so naively, was truly the woman's character flaw. Much worse, her husband's was to love so blithely that any wind could buffet his devotion, especially if it ruffled any portion of his overblown reputation.

Othello raved on about her crimes, which were such a sorrow to him, and though his wife did protest vehemently, he would not hear her chime of truth. Mourning his own need to destroy her, he wrapped his large hands around her neck . . . and wrung.

Rand closed his eyes, recoiling from death so needless, from murder so immoral.

He shifted, his gaze flying to Jess's hands. She clutched her parasol handle so hard the fine bones of her hand stood out in macabre relief through her thin gloves. Slowly, painfully, he raised his eyes to her face.

Tears rolled down her cheeks.

Sweet Christ. He never knew if he said it, he only understood he had to get to her. He dropped a hand to Amanda's arm—but the shock of what he felt petrified him.

The child trembled, groaned. Amanda's teeth were bared as she flung off his hand. *"Let me go!"* she screamed at him.

"Amanda!" Jess called as she shot up, her own tears glistening, forgotten on her cheeks.

The actors halted.

The crowd muttered their dismay.

The girls flocked around or fell away, a measurement of their horror.

Jess pleaded with Rand. "Help me get her out of here."

Chapter Eight

"GET YOUR HANDS OFF ME!" AMANDA RIPPED AT JESS'S fingers as she and Rand urged her toward the entrance of the tent.

"Come with me willingly, then," Jess whispered, brushing away her tears of compassion for Desdemona, murdered by her husband.

"I will not." Amanda said it with bared teeth.

"It's all right if you don't want to see the play—"

"I *hate* it!"

"Very well, but you must let the others enjoy it." Jess had to get Amanda home, quiet her, and try to discover what had sent the girl into this tirade. Jess had suffered such outbursts herself when she began to remember exactly how her father had killed her mother and . . . She paused. *No.* Though this child's tragic accident mirrored her own closely, no two head injuries were the same, and no two recoveries were, either. Yet the very possibility of more similarities made Jess examine Amanda carefully.

She was still fuming over the quality of the production and the acting. "How can anyone enjoy *this?* Othello forgot a line. Desdemona dies like a snapped twig." Amanda pushed past Rand and rushed up on the stage.

"This is how you are supposed to kill her," she reprimanded Othello and put both hands out to wrap them around Desdemona's throat.

The young actress flinched away from Amanda. "She's insane. Take her away!"

Othello lunged for Amanda.

She slithered from his grasp. In one second her mood swung from feral to indignant. Though tears sprang to her eyes, she focused on the crowd who pointed or shouted at her.

Jess mounted the stage steps, Rand at her side, and curled her fingers around the child's wrist. "That is quite enough. Let's go."

Patricia Mellwyn, who had sat behind the Farrell contingent, shot to her feet. "I have never seen such poor behavior in public. You will have to control your students, Lady Curtis, if you wish to receive the cooperation of these good people who are your neighbors."

"Amanda is not hurting you, Lady Mellwyn. I apologize for the interruption, but we are leaving."

"I go where I like," Amanda tossed back as she whirled to face Othello. "Let's see you do that scene again," she ordered.

Jess stood appalled. Her own ranting had never been so rude.

"Jess?" Rand asked quietly.

She understood he wanted permission to proceed. "Yes. Do it."

He lifted Amanda and clutched her to his chest. She screamed, she writhed, she beat him about the shoulders, and when that didn't work, she pounded his head with her fists.

When they got outside, Jess bent, hoisted her skirts, and tore off a strip of her petticoat. Rand was striding ahead, but even agile as he was, he had a hard time making headway with a rabid little creature in his arms.

"Wait!" Jess called to him. He paused, ducking the girl's blows. It gave Jess just enough time to wind the strips of cloth about Amanda's wrists.

The child bucked and Rand nearly dropped her, but he clamped her to his chest. "Pound away, my girl. You are going home."

Where Amanda got the energy to fight him, Jess never knew. She could only marvel that one so small could pummel one so huge.

Their ride home was a race by Rand's frightened coachman and a team of hard-put bays.

"We won't go to the dormitory but up to Farrell Hall," Jess told Rand as they left the main road for the school. "I want her with me."

"What makes you think I want to be with you?" spat Amanda as she yanked at her bindings. "You're cruel. Wait until I tell Pool what you've done."

"Pool?" Jess asked.

"Yes, *he* has become my true friend these past weeks. He'll yell at you. You won't like it." Her beautiful eyes beaded to slits. "He'll set me free."

Rand snorted, easily waylaying her from giving him a bonk on the head with her two fists. "A good idea and a poor one. She's not making sense, Jess. Is this a typical reaction? What cures have you got for this?"

"A few."

"One—let me go!" demanded Amanda.

Jess cut her a look of reproof. "Do try to be quiet, dear. You're not going anywhere, except with me."

"I'll write to my father. He will surely set you straight."

Jess pinned Amanda with a glare of remorse. "No, sweetheart, I don't think you really want to send for him."

"He'll take me away."

"He might." Jess grew colder by the second, recalling how her own father had tried to deal with her unruly behavior by sending her to the parish workhouse inhabited by derelicts and those of lesser intelligence. Her aunt Mary and Cat's father had objected so adamantly that they persuaded her father not to confine her to hell. "Would you want to go with him?"

Amanda pondered that for a minute, then shook her head.

"No? I didn't think so. So you will deal with me. The very first thing you will do is stop struggling with Lord Templeton."

"He's manhandling me."

"It is the opposite and you know it." Jess reached up just as Amanda would have lashed out a hand to hit Rand again. "Violence is not acceptable. I told you that the day your father brought you to us."

"I do as I wish."

"At your own risk."

"Do you want to call in that London doctor my father said would come?" she sneered, then paled. "I know *he* would take me away."

"I wouldn't send for him, Amanda." Jess turned to Rand. "The man wanted to commit her to an asylum for the criminally insane."

Amanda chewed her lip. "He had wet hands."

"*He* was the lunatic," Jess elaborated for an enraged Rand. "Emory had read an article about him in the *Times.* He was one of those spiritualists who believe in meditation as a cure, not earthly medicine or human therapy or even kindness."

"He was nasty." Amanda had retreated to a world far from here. "He came to our house after Mama died. He held my hand and stroked my cheeks"—she winced—"and told me I was pretty, but deserved to be put away. He said he'd come visit me often. I don't want to go there. Not with him."

Rand and Jess locked gazes.

"Not with anyone!" Amanda took Jess's hand and pleaded. "Don't let my father do that. I want to stay with you." She threw herself into Jess's embrace. Her fury died so quickly that Jess could see Rand jarred by the transition. Amanda clung tightly to her and cried bitterly.

Jess held her as she let out her woes. The first best cure she could give this child was the opportunity to drain all her emotions. "Cry, my dear," she crooned as she rocked. "Do it until you can't cry anymore."

When the coach pulled up to the front door of Farrell Hall, Rand took an exhausted Amanda from

Jess's arms and carried her inside. He followed Jess up to the chamber next to hers and waited outside the door while she helped the child out of her clothes and under the covers. She led him back down the stairs to the music room where she rang for Pool, the housekeeper, and two upstairs maids.

"When she awakens, I want to be notified," Jess told them. "Then we'll see if she is civil. If so, I want you to have a few things ready. She's to have a warm bath and some chamomile tea, toast, an egg custard—as much as she wants of those, but no other food until she is calmer." She examined Rand briefly. "And please bring me ice chips, liniment, and bandages for Lord Templeton."

"That kind of food helps such a condition?" Rand asked her when the servants had left them alone.

"I know from personal experience that those foods soothe overwrought nerves."

"This is worse than a case of nerves!"

"Yes. She experienced some . . . imbalance. I had a few such episodes myself in the first year after my accident. They are frightening. It's as if lightning has struck you and you can't control yourself. You understand what you're doing and saying, but you have no idea who has written the script or why you are delivering your lines in this terrible, wild way. You want to stop, change, sound and act normal, but you can't cease until you just deflate, like a punctured balloon."

"Good God, Jess. Then Amanda might say or do anything! Could she hurt someone or herself?"

Jess's mouth went dry. She would not lie to him. "It

is possible." She ran her hands over furniture and the mantel. "But not probable. She has never willfully committed any mean act, and—"

"She's never acted like a crude, spoiled child, either. Jess, a special diet of soothing foods can help, but it is not the total answer. Neither is understanding or commiseration. Not for a burst of temper like the one Amanda had."

"After my attack, one of my doctors told me he thought this kind of behavior typical of many victims of head injury."

"And where is this doctor? Can we call him in for Amanda?"

"He died years ago. And I know of no physician anywhere who is an expert on head trauma. Those who study it are few in number because there is so little to codify. A definitive set of conditions is difficult to define because every person's injury is so different." She sank into a chair. "My means are as limited as my knowledge."

"Mine aren't. I can help you. Let me."

"How?"

"I told you I know quite a few doctors. One in particular, a brilliant man, is quite gentle with children. I don't have any idea what he knows about head injuries but he is kind and methodical. He has helped me by seeing some of the boys in the London orphanage who have grown up alone and have engaged in thievery or cardsharping to survive."

"He has a sound education?"

"He is not one of those anthropologists or phrenologists whom Patricia Mellwyn seems to favor. His name is Johann Steineke. He and I have had lengthy discussions about the nature of the human mind. He is impartial, considerate, deliberate—all of the things a doctor should be, especially in a case like this. I know if I asked him he would examine Amanda."

"Would he come here?"

"I'm afraid not."

Her hopes, instantly high, plunged as quickly. "But why suggest—"

"He's ill. Dying. Bedridden for over two months now. If you'd like to see him, you'll have to take Amanda to London."

She paced the room, touching the piano and harp, wringing her hands. Dr. Johann Steineke seemed like a good peg on which to hang some hope. But she would have to stay in a hotel under an assumed name. A woman alone was welcome at few reputable establishments. But she'd have a child. Perhaps she could pretend she was Amanda's mother. She could not stay at Cat and Spence's house in Park Lane because the Lyonnses were living at the Red House in Richmond while their London town house was being painted and refurbished. Jess had no other relative or friend to ask such a personal favor. No one to ask . . . except Rand.

She halted and faced him. "I am tempted."

"What prohibits you?"

"Harrison Emory."

"You mean he wants Amanda to see only the physicians he chooses."

"Yes," she said ruefully. "But also if I took her to London, Harrison Emory might learn of it through rumor, and he could try to ruin me and the school. What's worse, I conclude from his speech that Harrison is motivated by less than purely paternal interest in his daughter's recovery. He seems too concerned with what society thinks about Amanda's condition. There was quite a bit of talk after his wife died. Why was an experienced horsewoman riding out—racing—on a rainy day? Why did she miss a hedge she should have cleared even though it was raining? Why was Amanda so close behind her?"

"My God, I didn't know."

"Amanda doesn't remember the accident, and so she can't tell us. Harrison found them both. His wife was dead, probably instantly after her fall. Amanda was in a coma, but very much alive."

Pool came in with his tray of medicinals and left Jess to her nursing.

She went to Rand and took his hands tenderly. "I'm so sorry for the way Amanda treated you. I think you are going to have a few bruises. Please sit down and let me tend to them."

She unbuttoned her cuffs, rolled up her sleeves, and began to treat his face and hands.

He sat, his head against the high back of the chair, his sweet blue eyes watchful and grateful. When he closed them to let her minister to him, she indulged her need to nurse him and thank him in some small measure for the multitude of things he'd given her.

With a lump in her throat, she bathed his scratches and bruises. The afternoon sunlight illuminated his stark handsomeness, gilding the tan of his complexion. Near as Jess was, touching him as she forever longed to do, she felt her heart break for this generous man who suffered for her sake and that of a child.

How fortunate she was to know him, have him for a friend, a companion. How humbling it was to merit such a gift from God as this caring man. How terrifying it was to simply adore him. How insane—ah, yes, "insane" was the right word—to avoid him . . . and the prospect of a normal, healthy life.

"You're staring at me. I can feel it," he said with that soothing voice of his. "Do I look that awful?"

"You could take a job with the fair as the Black-and-Blue Man and charge a hefty admission."

He grimaced. "A clown."

"The Strongman," she corrected.

He didn't move a muscle.

"How do I thank you?" she asked in such a way that she expected no answer.

He opened his eyes. "You thank me in a thousand ways silently, and therefore all the better for their eloquence."

She paused, one hand in midair.

"Like that," he mouthed.

"I don't deserve you."

"I have the same thought about you, darling. It makes me humble, but so proud and wildly happy to know you and learn more about you each day."

She went quite still. "You don't know everything. . . ."

"I know enough. Tell me what you will when you will. If it takes a lifetime, you'll learn to trust me, show me, tell me."

His endearments stopped her heart. Whether it was frustration, fatigue, or her old head injury that could not let her think straight, she could form no proper response. Instead, she dipped her fingers in a liniment jar and asked him to hold still.

He sighed beneath the pressure of her evasion.

"Very well. Tell me about Amanda, then. What happened to her in that tent that caused her behavior to go awry?"

"It's a jumble. I haven't had a chance to sort it out completely in my own mind."

"Why not start with me now?"

She took such comfort from his mellow gaze. "With you so much is possible. So much I never thought to sample or enjoy."

His piercing look told her he adored her comment.

She clamped the lid on the jar, wiped her hands on a damp cloth, then stood and turned toward the garden doors.

"It could have been any number of things that happened at the fair. I'll ask her, see if she knows."

"She might not?"

Jess crossed her arms and shook her head. "It's possible she understands nothing. Her behavior could be caused by internal conditions."

"Explain that."

"Perhaps the brain experienced some sort of change. You asked about the foods I requested for her. That is a good example. For if our bodies are representations of what we eat, so are our brains. It may sound like an old wives' tale to give a person who is agitated warm milk, eggs, and toast, but it works. I know. My aunt Mary—the lady I lived with before I came to Farrell Hall five years ago—understood such things and used such remedies for me."

She faced him because she owed him as much honesty as she could give him. "I was not fully in control of myself at times after my accident. My great-aunt Mary did as I did this morning and cut old sheets to wrap around my arms and legs so that I wouldn't hurt myself or others." Hot tears clogged her throat at these revelations. "I've never spoken of this because it's so dreadful."

"I feel it, sweetheart, and I'll stay right here. Nothing you could say would send me away."

"Oh, Rand! They are not pretty things to tell!"

"Darling, look at me. I've lived in Hanoi where petty thieves are caged in the streets and stretched out by their pigtails to rot in the sun. I've spent years in Calcutta where those who are not of the proper castes can beg for food but die for a crust of bread. I've lived in London where two-year-old children are left alone to fend for themselves by weary mothers who labor for twelve hours a day in a factory. Do you think you could tell me stories worse than those? What else is there about this morning and Amanda that I should know?"

Jess put a hand to her trembling mouth. To say the next few words meant she had returned to the similarities between Amanda's case and her own—the very parallels she told herself she must ignore in order to see Amanda's case as individual and separate from hers. It was the only way to help her.

"Perhaps . . . Amanda saw something in the play. I don't know what. She was quite an actress before her accident, and you saw how she pleaded, so excited, to go see the production. Why she would turn like that is a mystery."

"Is it?"

Jess very slowly raised her eyes to his and thanked heaven she was as far from him as she was. In his countenance, she saw the challenge. "You're referring to her disclosure to you the night she ran away—that she thought her mother and father had problems."

"Yes."

"It sounds similar. *Othello* is about a man hurting his wife."

"About a man who is jealous of his wife. Irrationally so."

Oh, how she hated this topic! But she had to go on, didn't she? For Amanda's sake.

She spun about, her hand to her throat. "But Othello strangles Desdemona. Amanda's mother died in a riding accident."

She heard Rand come across the carpet to her, felt his warm hands on her chilled body. "Christ, you're as cold as sin."

Rather than succumb to the comfort and the diversion of his embrace, Jess stepped away. When she turned at the other side of the room, he gazed at her shrewdly.

"What ails you, Jess?"

That gutted her. He was coming too close, and she must not allow him nearer. "Most men would leave. But you persist." She admired him with an overflowing heart and a fear so voracious it gobbled up whole any hope of having him as her own. "God knows I have never known a man your equal. You deserve a woman as generous, as gentle."

"I've found her."

"No! Don't say that!" She clamped her hands over her ears.

He had her by the arm before she could slip away. "Why can't I?"

"You're confusing me. My brain isn't thinking in

straight lines. There is too much happening, and I don't deal well with more than one problem at a time."

"I'm not a problem for you, Jess."

"No," she breathed and on impulse ran her fingers over his lips. "You are a joy, a glorious present sent to me, but I don't know how to cope with Amanda's unpredictable behavior while I confront the fact that I—" *Love you.*

She swallowed hard and headed for the piano. With a flick of her skirts, she sat down. Placing her fingers on the keys, she began to play "Für Elise." Loudly.

But putting music and distance between them did not deter him from his pursuit. The room reverberated with his dedication when he spoke.

"Please stop, Jess. I won't come near you to confuse you. I won't do anything to make you walk away from me. I want you too much. Don't, I beg you, ignore me by submerging yourself in the music." He strode over, pressed his hand atop hers on the keyboard, and sent discordant sounds banging against the walls.

She owed him much, but a note of honesty would have to suffice—and substitute for the horror of her entire sordid past. "I like it. It's easy. A child's piece."

"You play it because your mother liked it."

"Yes, just as she liked the Moonlight Sonata. This was a special tune for a moody, unhappy woman. A fragile creature given to excesses, exaggeration, swooning, and laudanum overdoses."

"Was laudanum the cause of her death?"

The subject had her groping for the keys and stumbling over the next few bars. "No," she said, avoiding her father's part in her mother's death. "She died in a riding accident minutes after she and I had had an argument. Like Amanda's mother, mine failed to clear a jump. Her horse went down. He broke two legs. My mother broke her neck."

His hands lifted hers from the keyboard to his mouth. Drowning in the need to feel more of him, she let her eyes absorb the tenderness of his lips against her skin.

"Is this emotion I see now grief over your mother's death or guilt that you argued with her before she died?"

Guilt over arguing with her mother was only a minor part of her problem!

He sat beside her on the piano bench and took her in his arms, tucking her head into the crook of his shoulder. "Jess, you were thirteen when your accident occurred—a year older than Amanda. So young to have your life change completely," he lamented and dropped a kiss into her hair. "Please tell me why you are so tormented. Because Amanda's situation reminds you of your own? Didn't you realize you'd remember it more vividly when you agreed to enroll her here?"

"Yes, yes." She clutched him close, inhaled his sweet scent and comfort. "The similarities astonished me from the start, but I had to dismiss them as coincidence. Then you told me that the night you found Amanda in your house, she revealed that her parents fought. Mine fought bitterly too. Often. Although Harrison Emory seems . . . well, saner than my father was at the time, I doubt . . . I doubt his veracity because I—I doubted my father's!"

Rand peered down at her. "In what way?"

"He said he loved my mother, but he—" Lord above, she'd come this far, too far. Now there was no way out except by way of a detour. "My father was much like Othello and Emory in that he was concerned about what society would think of my mother, what people would say about her fits, her moods." Her affairs. Her increasing inability to be discreet about them.

"Did he abuse her?" Rand examined her expression closely. "You told me weeks ago that you feared a man's touch. . . ." His eyes went wide with horror. "Or did he hurt you?"

She could scarcely breathe. "Not . . . sexually."

"I see," Rand said after the longest time and brought her back to his chest. "We'll deal with this enigma one element at a time. What did he do, Jess?"

She flew from his embrace with such force that Rand couldn't hold her. "I told you this morning outside the fair that I didn't want passion with a man. I don't want to be possessed. My mother was. By my father and by—"

Rand waited. She knew he'd wait an eternity for her to continue her disclosures.

"My mother was possessed by music."

The searing look Rand gave her told her he suspected more than that.

"It's true. She lived in a fantasy world. She was not stupid, not insane, but given to flights of imagination. She was a brilliant composer, boxed up by society's belief that women cannot be artists!"

"Hers was a mind that did not apply its talents."

"Oh, *yes,* Rand! She did! She told me that when she was a child she was so disciplined that she practiced for hours and hours each day, until her fingers ached and her wrists throbbed. But she was a woman from a respectable family in a society that did not permit women to express their passion, only to become part of a man's. She loved music, but her father would not allow her to become a concert pianist. It was not done. It still isn't."

Rand looked at her with sorrow. "Some men are brought up with more respect for others than your father or your mother's father. Some men adore their women, but they don't lock them away or put them on a pedestal. They love them as *equals.* The passion they have is gladly given, freely shared. And if, in the sharing, they discover a certain kind of possession, it is each heart's union with the other. The very sort, I think, you fear. Am I right?"

"Fear but want," she whispered. "Very badly."

"With me?"

"*Yes,* because you are not like any man I've ever known. Oh, but don't you see that your life would be simpler if you took me at my word and went away?"

He smiled and came toward her, winding his arms around her again and resting his lips near her ear. "I do take your word for truth, but I can't follow your instructions. I'm not one of your students, darling. I'm the man who is going to give you everything, remember?"

"I do." She bound him closer. "All I have to do is ask?"

"Take *me* at my word, darling."

"And what," she asked in awe, "can I possibly give you in return?"

His eyes narrowed on her mouth. *"This."* He

pressed his lips to hers and claimed her with brief ravenous hunger. "And this." He scooped her up and took her to a settee, where he laid her down and bent over her.

Dazed and needy, she expected him to take her with a kiss of possession, but his tender touch of mouths captured her more. She wound her hands in his hair and pressed against him, dying to offer more. As if he understood how torn she was, he strung a line of kisses down her throat, trailed one hand up her hip to cover her breast and tease a nipple. Then he nestled his mouth in the valley between her breasts and spoke against her heart. "I'm going home now, darling."

She stifled a whimper. "No—"

"I'm going to lecture myself on discipline." He grinned wickedly. "But I'll be thinking about how endlessly you and I are going to give delight to each other." He ran a finger along her brow. "I want you to remember that, dream of it, in your bed tonight. And accept the fact that in each way we give, darling, there will be passion like you've never known—and happiness that you so richly deserve."

She went to bed that night believing that happiness was possible for her.

Within the hour, Amanda awakened her and the entire household with her screams. At dawn, after she finally got the child settled, Jess dropped into her own bed. Exhausted but thrilled that Amanda had finally calmed down, Jess stared up at the ceiling, recalling Rand's parting words. They blended with an old belief she had long lived by—that happiness came to those who not only welcomed it but worked for it. Happiness was, for her, a choice, a state of mind more than a condition. A gift she had given herself. Because few others had or could. A treasure she had kept as a talisman so that when the challenges of daily life came again, as they always did, she knew the sorrows would pass, life would go on, and she might find some small joy again.

Jess hugged herself.

For her, she prayed, the day had come when she had found the greatest joy of her life. Love. With Rand Templeton.

Chapter Nine

SLEEP DID NOT COME EASILY IN THE NIGHTS WHICH followed.

"Why should tonight be any different from the others?" Jess muttered and peeled away the covers.

She lay there, flat on her back, arms out like a butterfly, listening to the hush of wee morning.

Like two concurrent refrains, sorrow over Amanda's condition resurrected memories of her own past while joy that the child had lucid hours gave hope that Amanda might still lead a normal life. Such dichotomies were not ordinarily found in one event.

Jess laughed into the soft dark air. One of her former doctors would have declared her officially insane. "No one," he had once told her father and her great-aunt Mary soon after one of her episodes, "can laugh and cry at the same time."

But she had then. Could now. Inside, where no one could see—and yet she considered herself normal. If indeed fear over Amanda's intermittent ravings coupled with pleasure over her relationship with Rand could be called normal.

Jess was bone-tired of enduring the extremes of Amanda's mental condition. In the daytime, she would go on endless walks with Amanda when the child's energy overflowed. They'd talk when the girl was inclined to discuss any issue in a conversational tone, which was increasingly common, thank God. Jess had even managed to persuade Amanda to review a botany lesson, though she suspected that Amanda absorbed little substance. Frustrated in those times when Amanda napped or haunted the rear of classrooms, Jess occupied herself—*threw* herself—into teaching her classes and doing her bookkeeping or any activity to keep her mind off her own past. Then she would allow herself to enjoy Rand in the few minutes she spent with him each day.

Although Amanda refused to practice the piano, Rand would arrive every morning in the hope the child would change her mind. She never did. She would not even speak to Rand, but sent word through Pool that she was indisposed. When Jess asked her why she did not explain herself in person to Rand, Amanda said she was certain that one day she would like to, but right now she was too ashamed of her behavior at the play to face Lord Templeton. She declared she was so upset with herself that she had to force herself to speak even to Jessica. So Amanda's social conscience had returned, and for that, Jess was pleased and waited for the day when Amanda might forgive herself her actions.

In the meantime, Jess took the opportunity to see Rand. For the hour in which he would have tutored

Amanda, he and Jess did the ordinary things courting couples do. He brought over the purple parrot he'd bought at the fair, and they introduced the bird to the Farrell trio of cat, dog, and monkey. Rand took Jess riding over his estate, pointing out his favorite places including the man-made lake and the Greek temple where Rand had played hide-and-seek when he was a child. He advised her on the sensible purchase price of Madras cottons for a sewing-class project. With tears of gratitude in her eyes, she accepted a bolt of aqua Bangkok silk.

"I'll grow greedy if you keep giving me such lavish gifts," she said as she rubbed the incredibly delicate fabric against her cheek and down her throat.

Slowly he lifted his eyes from her cheek and locked them on hers. "Become whatever suits you, my darling. What pleases you makes me happy."

So in the subtle sweetness of the spring nights, her mind gravitated from Amanda to Rand and this wonderful period in her life. A time like no other she had known. Days of delight brought on by this love affair of hers, so pure in its clean-burning fire, yet becoming more passionate with every word and look, and each wet, trembling kiss.

The need for more would make her toss off her covers, leave her bed, and read or write. When that failed to distract her, she'd pace her balcony, look at the tree line toward Rand's home, and pray this blessed period in her life would never end.

"But Amanda's agony must end," Jess said aloud. "*Will* end," she affirmed, counting yet again the dwindling number of outbursts the child suffered each day. Taking comfort from those statistics, Jess thought this irrational behavior would end soon and called in no doctors.

Most doctors had been unable to give her help when she was young. Because many victims of head injury died immediately or could not communicate the extent of their incapacities afterward, little information about such conditions existed. Doctors lived in a twilight world of half-told facts and were unable to compare one case to the next. The subject of head injuries was therefore a fertile field, untilled except by the brave, the tenacious—or the cavalier.

In fact, the only doctor who had ever helped her piece together her fragmented past had been found by her great-aunt Mary two years after the accident. Dr. Robert Tillingsworth had made head injuries his life's work, but he had died eight years ago. Before that, he had helped Jess understand her condition, work within her boundaries, and then exceed them in novel ways. He had worked off her energy with long walks and runs through the countryside. Encouraged small-muscle coordination in her hands with finger games, piano playing, and violin lessons. He had demanded that she write down her thoughts whenever she had an impulse to do so. In that way she had collected proof in black and white that her thought processes could be complete and logical. She gained courage to do more. And to hope.

But few recollections were as wonderful as those elicited by Dr. Tillingsworth. Most of Jess's memories were of the parade of doctors, whose examinations, prognoses and suggested cures ranged from the ridiculous to the sublime. Like that hideous creature who wanted to commit Amanda to an asylum, two physicians had called Jess a hopeless lunatic. Another—who she doubted had ever opened an anatomy text—claimed that her "humours were off-balance" and, like a medieval surgeon, called for leeches and a bloodletting, to which her father in his abject frustration agreed. There were the others, too. The oily one who prescribed laudanum daily when she was agitated. The thin one with liquid gray eyes who decided Jess was possessed by the devil and needed an exorcism—by him, of course. So yes, she trusted her own memories as good enough, perhaps the best equipment to help the child.

Meanwhile, Jess clung to what hope she could and muddled on with the challenge of aiding the girl who was so much like her.

"Best to wear yourself out, then, old girl." Jess rose, donned her robe, and descended the staircase. She crossed the hall, chose the library as a likely source of diversion, and noted as she passed that the door to the music room stood ajar.

No light gave evidence of an occupant. Yet Jess could feel the breath of life inside the room. Then she heard it.

A metronome ticked.

Facing it and the piano she had not played in over a week, Amanda did not turn when Jess crossed the threshold.

"Are you angry with me?" Amanda asked from the shadows.

Jess walked toward her, took a chair close by, and saw a flash of white stretch upon the child's lap. The sound of Precious's purring could have made the floorboards vibrate. "No. Should I be?"

"I can't sleep."

"That's not unusual for someone with your condition."

"Is that why you are awake? I mean, should I expect that for the rest of my life I'll not rest?"

"You'll learn ways to deal with your restlessness appropriately."

Amanda had overcome so much already.

Just as Jess herself had. The monotone. The inertia. The slow flowering to old joys and a new life. And then the terror of irrational behavior. Wild and rude. "The nerves realigning themselves—adjusting, if you will—to a new set of circumstances," Dr. Tillingsworth had told Aunt Mary.

His ideas were radically different from those of the first physician who had examined her immediately after her accident and predicted a somber future for her: "Perhaps paralysis, seizures, no memory of the accident."

But she had proved him wrong, hadn't she?

"You're recovering well from your fall, Amanda. You walk and talk. You read and run, do your lessons, all things your father thought you'd never do. You even play the piano, which requires dexterity in many tiny muscles. These are extraordinary achievements for one who has been through what you have."

Amanda sighed and stroked the cat. "I have been horrid these past few days, haven't I?"

"Your words and deeds have not been pretty."

"I'm sorry," Amanda whispered to the cat. "I've made things a mush."

"You are a precocious young woman, Amanda."

"Thank you. I haven't been wonderful lately."

"But you are worried. What about?" When she got no answer, Jess leaned forward in her chair. From this proximity, she could see the shadows of regret mar the elegance of the child's face.

"My father loved my mother dearly, you realize. When she died, he cried for days. I never saw him. I was confined to my bed because of my fainting and dizzy spells, but the servants told me, and so did the doctors who came to see me."

"You are worried, then, that your father won't recover from his grief?"

"I suppose so."

To continue in this vein meant Jess might discover family matters too intimate for the ears of a schoolmistress. Yet not to pursue Amanda's need to discuss this aspect of her life might mean the child would remain stuck on the tragedy of her mother's accident. To recover fully from this cataclysm, Amanda needed to come to terms with it, even though she might never remember any of it. Only then would she put behind her any grief or misplaced guilt associated with it. "What else troubles you, then?"

"I know he loved her!" Amanda proclaimed vehemently, her strokes of the cat halting. "He doted on her. Presents of jewelry and lavish dinner parties and tours abroad. She complained that he did too much, and she wanted him to stop. She said he could not buy her affection."

"Was that the only thing they argued about?"

When Amanda turned shocked eyes to her, Jess explained, "You told Lord Templeton the night you ran away that your parents were not completely happy together and that your mother played the piano incessantly. I hope you aren't distressed that I bring this up. I mean to help you."

"No, I'm not upset." The child sighed and resumed petting Precious. "Our servants knew, and the vicar's wife. I don't think anyone could miss noticing. When my parents were together, my father watched her too closely. She fought back by talking too gaily or playing the piano badly. Too forcefully. The air banged with it." She shivered.

Jess fought the urge to imitate her. Memories hovered over her, violent and nauseating.

"But in the past few days, Miss Curtis, I have been afraid of other things. I . . . I don't know what's the matter with me." She bit her lower lip and nuzzled the cat to hide her tears.

Jess went to her knees before her, a hand brushing dark burnished curls off her cheek. "I think I know. You are suffering from an ordinary event in the recovery of a head-injured person. Your brain is mending, just as your knee does when you have a bruise. You are experiencing the reconnection of old nerve endings or perhaps new ones."

Amanda cast miserable eyes to Jess. "Do you think I am insane?"

"A head injury does not make one insane."

"But I can't control what I think!"

This put Jess on guard. "What do you mean?"

"What is your definition of a person who is mad?"

"I can't define it. I am not a doctor."

"No. But tell me your definition anyway. You know more than most about such things."

"A person who exhibits insane behavior is incapable of reason. He cannot control himself."

"That's me since that day at the fair. I wanted to stop raving, but I was too angry."

"At what?"

"Othello. Desdemona . . . But now . . . now I see *things.* That play—"

Jess's flesh crawled. "What about it?"

"The entire time I saw Othello arguing with Desdemona . . ." Amanda's face filled with hatred, and for a desperate second Jess feared she'd have an irate child screeching again. What she got was an explanation uttered through clenched teeth: "I thought of my parents. The way my father looked at her, like a hawk. The way she fought back, but was so weak. And when . . . when Othello leaned over to strangle his wife, I didn't see the actors. Instead, I saw . . ." Amanda clamped a hand over her mouth.

"What?" Jess urged, remembering the scene at the fair.

"Oh, Miss Curtis," Amanda wailed and nailed Jess with wild eyes, "I think I must be insane, because all the while that man was killing that woman, I thought I saw my father strangling my mother!"

Jess gaped at the girl.

"Don't you understand, Miss Curtis? I'm frightened! I'm seeing things that couldn't possibly have happened. And that's insane, isn't it?"

At the indecent hour of seven in the morning, courtesy of his butler's directions, Jess found Rand. Sprawled in the grass, legs stretched out, he was examining the sunrise reflected in the pool in his garden. His stallion nuzzled grass nearby and took note of her and her mare's arrival with a whicker.

Rand no sooner turned than he was up, hands around her waist, helping her dismount and sliding her slowly down his body while his lips captured a languid sample of her mouth.

"I have never tasted anything for breakfast that remotely resembled this," she told him with her eyes closed, drifting from one succulent kiss to the next.

"Ambrosia," he growled. "The food of passion."

She chuckled. "You think of only one thing lately."

"Do I? If so, perhaps it's because I hear this siren calling me, and she's got the sultriest voice and the softest hair and these silken lips." He licked his own. "From the first, I wanted your mouth, Jessica Curtis. Give it to me again, will you?"

Groaning, she wound her arms around his neck. "*I* want more than a nibble, my darling Rand."

He gave her a feast of spicy short kisses and long, hot ones, each a delicious appetizer for more of him, sans clothes and propriety and the world's demands.

"Someday," he said gruffly, when the two of them were breathless, "we're not going to stop with kisses."

"I know," she sighed and nuzzled her nose into his chest, "and I won't want to."

He caught her face between his warm fingers. "Do you want to now? I'll make it perfect for you. You won't be sorry, sweetheart."

She shook her head, but said, "That I know in my heart. I came because I need you to help me."

His hot blue gaze flowed over her unbound hair, took in her unbuttoned riding jacket, and then examined her eyes. "In any way I'll help, my sweet Jess.

You appear to have had a worse than usual night. What's happened?"

She told him that Amanda and she had talked in the middle of the night and as a result, "She wants help—any help that I approve. I know of none except your friend, Rand. I want to take her to London to the doctor you told me about. I doubt her father would approve, but I question his real intentions toward her recovery, so I won't ask his permission."

"We'll go under the tightest security. Amanda has become worse, then?"

"In one way she appears better. She is less angry at others, quiet and conversational. But she is frightened by a new occurrence."

He shifted, rays of sun highlighting the sharp bones of his cheeks and jaw. Worry lined his mouth. "Which is?"

"She may be having delusions."

"Are delusions what one might expect with a head injury?"

"I'm not certain. That's why we must see someone who knows more than I. Please, Rand." She put a hand on his arm.

"This won't be easy on you."

"My primary concern is Amanda."

"Mine is you. This experience with her is tearing you apart, but I think it is necessary to your well-being, because—"

"Without reexamining my own experience, I can't proceed with my life. Yes, that's true. I have recently begun to see so many new possibilities for my life. New reasons to view my past, hopefully in a more circumspect way." She smiled serenely at him.

"Amanda's recovery is important to me. I must help her. My accident happened long ago, and my parents are dead."

"But there are even more similarities to Amanda's accident and recovery than you've told me, aren't there?"

She stared at him.

"It's true, then. These secrets keep you from me. I want you too badly, Jess, to sit by and allow you to ignore them."

"I have learned that cowardice eventually costs you your self-respect."

"A huge price."

"I have paid it for many years. I want to be proud of who I am when I come to you for—"

He plunged a hand into her hair and lifted her face up to him. "Anything."

"Everything," she whispered.

"I'm proud of you, Jess. I need you, darling. All of you, naked against me, skin to skin, heart to heart."

"I won't disappoint you, Rand. I promise you."

He kissed her madly, swiftly. "Go home, my love, and pack. We leave for London at midnight."

Chapter Ten

"DON'T LEAVE ME."

Jess peered down into Amanda's worried eyes.

"Please." She crushed Jess's hand.

The elderly doctor in the huge four-poster chuckled, then coughed. *"Bitte,* do remain, Lady Curtis. I think you want to, *ja?"*

"Yes, thank you," Jess affirmed. She wanted to be beside Amanda when this man asked her questions about her past and her injury. She wanted to support Amanda if she should falter in her courage to confront her problems. To hear them discuss a case similar to her own would be wrenching, and God knew, she would have loved to run from her own challenge—reviewing the details of her own mother's death and her father's . . . and her own part in both. "I want to stay," she said, because bravery might take her past the traumas of remembrance to a new, exciting life.

Amanda would not look at the elderly man propped

up in the bed. He was dressed in shirt and waistcoat, ready to receive, covers tucked up about his slight form, although he was obviously very ill.

"Mein freund," Dr. Steineke rasped to Rand who stood at his side, "help her to know I am not as frightening as I appear."

That was not the half of it, Jess thought. He looked ready to be carried off by his Maker. With yellowing skin and nails but no hair, the emaciated man could expire any minute.

"Bitte," he beckoned with a curl of his bony fingers. "Come, Amanda. You will sit here on this side of me with Fräulein Curtis. And Rand, resume your chair, *mein herr.* We are friends, bound to the same goal, so we will speak truth that goes no further than these walls." He wiggled his spectacles on his nose as he saw what reaction that might bring from Amanda. "Do you believe that, *liebchen?"*

"Yes, sir, I do," she replied with a smile that grew and made them all grin and relax into their chairs.

"Ach, so. I am told that you speak German, Amanda. How is that?"

"My mother had a music teacher who was from Düsseldorf, sir. I sat in on her lessons with him. He used many phrases, and I found that German is not so difficult to learn."

"I see, and did he teach music in a way you enjoy?"

"Yes, sir."

"Bitte, tell me."

Jess tilted her head at Rand, who sat across from her, on the other side of Dr. Steineke. Had Rand told his friend on his early morning visit here about the connection between music and Amanda's behavior?

As if he felt her scrutiny, Rand turned his dark blue eyes from the girl to Jess, then stuck there.

Yes, of course. He had told the doctor everything about Amanda.

And about her, too?

Definitely, because the doctor would need to know that she had suffered a head injury and that, with such knowledge, she had tried to aid Amanda's recovery—until she ran out of solutions and became frightened by Amanda's hallucinations. At that point Amanda had questioned her own sanity, and the only hope Jess could grasp was with Rand. Rand who had vowed to help her with Amanda and with her own progress in becoming a woman who could give love and accept love fully.

Jess shifted in her chair. Uneasy with the terrors this session with Dr. Steineke might bring, she scanned the large and heavily furnished bedroom of this doctor who was so kind as to try from his own deathbed to cure a child.

The room was appointed in rosewood with drapes of mauve and walls of beige, masculine and muted. So very different from the bedroom she occupied in Rand's town house on Grosvenor Square. A gold-and-white neoclassical style graced that home, where kings and queens had dined and danced, and now she occupied the marchioness's bedchamber.

At first sight of the room when they arrived from Farrell Hall, Jess had been entranced. Who wouldn't have been charmed by its creamy simplicity? But she had balked, standing there with Rand and his young butler.

It wasn't proper that she sleep here where the mistress of the house belonged. Well, what the devil, it wasn't proper for her even to *be* here in London with a child who wasn't hers . . . and a man who wasn't hers . . . and a secret that drew her in sympathy to the child and blocked her future with the man.

Rand insisted she use the bedroom. "With a large bath and decent dressing room, this is the most comfortable chamber in the house aside from my suite, through that door." He nodded at the far wall, then turned to the one opposite. "It also has a connecting door to the nursery, which will be Amanda's room. The better reason for you to remain here, Jess."

When she had flinched at his use of her first name in front of his servant, Rand hastened to add, "Reynolds will say nothing of you and Amanda being here, Jess. No one on my staff will. I hire people who are dedicated to me and my wishes, and I demand they be discreet at all times."

With that, Rand had turned on his heel and shut the door soundly between them, leaving Reynolds to explain the particulars. "I'll send my wife up to you, mum. She's the housekeeper and she'll bring a maid, too, to help you unpack. Will there be anything I might bring to you or the young lady before you retire?"

"Yes, please. Two glasses of warm milk." *Courage. Buckets of it.* "And a saucer of it for the cat Amanda brought with her, if you will."

Blessedly, Amanda had fallen asleep quickly. The

carriage ride in the middle of the night had been exciting to her. The idea that she was doing something clandestine stirred the child's imagination and hope. It was exhilarating to take a trip of which her father would not approve and to seek the help she so dearly desired. Ah, yes, she was weary of her delusions and their toll on her.

Amanda had welcomed this opportunity—at least until she was faced with the sickly doctor and, like all children, momentarily taken aback by physical disease. In fact, they had spent a pleasant morning enjoying the amenities of Rand's town house. The library. The billiard room. Then before luncheon, Amanda had faced Rand as he returned from a brief meeting with his friend Dr. Steineke.

"I wonder, Lord Templeton," she had asked, focusing on his cravat, "if you happen to have a piano in the house."

When he told her one stood in the front drawing room, she asked if she could see it and, having received permission, went off by herself to inspect it.

"Thank heavens, she is at least curious to know if I own one," Rand said.

"We'll see if she has the urge to play it," Jess mused.

"I hope she'll have more reasons to indulge herself soon. I spoke with the doctor. He is very sick, in the last throes of consumption, but he wants to help us if he can. He will see us tonight at eight o'clock."

"I'm eager to go," Jess told him.

Rand took her in his arms. "I know you are." He hugged her in such a comforting way that she understood he perceived her trepidation, too. "So that Emory and others will have no idea what I am doing here in London, I'll have my coachman come by at seven o'clock. Reynolds, dressed in my dinner clothes, will go to my club, enter the front door, then enjoy a repast with a few of his friends among the staff. Within ten minutes, a public brougham will come around to the front door here for us. I will be attired like Reynolds and you, as his wife."

"And Amanda?" Jess asked, finding the fun in his skulduggery amid the terrors of what they were about to do.

"Why, didn't you know that a young cousin of Mrs. Reynolds came up from the country only this morning?" The twinkle in his eyes dimmed as he asked, "Did you bring a veil?" At her nod, he lifted her chin. "Such a shame to hide such beauty. Someday soon you won't have to."

His words, a reference to a time when she wouldn't want or need to hide anything from him, pacified her jumping nerves. But at seven-thirty when she descended the staircase with Amanda to see Rand standing in his white marble foyer, Jess panicked.

While she climbed into the rented carriage, she pulled the black veil securely down about her cape collar. Feeling strangled with the tension of the coming meeting, she had sat in that coach, listening to the clomp of the horses' hooves as they made their way across town to . . . to Harley Street, she supposed, and knew she had forced herself to take the logical action that would free her from the shame of her most illogical one—the day she'd faced her father with a gun in her hand.

Jess clenched her hands.

"Und so, Amanda, you have brought your pet with you."

"Precious belongs to Lady Curtis, sir. But I like her." Amanda hugged the white angora, who purred her delight.

"Does she soothe you?" he inquired.

"Yes. She likes music, too."

"Any piece in particular?"

"I don't think so." She grinned.

"I understand you like Beethoven."

Amanda listed the works she enjoyed playing.

The doctor nodded. *"Gut.* But tell me how you feel about Chopin's Minute Waltz."

Ah, thought Jess. *The issue at hand, finally.*

"I'm not certain lately," said Amanda. "I think I like Beethoven's Moonlight Sonata better."

I don't, Jess answered for herself. *I hate it.*

"Explain yourself, *liebchen."*

"In my visions of my mother, I see her playing it over and over. I am sick of it. But she looks scared and . . . and scary."

Possessed by a demon.

"What happens in your vision after that?"

Amanda shivered. The cat jumped to the floor.

Jess quaked.

"Tell me, *liebchen."*

"My father comes into the room."

Yes.

"He has something in his hand."

"Und was ist das?"

"A newspaper."

A calling-card case. Beautiful porcelain. Ugly.

"He's angry, yelling." Amanda lurched from her chair, and Jess watched her with dead eyes. The child paced, wringing her hands. "He says he is ashamed of her. How could she do this to him? He'll be the object of jokes. So will she. He'll have to call in her doctor again. Now he will send her to that spa in Alsace, no matter what she says. He'll tell everyone they're going abroad for the Season. That way they won't have to face anyone while the whispers go around about them, about *her.* Doesn't she care? He's shouting at her. She's said nothing, you see. She has let him rave on. But then she . . ."

Laughs at him.

"Laughs at him."

Jess's vision cleared. Amanda had spoken her own thoughts. No. She couldn't have.

"She goes on as if she doesn't care what he says," said the child, like one in a trance. "As if she's . . ."

Insane.

"Mad."

Jess felt perspiration bead between her breasts. The lovely room before her paled, misting in a yellow misery.

Amanda blinked and seemed to fix her sight on something pathetic. "But my mother just sits there, laughing and playing the piano. My father is furious and throws the paper down. It's then that he sees me. He hasn't before because . . ."

I'm cringing. Shrinking into the draperies.

"I've been reading in the inglenook and only just come out now that he sounds so angry."

"*Und* what does he do, your father?"

He hits her.

"He leaves." Amanda walked back and forth. "He leaves." She grew pensive, watching her inner drama.

"Und your mother, *liebchen?* What does she do?"

"She watches him go and then turns to me. But she . . . looks odd."

Blank. Like a porcelain doll.

"Und does she say anything?"

"Finally. Yes. She says I must grow up to be a better person than she is. A better wife and mother." Amanda stopped to face the foot of the bed. Her skin was ghastly white, her eyes huge. "I tell her that she is a wonderful mother. The very best. But she says she's going to leave me. She must. 'Your father is right about that,' she tells me. 'I cannot let you pay for what I've done.' But I—I don't know what she's talking about! She doesn't make any sense to me, except I know she's leaving . . . leaving *me* . . . and I don't want her to go. I love her! I don't care what she's done or what he thinks she's done."

She was the world to me. She taught me nursery rhymes and pretty poetry. She taught me the recipe for taffy and how to pull it till it was the right mellow color. She endured my rough efforts on the piano and ignored my failures. She combed my hair, recited family stories that made me chuckle at my ancestors' foibles, and told me how flowers grew. I learned from her so many things, the most important of which was how to love.

"But it didn't matter what I said or how I cried. She put her arms around me and hugged me, and then she rose and left me."

And no words or tears could bring her back.

Amanda stared at Jess. "Oh, Miss Curtis," she pleaded, "don't cry! It's only a vision. It's not *real.*"

Jess sat in the double chaise before her chamber fire. She glanced up at the clock and realized she'd been here more than an hour.

Amanda had gone to bed quickly, utterly exhausted. She seemed unaffected by her ordeal, as if she had viewed a play with actors. As if the scene she had related were an impersonal presentation by people she did not know or care about. Jess still did not know if Amanda's story was real or imagined.

In her own mind, Jess replayed the scene in the doctor's bedchamber with precision. It had been at least five or six years since she had relived her long-ago experience.

She'd thought she didn't have to. She assumed she had learned everything there was to learn from it. That her mother had disgraced her father by her liaisons. That one of her mother's lovers had committed the unpardonable sin of publicizing their affair in a lurid manner. And that when her father learned of it, frustration consumed him and he became physically abusive. Jess had shut the scene in a dark closet of her mind.

But her visions *were* real memories. She knew that. Had always known it.

What she had not recalled until tonight was that she had adored her mother. Immoral and irresponsible in her role as wife, Elise Leighton had been a mother whom Jess mourned with all her heart. For the endearing reasons every child craves a mother's love,

Jess had wanted Elise's—and she had received it. Lavishly. Elise had bestowed on Jess her time, her attention. Elise had schooled her in piano and poetry, personally chosen tutors for her, and encouraged her toward excellence in any endeavor. Now, as headmistress of girls whose mothers were not often involved with their offsprings' lives, Jess knew what she had not understood as a youngster: Elise was unique for her time and her class. She took an avid interest in her only child, her daughter. Elise had spent hours teaching her music, poetry, painting, the skills of horsemanship. She'd demanded that Jess learn to jump posts, gates, hedgerows. And she had told her—*ordered* her—to remain at home with her father when he learned of the sordid excess of her passions with her last lover.

But Jess had forgotten the good portions of her mother's character because of that last awful scene scarce minutes before Elise died. Jess had thought the lesson to be learned from her mother's death was that passion was to be avoided, lest she lose her soul and her life.

But Jess had not lost herself. She had found a passion in her teaching and her students. She discovered a zeal for administering Farrell School. And finally, when one day her fervor to accomplish both those goals led her to Rand Templeton, she learned with Rand that the greatest passion of her life awaited her.

Elise had suffered and died and, in so doing, had set an example for Jess. But Jess had viewed only one facet of the lesson. Tonight she glimpsed the other. And with that in her sights, she seized her courage, rose from her chair, and went to knock on the connecting door to Rand's bedchamber.

To her amazement, he opened the door instantly. Dressed in a red brocade robe and black pajamas, he balanced a tray with cups and saucers and a pot covered by a cozy. "Here is your cocoa, more milk than anything, like your recipe for Amanda. I kept hoping you'd invite me in." He scanned her features for evidence that she would open more than this door to him. "Bringing you something warm and soothing seemed like a way to bargain." He looked worn with worry.

"You need never bargain," she confirmed, suddenly greedy for him, the only comfort she'd ever craved. "Let me show you," she whispered and took the tray from him, pulled him inside, and indicated the double chaise before the fire. As she poured for both of them, she felt his scrutiny. Giving him his cup, she sank beside him on the chaise, sipped the warm brew, and closed her eyes.

She heard him put his cocoa down and felt him turn to wrap an arm around her back and draw near. "You're as hot as Hades."

"Your footman built a good fire for me."

"I'll increase his wages. I wore a hole in the carpet pacing in there," he said, inclining his head toward his bedroom, "because I did not want to be presumptuous and intrude on your reverie."

"Analysis," she corrected him. "And you could never be presumptuous."

He arched both brows. "No chills?"

"No," she said, surprised, pleased. She put her cup and saucer on the side table. "Tonight I am not afraid—or not so much—of the awful scenes I remember. It is my memories that couple with my head injury to cause the chills."

He brushed his thumb across her lips. "I thought so. I want to help you, Jess, so that you're not afraid of anything—past, present, or future."

"You have helped me. You never get angry with me, even when I frustrate you so with my lack of progress."

"If I were prone to anger, the sight of you when Emory attacked you with that cane and when Othello killed his wife would cure me."

Jess chewed her lip. "I wish I'd never witnessed those scenes. I'm not very strong when it comes to things like that."

"No, you are too kind to believe others could be like that. It's not a surprise to me that you do well with children, darling. I have this vision of what wondrous things you can become. The famous headmistress."

She chuckled, thrilled at his compliment. "An archer of promise?"

"A pianist of great accomplishment."

"I could say the same of you."

He cupped her chin. "The only thing I want to hear is what I can become to you, darling."

"Oh, how I want to do that, Rand. But first I must explain why it has taken me so long to come to this point. I have wished so often that I could tell you about myself, about my past, but I have made a habit for many years of ignoring the facts of my mother's death. It was simpler."

"And safer, too?"

"Oh, yes. Definitely."

"You are safe with me."

She settled against him, reveling in his solace. "I have learned that."

This movement into his arms meant that now they were both stretched out on the huge chaise, facing the flames of the fire. Embraced by him as she was, he placed his lips on her temple and told her she was wrapped in his cocoon. "I will care for you, no matter what you have to tell me."

"I know that, too," she murmured. "You planned it so that I would be there when Amanda recounted her visions. That was wise of you. But then, you have been so much more rational about this than I from the start."

"That's not true. For the longest time I had no idea what problem we confronted."

She smiled at his use of "we."

He turned her a bit to see her expression. "That's better," he said with satisfaction on his face and settled her again into his arms. "I thought it practical for you to be present with Amanda. She is only a child, and when she was presented to a stranger, especially to a man with a foreign accent and unhealthy as Dr. Steineke is, Amanda needed to have someone there who loved her." His mouth rested on her cheek as he whispered, "Just as you did."

Jess covered his arm, which was wrapped about her waist. Lacing her fingers in his, she said, "You have thought of everything."

"Not really. I didn't think the afflictions caused by a head injury could be so great."

"That was because you had no experience with the

repercussions of them, and also because you and I had seen such progress with Amanda that we were not prepared to deal with her setbacks—that scene at the fair, and the visions."

"Are they really visions?"

Ah, the crux of our mutual dilemma. "After tonight I can truly say Amanda told us what she really saw. But whether she saw it in her head or in her home, I do not know."

"Neither does Dr. Steineke."

"For that, for his lack of readiness to jump to a conclusion, I liked him."

"He is wonderful."

Jess swiveled her head around to look at this man who was God's finest gift to her and said, "For him, I am grateful. For you, I am—" Tears clouded her eyes then.

Expectation drained him of color.

"Honored."

He framed her face with shaking hands and kissed her soundly. When he secured her back into his arms, she felt him swallow and recompose himself. "Perhaps tomorrow's session will tell us more."

"Amanda seems so calm about it all. As if it occurs outside of her. As if it is happening to someone else."

"But it *lives* inside you, my darling."

"Yes." She pushed back against his chest, as if in some instinctive way—what?—to be absorbed by him? Or to hide from him? From herself.

No. Not anymore.

"The same sort of scene happened when I was young," she told him in a rush. "The picture Amanda painted was a reproduction of one I saw between my parents, not just once, but many times. My mother was, in many ways, everything a parent should be. She was an angel—gay, tolerant, willing to play child's games in the nursery or our version of hide-and-seek on horseback. She had a mellow voice, hair of sunburnt gold, and eyes like the most costly aquamarines. I loved her, as a child adores her mother—completely, without knowledge of who she was or what she was to others or to herself. My father said he loved her. He doted on her. But he smothered her.

"She had wanted, ever since she was a child, to be a concert pianist. I remember her talking about it. She'd get this expression of bliss on her face. I didn't understand it, I was a child. But last year I read her diaries. I have had them for eleven years, but I had never read them. It wasn't until a year ago that I thought I could finally cope with her thoughts about her life, you see."

"I do."

She inhaled slowly. "My grandfather thought acting, singing, and composing were simply not done by a viscount's daughter. Cat's mother, who was my mother's older sister, led a life acceptable to my grandfather. She had met Walter Farrell when she first came out and she had loved him from the minute she met him. My mother evidently loved only music long before that, but my grandfather restricted her from practicing and composing. So what could she do? She conformed. She met my father when she was nineteen and married him. I think, from the way she wrote of her attraction to him that she loved him, but as a friend, not as a mate."

"What was his opinion of her delight in music?"

"He was—what can I say?—a man of his time and place. He allowed her to play at dinner parties. To occupy herself with her music. He treated her like a fragile doll."

"What happened?"

"She became obsessed with music. I remember her being constantly at the piano in the music room, night and day, at any time, at odd times. She'd hit the keys so hard the house would shake with it. My father would go to her. They argued, sometimes wildly. After such episodes we sometimes traveled to Paris or Rome. They went to the opera and the symphony and scandalized everyone by taking me—a mere child—along, even to bistros. One time we went to Vienna. I loved it there. So did my parents, for some reason which I'll never know. But, oh, we ate like gluttons—pastries and cakes made of thick chocolate and cream and giant black cherries drenched in liqueurs. And every night we waltzed in tiny cafés to violins and pianos."

"You like to waltz, then?"

"Yes, but I'm not very good at it. I haven't had much practice."

"Why did you travel with them? Weren't you given to governesses or sent off to school?"

"I had been, but like Cat, I was so active that I was always a challenge. I was, they said, too whimsical, too volatile, 'a difficult child.' Soon my mother hired special tutors for me. When we went abroad, I had new ones. I liked the change, the excitement, of new people and new places. But the idyll always ended. We'd come home. Then my mother would return to her old habits, and the joy would end. She and my father would fight. Finally he called in doctors." Jess shivered.

Rand bound her closer.

"He began to send her away alone. At first, I had no idea where she went. In my child's way, I knew only that I missed her and I hated the governesses, who could never equal my mother or tolerate a child who was overactive and lonely. From one of my governesses, I soon learned that my father had been sending my mother to women's lodges, rest homes, spas. Pick a term that means . . ." She bit back great pain.

"Asylum."

"Yes. She would come home looking grayer, weaker, smaller than when she left. She also took potions. She carried a little blue bottle around with her, patting it in her pocket as if it were her companion, drinking from it as if it were water."

"But it was laudanum."

"Yes, the remedy that was no remedy at all. She seemed serene, but she walked in a fog. I know now that she was addicted to the drug, but he . . . he encouraged her. When she used it, he knew she'd be docile—until one day, she wasn't. They fought. I watched them from my nook in the music room. He had come in, furious at her for some behavior, I don't remember what, and she laughed at him. He struck her across the face. But she hit him back! I cried out, and they paused. The next day she went away by herself, to Paris. My father went wild, packed me off to Uncle Walter and Cat in Kent." Jess grew silent, trying to summon details she had so long ignored as unnecessary to her well-being.

"Did your father find her? Bring her home?"

"No. He didn't. He . . . tried. I recall him telling Uncle Walter while Cat and I eavesdropped from the stairs. My mother would return to England for two weeks or more at a time. Each visit was a nightmare. They argued. She'd leave for the country house in Lancashire . . . or so she said. Every time she left, I begged to go with her, but she wouldn't let me. And every time she returned, she was different."

"Worse?"

"No, better. She was happier than I had ever seen her."

"Why? What happened?"

Jess could not halt the flow of tears that welled up, it seemed, from the pit of her heart. They rolled down her cheeks while she silently convulsed in his arms. "Oh, Rand. We did not know it then, but she had great reason to be happy. She had found remedies for her problems. A submersion in composing and . . ."

"And?"

"Lovers."

Jess sat forward then, her eyes on the fire. "The scene Amanda recounted tonight may have been her vision, but it was one I saw myself with minor differences. My mother decided to immerse herself in her passions, in her art, and in her love affairs. My father knew about the lovers for the longest time, or so she wrote in her diary. She thought he tried to dismiss her infidelity, live with it. But she became more open about her meetings and rendezvous. She *wanted* him to learn and to be disgraced. She had given up the laudanum and the wild laughter, and she now devoted herself to composing. She created over twenty pieces. Ballads and nocturnes and sonatas that would sear your soul. I have kept her score sheets. The works are incomparable . . . but in between creating her own compositions, she'd play this piece by Beethoven constantly."

"The Moonlight Sonata."

"I began to know each note, every crescendo, and I irrationally adored it or loathed it. I knew what her playing it meant." She looked over her shoulder at Rand. "She felt trapped by him. She played the sonata to annoy him. It was one more weapon she had until . . ."

She snapped her gaze to the fire.

"Until one day she sat composing in the music room and he found her. She and I had been riding minutes before. I sat in the inglenook reading, and my father had no idea I was there. When he burst in, he was shouting. He had something in his hand which I couldn't see at first."

"A newspaper?"

"No. A calling-card case, hand-painted by an artist who was well known for his risqué works. The calling-card case was one made for gentlemen who collected the . . . unique in art."

"Erotic, you mean."

"Yes."

"And the picture on the case was of what?"

"My mother."

Rand waited.

"Naked."

Jess rose then, unable to sit there. "She had posed for the artist, and he had taken advantage of her to put her likeness on card cases! He used his art to disgrace her! What a travesty," she said and contemplated Rand. "You are such a good man to sit here and listen to this sordid tale."

"I'm here. For you. Tell the rest of it, Jess."

"Until that day, my mother evidently didn't know about her lover's use of her portrait. Despite her own immoral behavior, she had enough innocence left to be shocked, appalled, but then when she saw how furious my father was, she enjoyed his shame and bitterness. Suddenly she'd found a way to repay him for that portion of her torment for which he was responsible. She simply stood there in the middle of the room and laughed at him. He advanced on her and hit her. I stepped from the curtains, and he froze.

"He left then. Undone, he simply turned on his heel. She stood there, continuing to laugh hysterically, as if she'd never find the end of her mirth. Two days later she was dead, thrown from her horse. But until the day she died, she chuckled to herself like a madwoman. She *was* by then, I think, insane."

"She was a person who had been denied the full use of her talents."

"Yes. Her personality became warped by it."

"Thank God you see it, darling."

"Oh, I do. There are ways to survive with your self intact."

"You know those ways, Jess. I see the product before me."

She faced him, tucking her legs beneath her. "But I didn't know how to flourish. I didn't possess the desire or the courage. It's terribly frightening to view the possibility of living passionately, wholly. But my worry—over friendship and intimacy with a man—has been overcome by you. I am so thankful for you, Rand Templeton. And now I want to be fair to you."

"What makes you think you haven't been?"

"I continue to be afraid of the intensity of what I feel for you."

"That has been the problem from the start."

"My mother lost herself in passion. Passion for music, for men, for . . . sex. My mother was not allowed to develop as she should have. Her father and her husband caged her in society's rules. She seized her freedom from them and their restrictions."

"By overindulging."

"To the point of shame and degradation. So then," she explained, "you can see that the example I had before me was that an excess of passion can bring suffering and sorrow. I understood what it was to work hard, attend to a thousand tiny details to make your work as perfect as possible. But I did not think I could ever experience a desire to apply the same devotion to a personal relationship with a man. And do you know why?"

"I must hear you tell me that."

"Because I had never seen any man I cared for, I did not need to confront the issue."

He stared at her, barely breathing.

"Then, when I did encounter the issue, I saw more problems loom. I was afraid that, like my mother, I'd make you hate me because I'm not a woman to simply run a house and take tea with the ladies or live totally through my husband and children. I feared you could come to resent the time I spent at the school.

"But you never questioned anything I did. You supported me in what I wanted, what I did—*had* to do—with my life. The last hurdle I had to surmount was cleared swiftly when I realized tonight that I not only loved my mother but that I would not go mad with my work because it is not an obsession. I love my work the way she loved music. But I can control my obsession, not let it possess me. Then, too, I began to care for you, Rand, in dimensions my mother never discovered with any man. And that presented me with my final questions: Would I, if I went to your bed, never want to leave? Would I become a hedonist?"

"What was your answer?" he asked raggedly.

"I think that taking and giving pleasure with the one you value deeply is not hedonism."

She spread her hands wide and let her whole body express the wealth of what she felt for him. "Oh, Rand, I'm not ashamed, and I'm not in despair. I have found my own delight in educating children, and no one has ever tried to dissuade me from it. Since my parents' death I've been fortunate to live with affectionate people who nurtured me and assisted me, encouraged me in any endeavor I thought worthwhile. My aunt Mary. Uncle Walter. Cat. And now"—she placed her hand on his cheek—"my sweet man, there is you." She moved closer, her fingers outlining his handsome lips. "Rand, I want you to know why and how much I love you."

As if she'd cast him in bronze, he simply looked at her.

"Debonair Lord Templeton." She felt a smile curve her mouth as she leaned forward and trailed her nose down along his. "Please talk to me, darling, before my courage fails me and I feel a need to fly about the room and touch things to keep my fears at bay."

"Touch *me!"* He gave a shout of triumph, grasped her hand, and pressed it against his frantically beating heart. "Say it again," he demanded, his voice rough.

"I love you. I have for weeks. Years. My whole life, I think sometimes when I want you and you're not near me. I love your concern for children—anyone's, everyone's children. I appreciate your dedication to any cause you take up."

"You're speaking precisely the right words. Tell me more."

She grinned, circled her arms around his neck, and declared, "I need you, Rand."

"For parrots and May Fairs?"

"And piano playing and—"

"Children."

"The very reason I came to you in the beginning," she confirmed on a thread of sound, "and the way I learned how patient and gentle you are."

"The reason I came to you at your request, and the way I learned how persistent and unselfish you are. So dedicated and magnanimous that you would face recalling the terrors of your past to help a child overcome hers. Jessica Curtis," he whispered reverently, "my generous woman, I love you."

She trembled. The declaration she had wished to hear, she now savored. "Kiss me a few times and repeat that, will you?"

"Gladly." He slid her down to the chaise and covered her body with his. "I'm yours."

His lips tasted softer than they ever had before. But

she was hungry for molten expressions of his love and gave that in return. He groaned, crushing her close, and she arched against him. "Like this," she revealed, amazed at the enormity of her desire for him. "I always wanted you totally."

He drew back. "This grows too hot too fast, darling. We can't go on," he protested and rose.

The shock of love offered and accepted, sealed with a kiss of passion and then abandoned, had Jess blinking at the ceiling. "Rand, don't leave. I want—"

He came to stand over her, misery lining his features. "If I stay here, I know what will happen. I let my body overrule my heart with one woman, who paid a huge price for our ecstasy, and I won't allow you to be hurt. I love you. Adore you. I want to marry you. But we are going to wait until we're married for any more of this. I will *not* lose you, Jess." He turned toward his room.

For once, her mind worked mercifully fast. She caught his sleeve before he could make it to the door. "I can't let you leave, Rand. I think you must make love to me, my darling, because I must demonstrate how I welcome the passion we can create together—and because you must learn that I am not like Susannah. I believe every word you say, and I love you unconditionally, Rand."

Chapter Eleven

SHE WATCHED HIM DELIBERATE FOR HALF A HEARTBEAT— until he took two steps and scooped her up into his arms. "I want you beyond your past and mine as well. Tonight we'll begin our future."

"Yes, please, Rand!" She wound her fingers in his hair and held him still to demonstrate the budding of her fervor for him.

He received her kiss with a patience that swiftly died as he dipped his tongue inside the seam of her lips. When she opened wider for him, he took more until he robbed her of her breath and her sanity.

"Your passion tastes intoxicating," he told her as his lips sipped at the skin of her throat.

She writhed against him, lost in sensation.

He began to walk with her, but she was intent on trailing molten fire along his throat. "You burn high and fast, Jess. Wait until we get to the bed before—"

She couldn't stop. She had to feel his shoulders and his arms. She slid from his embrace. Her hands couldn't seem to cease their journey, and he groaned, bracing her against the wall. The contrast of cool, flat wall and hot, muscular man sent jolts of desire through her. With her body, she could tempt him, tease him, please him, pleasure him. Oh, that was such a heavenly idea. . . .

"My love," he said gruffly, his mouth pressing fervent kisses down her throat to her breasts, "I will not take you standing up. Not your first time." Somehow he caught her wrists and cuffed her with determined fingers. "This will be long and sweet, Jess. We have no need to rush"—he assessed her with smoky eyes—"and I will delight in giving you hours of enjoyment."

"What will make you happy?" she asked, her vision of him dreamy.

"I'll have you, naked against my skin, your heart to mine."

Mad to have that occur now, she slid out of his arms and reached for the brocade frogs on her robe and the satin ribbons on her nightdress. She watched him, his expression fierce and urgent. Suddenly shy, she halted, wondering if she was too brazen. . . .

"Go on, darling. Impetuous is how you are—and always for the right reasons."

"Being unpredictable is—"

"Very exciting."

Her eyes misted. "I can't believe how fortunate I am that *you* are so predictable."

"Continue, sweetheart, and learn new aspects of my nature."

His statement propelled her, and her fingers plucked at the last ribbon near her breasts. The cotton parted, and the subtle enticement had him flaring his nostrils and waiting . . . waiting. . . .

She stepped close, ran two appreciative hands up over his chest, realizing, admitting to herself, what else he wanted. Summoning more courage and a smile, she unlaced his sash, pushed his robe down his arms, and then undid the buttons on his pajamas.

She almost cried. In the sepia gilding of gaslight, Rand Templeton surpassed archangels she had seen in churches. His skin was bronze, smooth, and solid as stone, roughened by hair as black as coal and tapering from massive proportions to a lean waist. His arms were carved marble, trembling as she ran her fingers down them from his shoulders to his caring, waiting hands. She lifted them and brought them to her lips. When her eyes closed, she could still see him. But, oh . . . she needed to feel him.

She sent his two hands along her arching throat, inside her gaping gown, across her shoulders, down to her waiting breasts, and she looked up. Caprice said to kiss him, claim him as if yesterday had never been, tomorrow would never come, and only this, "Only *now* matters."

In a minute's melting of flesh, her bare skin met his. The conflagration made her gasp.

He pressed her against his arm and sent his hand down her hair, to her lips, past one breast, to her legs. "Darling," he whispered, "you are exquisite. I've been crazed with the desire to feel you ever since that night we found Amanda. I wanted your hair wrapped around me"—he draped one long tress over his shoulder—"and your legs between mine." He squeezed her close. "Your lips on mine." He kissed her hard and then moved to her breast. "Now I must have you in my mouth. Invite me, sweetheart."

"Oh, please. Touch me everywhere, or I think I'll die."

"Live with me, Jessie," he entreated, a devastating tenderness in his deep blue eyes. "Delight in me as I do you. Let me teach you."

He anchored her to him, bent over her, closed his mouth upon her needy nipple, and her whole body sank into his magic. He took her delicately, his lips a blessing to her ravenous hunger. He had her wildly, drawing her into his mouth with such a storm of care that she swayed and grabbed his hair.

"Oh, Rand! I never dared to dream of you!"

"No need to dream, darling. I'm here. I'm real. I want you. And you are the sweetest flesh and blood. Enjoy me," he crooned and shifted her in his arms so that he cupped her other breast. With a look of promise, he laved the other crest.

Fused to him, she writhed. She rubbed her legs together while some fury built inside her belly. His hand traced her ribs and curved over her gown along her hip and thigh. The cloth became a torture that separated her from his skin. Her every nerve screamed to tear it away.

She ran kisses over his jaw, calling his name, urging him on for some inevitable and indefinable joy until his hand rested at the place where she needed him most of all.

"I mean to make this unforgettable for you," he vowed as he dipped his fingertips inside her, and the two of them gasped.

"You opened places in my heart," she whispered as she undulated into his inspiring touch.

"Let me open your body, darling," he promised as his fingers parted her, the friction of the gown making her moan as she felt the cloth absorb her flowing need of him. "God," he said, nipping her earlobe, "you're burning up."

She froze. "Is something wrong with me? Am I—"

"You are perfect! Everything about you is so right." His eyes praised her from hair to breasts. His fingers swirled, summoning more admiration for his ardor. "For me."

Her heart soared and she pulled backward. In one lithe shrug of her shoulders, she let her gown fall to her waist. Her reward was a fierce narrowing of his eyes. She vibrated, his glance sending waves of desire along her spine. He leaned near to circle her burning breasts with his talented tongue while she shook her hair back and praised a god who had decided humans could feel such pleasure.

His tasting of her skin had her convinced she needed to sample more of his delights, and she shifted. Her gown slithered down her hips and legs. She smiled and knew, from the way he stopped breathing, then cherished every naked inch of her, that she had done the right thing.

Dragging in air, she thought he would take her in his arms.

He only stared into her eyes.

She thought he'd at least say what he thought of her body.

He stepped out of his pajama bottoms.

She thought she should run, unable to stand so close and not reach out to him.

"Look at me."

She fastened her gaze to his and couldn't speak.

"All of me."

She did. Oh, she did. She skipped those marvelous assets she'd glimpsed before and examined the one part of him her every instinct demanded she possess now. She whimpered, unable to believe how much man he was. Long and wide and hard and hers.

She bit her lip while her fingers tingled to touch him. "I—I never imagined you could be so large."

He barked with laughter, which quickly changed to ardent appreciation. "Thank God for that. I don't want you to run from me but to come to me."

"You are very big, and I—" One of his hands drifted over her hip, across her thigh, into her hair. She blushed, she was sure, to her toes. "I have no idea if I can—"

"You'll hold me, sweetheart. I'll caress you and pet you until you're more than ready for me." He extended his hand.

She took it without hesitation. Because she needed to know if paradise began and ended in his arms, with his kiss, against his skin, she followed him like a sleepwalker.

Beyond their connecting dressing rooms and bath, his bedchamber was twice the size of hers. So was his bed.

The sight gave her pause.

Filling suddenly with alarm, she stood at the door and watched him walk like a sleek giant animal to the center of the huge pastel Chinese carpet. The medieval canopied four-poster on the dais beckoned.

Rand turned, his eyes ablaze. "Do you like it?"

"Yes, I— It's lovely."

"I intend for us to have each other there."

She examined the ornately carved oak bed with its royal blue coverlet and creamy sheets, turned down for him—and now inviting her. Feeling his eyes on her, she turned to probe his gaze. He meant for her to continue. He wanted her absolutely sure of this—and of him.

She crossed the room like one possessed, mounted the two steps of the dais, slowly faced him, and sat down, sliding back along the mattress to the center of the impossibly huge bed.

"Come share it with me," she said, not knowing if it was her voice or her heart that spoke.

He strode to the edge of the bed, and though his eyes devoured her, he did not draw nearer. "Lie back." When she let her fear of such boldness flash into her eyes for a second, he was fast to whisper, "I want to see you against the blue coverlet. The strawberry of your hair and the milk of your skin. You can't know, darling, how delicious you look. Lie down, and I promise I'll reward you. I want to eat you up. . . . *Yes,*" he rasped when she eased herself back on her elbows and then down to the slick coverlet. "Close your eyes, love of mine."

Recognizing that this act would be the final commitment of her body to his soul, she did as he requested.

She heard his feet pad upon the carpet. In seconds he returned. She felt his knee sink into the mattress as his body heat warmed hers. For a spellbinding minute, she knew his eyes consumed every part of her until he spoke.

"It is a four-hundred-year tradition of the Templetons that every marchioness comes to her husband for the first time in this bed. But this treasure is even older." He took her left hand and slid a small cold object onto one finger. "It is the betrothal ring of the marquesses of Ashford. Open your eyes, Jess, and look into mine. See what you are to me. Then say you'll marry me."

Words fled before the beauty of his present.

"Yes is the only answer I will accept."

She raised her hand and studied the ring, a shimmering circlet of sapphires and diamonds. "You didn't have to do this now . . . before we . . . Why?"

Compassion surfaced in his eyes. "You know."

She studied him. "I do," she murmured finally, pushing back the black hair from his brow. "You're proving to me yet again that you are not like that artist or my father or grandfather. You're trying to show me how honorable you are." She caught back a sob of joy.

"Say you're going to marry me."

"I'm going to make love with you, darling," she told him with a teasing lilt, "and afterward"—he gripped her shoulders—"I'll spend my life doing so, as your wife."

Whatever she had felt before in his arms—desire, fear, delight—paled in comparison to the swift ecstasy her commitment to him brought.

With an oath of joy, he seized her. Kissed her hard. Arranged her purposefully, and then straddled her.

With a devil's grin, he ran his big hands from her crown down to her needy center, and stopped.

He dropped kisses over her breasts, her belly, and her thighs, then into her curls, where he spread her wider for the most tender exploration she'd ever known.

She soared into a new realm where sight and sound blended to show her only him. Her ears rang. Her heart pounded. Her hips lifted from the bed. His mouth composed a wild prelude to his possession of her, and she could do nothing but follow.

Then suddenly he left her.

She demanded to have him back. He soothed her by trailing a hand from her throat past begging breasts to waist and belly, and there where her body cried for him most he parted her to trace every fold, each burning inch. "Sweet Jessie, you're so beautiful, my love." He inserted one long finger, and she rose up off the mattress. "So giving." He bestowed a deeper thrust with more fingers. The sound of her liquid need of him consumed her senses in flames.

She reached for him.

"I know what you want." He led her hands around the silken part of him, which she had to have or die. At her touch he shuddered. His surrender granted her courage, and she gazed at him.

He was beautiful. As God created man, this creature was by design hers. Tenderness cloaking strength. "I want you inside me." She led him on with words and strokes.

He swallowed and arched into her caress. "There'll be babies. You'll have to marry me soon."

"Yes, *yes*. Tomorrow. Next week. Just *not now!*"

He snorted. "Next month," he demanded and urged her hands away from him so that he could place himself at the entrance to her body.

"You are a terrible man to take advantage of a woman when . . . *ohhhh, Rand . . ."* He gave her a sample of his length, and she moaned, "Yes! In June!"

He halted. "The first day available. Say it," he ordered between clenched teeth as he slid into her and tempted her with "We'll do this often."

"In the Tuttle church!" She beat the mattress when he stopped again.

"How novel, darling." He gave her another inch. But paused. "Who'll be there?"

"The vicar! *Oooo, yes, more, you wretched man!* All right, the whole village!" She sank her nails into his hips.

"Wherever I say. Whenever I call."

"Piccadilly Circus, Albert Hall—at *teatime."* She smoldered. "Any nook or cranny in the whole of bloody England!"

He chuckled. "Anywhere on earth you are, I love you."

She struggled to sit up. "If you don't do this, Rand Templeton, I may leave you this minute!"

He offered another sample, and her head lolled in ecstasy as he returned with a long, slow thrust that made her groan. "Don't ever leave me," he urged.

"I can't."

"I promise satisfaction."

"Just give me yourself."

"Yes, love. Now."

And so he took her up and into a crescendo that freed her of her body's last impediment to their union. She gave it gladly, with no remorse, no regrets. Seated at the door to paradise, he pressed against her with honeyed torture. "Do you feel pain?" He brushed her hair from her face.

"No, no. Only joy. Oh, Rand, Rand," she plunged her hands over him, "what is this driving need?"

"The mystery," he said, flowing in and out, "and the madness of what we will be together from now on."

With him inside her, he sent a gentle hand between them, and there he found some sorcerer's point that drove her up into his arms and made her crazed for the harmony she'd barely heard before.

He kissed her, caressed her, and took her higher to some astral hall where the black of heaven beckoned and the stars danced in concert to their ecstasy. Above the cares of yesterday and beyond the fear for tomorrow, she rose with him, his arms securely around her, and together they found the unison of passion and release.

The drifting back to earth was a lullaby. His body, hot and hard, became her only reality, her every peace. She moved against him in languid ardor, spreading kisses down his throat and across his marvelous chest.

"You're beautiful," she told him.

He barked in laughter. "Darling, you are supposed to feed a man's vanity with virile words."

"Those are too simple for you." She sat up and swung a leg over him, running her hands over the flesh that had brought hers such freedom.

"I prayed you'd come to me."

She chuckled, an airy trill to her own ears. "Prayers

come true, then. From the beginning I was enchanted by you."

"You looked so much like the indomitable headmistress, but so scared and so delectable. Like now." He pushed her hair away from her nipples and cupped her breasts, thumbing the points to sizzling peaks.

"Oh, ummmm . . ." She knew she was purring as he replaced his thumbs with two suckling kisses. "I think I wanted to do this long before that morning weeks ago."

He pulled away. "How long?"

"Since I saw you at Cat and Spence's wedding."

He pressed her breasts together and plumped them to receive the velvet swath of his tongue across their crests. "Hmmm, to think we wasted those years when we could have been doing this."

She frowned.

"What's wrong?"

"You asked me to marry you," she mused, considering his ring and his beguiling eyes.

"And you consented." He tensed.

"Yes, but—" She raised her face to the ceiling as he gripped her arms and sank beside her.

"I won't let you walk away now, Jess."

"I want to know . . ."

"Ask."

"Why did Susannah not believe you would return and marry her? I cannot imagine anyone unable to see how honest you are, how forthright."

"I asked her that question as she lay dying. She said no one had ever kept a promise to her and she had no reason to think I would be different. When her pregnancy began to make her sick each morning, and when she grew big so quickly, she could not bear to face any social criticism. Her parents, of course, were missionaries and were opposed to passion expressed before marriage. In Susannah's convoluted logic, she thought if she no longer had the baby, she'd wipe her so-called sins away. But she only added another when she took that drug and drank too much of it. She suffered the agony of a slow poisoning. She aborted the baby as I sat there with her. She followed him within hours." He shot a hand through his hair. "I thought myself responsible because I did not return to Calcutta sooner and couldn't find her in London, despite clues to her whereabouts, until weeks after I docked. I was also angry with her for killing our baby. He was my baby as much as hers. I thought of a thousand things she could have done—sent for me through my Calcutta agent, used her meager savings to come to me in Annam. I was bitter at her that she had acted so independently. But most of all, I missed her. I had dearly wanted her—and my baby."

Jess sank into him. "Give me your sorrow over them. I'll help you bear it, Rand."

The vise of his arms clamped about her and tucked her beneath him. "You, Jessica Curtis, are so very predictable." They both grinned. "I need you, adore you, and I admire you for your bigheartedness, my darling."

Her mind stumbled over the word "admire" for one syncopated second, and then she moved against him in the age-old promise of a woman to her beloved. "We will become all things necessary and divine to each other."

He made love to her again then, their union a

rhapsody of new delights. The novelty of happiness shook her to the marrow of her bones, and when she felt the first note of terror over it, she wept quietly.

He kissed away her tears, which he thought were tears of joy. She did not dissuade him and soon feigned sleep. Content at her rest, Rand found his own.

The hours ticked by, and she reclined there in his embrace, listening to the tempo of his satisfaction and reciting variations of how to reveal her last secret.

Her lie.

No matter how she said it, one thing would be true. Once he knew, he could not say he admired her.

She gave a silent cry of despair at the thought of hurting him so.

After all is said and done, you are still a coward, Jessica Curtis.

Even in sleep, instinct had Rand curling her closer.

Ironic, isn't it? The very thing you feared has not occurred.

Her hands drilled into the sheets.

No, dammit! She had not lost her total self inside their love!

If she had, she wouldn't now be riddled with the secret that commanded her to tell him or leave him.

Chapter Twelve

"SO THEN, *LIEBCHEN*, WHAT ELSE ARE YOU AFRAID OF?"

Ah, yes. Rand heard Dr. Steineke's words with a grim firming of his lips. *The question that I, too, would like an answer to.*

He detected only silence from Amanda.

And the same from Jess.

Rand didn't have to look at either of them to know their problem. It was reluctance. Fear of telling all and allowing someone else intimate knowledge of the self.

Rand drew back the drapes with one hand and braced himself against the windowpane. Below, a heavy spring rain painted the street in black ink. Reflections of the gaslight flickered across the sidewalks as a few brave souls scurried to get out of the downpour.

Just like you. Rand set his jaw. *Can't find a way to permanently unlock Jessica Curtis's heart. Despite last night's intimacies, she runs from you.*

He could feel it. Had known it like lightning at dawn when she had begun to remove herself from his arms without a word. He'd swiftly caught her and brought her back.

But his kiss was too little and perhaps too late to counter whatever tragedy lurked in her eyes.

He'd thought at first that her reticence was virginal innocence, natural shyness the morning after her initiation to the art of love. He concluded that the solution was to give her more evidence of how they were so very right for each other.

He'd given it.

He shut his eyes now at the memory of how rapidly Jess had come to him, with him. Like molten gold, the vision of how Jessica Curtis made abandoned love to him poured through his mind and filled his veins with fresh desire.

He shifted, his shoulder touching the parted drapery, and glowered at the street.

He had only himself to blame.

Too simplistically, he had assumed that her revelations last night—and her surrender to their passion for each other—had resolved whatever her conflict was.

You were so wrong.

If he had been too overcome with joy to recognize that before sunrise, he had seen it at his breakfast table. Noted it in her finicky eating. In her need to fly from him to see if Amanda was up and to continue with her lessons.

He had let her go. Christ, how could he keep her? No mere kiss would do. He had only to brush his hand against hers while reaching for the marmalade and she jumped away from his touch.

He crossed his arms and scoffed at his inadequate alternatives. He'd offered her the daily newspapers. When that failed, he'd tried an invitation to his study and a look at some sketches he'd done of Asian flowers. She had examined them with interest, but then said, "Amanda must be awake by now and I know she would really enjoy being shown to the drawing room and your piano."

Amanda appeared minutes later and was thrilled at the chance to play. What had he expected? The child needed to amuse herself. She was confined here for fear her father might discover that he and her schoolmistress had smuggled the child into London to visit the most renowned brain specialist in Europe.

Rand had shown Jess and Amanda to the drawing room, a ball of contradictions. Dejected that he hadn't gotten Jess to warm to him, he was also damned happy to give her and Amanda the means with which to occupy themselves until they could once more step into his carriage that night and ride off to see the doctor. He decided he would throw himself into increasingly urgent textile business and estate management issues, which he had sorely neglected lately while he assisted Jess and Amanda. He could not continue to do so without consequences to his prosperity and that of his mill laborers and farm tenants.

But Jess had caught him as he reached the hall and stopped him with gratitude shining in her gorgeous aqua eyes.

"Thank you," she had offered in a way that sounded like the dulcet tones he had evoked from her last night, when she lay naked in his arms.

"You're welcome," he had replied, replaying memories of her cries of ecstasy when he was inside her. "I want you—" he had said in a way that made her redden down to her prim neckline—and beneath, he prayed, to the part he needed now and forever. "I want you to have a pleasant afternoon."

"I know I will."

He needed to crush her to him and carry her off like a pirate with a prize he must steal to gain. Because Amanda might be within earshot, the most he could do was to take Jess's hand. But when he raised it, he saw she did not wear the Templeton family heirloom he had given her last night. "Your day will be better than mine. You removed my ring."

She cast her eyes to her bare hand. "I took it off this morning. I did not know how to explain it to Amanda."

"It requires only a few words of truth."

"I don't want her to know that I . . . that we—"

"The child is innocent of what occurs between men and women, I think. Yet she knows—as your students seem to, and you don't—that you and I are committed."

"Please," Jess whispered with a glance over her shoulder to locate Amanda. Rand could hear her as she trilled a few notes on the piano.

"She can't hear us, Jess. But the child has eyes to see, as I do. So tell me what is wrong in the light of this day, darling."

"Let's go into another room."

"I'm not budging, Jess."

She bit her lower lip. "I'm questioning what we did last night."

"And?"

Her huge eyes swam with tears. "I want to marry you."

"But?"

"There are more things you do not know. You deserve the best of one who cares for you. In my humility, I hear you say you love me, and I want to be worthy of that."

He wondered what he had failed to do to convince her that he loved her without reservation or conditions. "I know your worthiness, Jessica Curtis. You need to see it. Whatever it is that calls that into question, I want it out. Tonight."

She hadn't responded or nodded. Hadn't even blinked. She had simply stared at him for a long minute. Then she had returned to her student.

He hadn't seen her since. He refused tea and took supper at his club. There he had the good fortune to find a friend with whom to dine. John Marlow had been a business associate of Rand's for over ten years. As such, he was instrumental in helping Spencer Curtis three years ago when smuggling and blackmail had clouded Spence and Cat's future together. John, who was also the father of one of Jess's students, Corinne Marlow, now bluntly told Rand of a rumor circulating about him and Jess.

"Glad to see you tonight," he said. "Heard you were up from Kent and I would have come around to call tomorrow to tell you this. It's unsavory, I'm sad to say, but I will tell you. Harrison Emory was in town briefly last week before he gadded off on his perpetual rounds to God knows where. Trying to forget his wife, my Edwina says. Whatever his problem is," John continued, taking a swallow of his Bordeaux, "Emory drinks too much and wonders aloud—and in my drawing room, I'll add—what your intentions are toward Cat's cousin."

Rand had put down his fork to listen to John's story.

"The man says you are with her night and day. He implies . . . certain breaches of propriety."

"None have occurred. I have gone to Farrell Hall to help with a student."

"Emory's daughter. Corinne wrote about her. What's her name?"

"Amanda."

"Yes, yes. But, Rand, let me put this to you. Corinne also writes that you are there often. If Emory knows about your presence there and I do, how many other parents of students do? And you know what mischief idle minds can get up to, Rand."

"They can't indulge in much gossip about my actions at Farrell Hall, John. Jessica and I are engaged to be married. We haven't announced it because Jessica wants to wait a few weeks." But *why* did she insist on waiting? That was the question for which he had no answer.

"I understand. Cat is very near to term with these twins, and Spence tells me he doesn't want his wife excited in any way. Are you saving the news until after those babies are born?"

"Not that long," Rand said, hoping he was right

about the timing, grateful he had this excuse about the twins to please the wags.

But it galled him that it was now public knowledge that he pursued the headmistress of Farrell School for Young Ladies. To waylay further speculation and any damage to Jess or her school, he had to make her see the need to marry him—and as quickly as the social code permitted.

Within minutes, Rand had abandoned John to his port. Climbing into his coach, he ordered his driver home while he brooded over what he had learned about Emory—and what he still needed to know about Jessica.

Rand was tempted to find out more by himself. Certainly he could return and ask discreet John Marlow if he had ever heard rumors about the Curtises. Better—but worst of all—he could visit Spence in Richmond. Cat might have told Spence about the horrors Jess was hiding from him—and from herself.

But hell, to skulk about was not his style.

Besides, he wanted Jessica to tell him.

He'd arrived home, resigned to ask her to reveal her secret. He wouldn't demand or push, but simply state his case while he waited for Jess to discover the next steps on her own. The frustration of merely passing time was killing him, especially when he needed to make an engagement announcement soon to squelch budding rumors.

Within minutes he had gathered Jess and Amanda into his carriage and they had headed for Harley Street.

In a repetition of last night, Jess and Amanda sat

near Dr. Steineke's bed. Tonight he coughed more frequently and looked even paler.

Rand turned and lounged against the window frame.

Amanda appeared nervous, shy of the doctor whom she had liked before. She petted Precious with rough strokes, which made the cat so uneasy she jumped down to roam the room. Though Rand wondered what had happened to rob the child of the serenity they'd seen less than twenty-four hours ago, he was more taken with Jess.

She appeared . . . what could he call it?

Shattered.

Tearing his gaze from the torture in her face, Rand focused on her white-knuckled hands and listened to the rain outside.

"I repeat, *liebchen,* what is your trouble?"

"I don't know what you mean, sir."

"Bitte. Of course, you do."

Amanda scowled at the kindly doctor. "I saw my vision in full when I was here with you, and . . . and afterward I slept the whole night through. I haven't done that since before I saw the play at the fair."

"I see." The physician trained his overly bright eyes on the child's. "You had a good day today, *ja?"*

"Yes. We . . . Lady Curtis and I read *Ivanhoe.* We played the piano. Even the Minute Waltz, and I was good, wasn't I, Miss Curtis?"

Jess nodded, but Rand saw the shadows loom in her eyes when she gazed back toward the doctor.

"Don't you think it odd that you would play that waltz, *liebchen?"*

"No." Amanda folded her arms and looked longingly toward the door.

"Why do you want to leave?"

"Because you are not being nice." Amanda pouted.

"Or is it because I won't let you tell me lies?"

At the doctor's bluntness, Jess's mouth dropped open.

"I'll tell you what I want," Amanda vowed.

"That will do no good. You must be honest, *liebchen.* We agreed. It is the only way to—"

The child shot from her chair, which crashed to the floor. "I *am* honest!"

"Nein, liebchen. Das ist nicht so. Your foot taps. Your hands open and close, like so . . . and your eyes go to the door. You do not have courage to look at me in the eye. What bothers you?"

"I . . . I'm not feeling well. I ran to my room this afternoon to get a bit of music and sprained my ankle on the stairs."

"Is that so?" Dr. Steineke asked, as if he did not believe her. But he checked Jess's eyes. When she shrugged, perplexed, he focused on the child. "You did not reveal this to your Miss Curtis."

"I did not want to bother her. She has been very sad today with her own memories."

Rand shot a glance at Jess who suddenly had a terrible time swallowing. Sad?

No, more like terrified. Of me? Of marriage? Why, dammit, why?

The doctor coughed violently and wiped his brow, but went after Amanda with a tenacity gloved in tenderness. "You are with friends, Amanda. They take great trouble to bring you to me. In order to help you, they avoid your father and ignore what others might say about you. You must give back with both hands those things which you can."

Amanda faced Jess. "I want to leave."

Jess examined Amanda for the longest time, as if she too sought a reason for her sudden demand to depart. Whether she found a cause for the child's behavior, Rand could not say. She did smile slowly with sympathy. "That will not solve anything, dearest. Believe me, I know this to be true."

How? Tell her how. Tell me!

Jess reached out a hand to Amanda.

The child sidestepped her. "I said I want to go home. Back to school. I'm fine. I'm better now. There is no more to reveal, and we are finished."

"So. It was only a vision," said the doctor.

"That's all. A vision." Amanda nodded.

"You did not replay it in your mind today?"

"No."

"Not last night in your dreams?"

"No."

"Should we invite your father to hear about this vision?"

"He doesn't need to know."

"Does not *need* to? Excuse me, but I thought I heard Fraulein Curtis say your father wants you to remember, if you can, what happened to your mother on the day she died."

"Yes. He does. He wants me to get well," she offered with hauteur.

"So would any parent. But you do not remember. Therefore you are not better to his satisfaction."

"Of course I am!" She flapped her arms at her sides.

"See. I walk and talk. I may not remember much about the day she died, but I am well, I tell you."

The doctor widened his rheumy eyes. "So you *do* remember something about that day."

Amanda looked as if someone had stuck a dagger in her. "Yes," she said in a small voice.

"What?"

"Well . . . well . . . that she was angry with me."

"Are you certain this memory of her anger is one of the day she died?"

"Yes, of course. We never argued before."

"You were always an obedient child?"

"Yes, yes! You doubt me! Why do you torment me?"

"Describe this argument."

"I see only pieces of it."

"*Gut.* That is a beginning."

"They don't make sense. In the first piece, she said she was leaving me. She had never left *me* before. I was crying. She said she couldn't come back. Why not? I wanted to know. But she wouldn't answer me. And in the next memory, I see her mounting her horse, spurring him on, and—"

"*Nooo!*"

Rand's heart jammed in his throat when he realized the one springing to her feet, objecting with tears running down her face, was not Amanda but Jess!

He strode to her, though the doctor waved a hand to ward him off. Rand took her arm. She yanked it free.

"Take us home, Rand!" Jess pleaded. "Take us out of here."

"That is not wise, Fraulein Curtis. You make of yourself a poor example."

Jess shot a look at Amanda. "I have my own issues to conquer here. Forgive me, but I cannot listen to more. Not today. I simply must deal with this in my own time, in my own way." She looked at the doctor. "Do not push me."

"Nein, Fraulein."

Jess spun to face Rand. "I cannot hear any more."

With apology in his eyes, Rand bade the elderly man good-bye and opened the door for Amanda and Jessica.

At the stroke of three o'clock in the morning, Rand looked up once more to the connecting door to Jess's room.

Sleep was a phantom he had not even bothered to seduce this hellish night. He had tried reading. Every word on the page repeated the dialogue he'd heard tonight on Harley Street.

He'd tried sketching, a skill he had not used since that terrible day three years ago when he had drawn a portrait of Susannah and another of Jess. Tonight, each one was Jess. With tears in her eyes, of course. In the end, he simply sat before his bedroom fire with a bottle of brandy by his side and considered the door between his chamber and hers. But he had no taste for liquor to blur his mind.

Her door could be unlocked, but that was only one frail impediment to their happiness. Others were stronger. One Rand recognized in those few minutes earlier with Jess and Amanda and Dr. Steineke. There something had occurred—or *re*curred—that blocked Jess from him. Something else had happened—or been confirmed for Jess—this morning in the hallway when he'd shown anger that she had removed his ring. If he hadn't demanded . . .

He had pushed her, done the very thing he said he wouldn't. He allowed his frustration to rule his actions and demanded she tell him what bothered her. He'd even given her a time limit of tonight. She had retired to her shell. Her cocoon. And his beautiful butterfly flew to him no more. Because he hadn't performed the very service that made love mutually rewarding and sublime. He had tried to pin her down, cage her. True love required that each partner be free.

He strode across the room and knocked gently on her door. She didn't answer, and he tried again. No response. Instinct told him she was awake but not able to talk to him.

"Jess, please let me in. I won't make any demands. Jess?"

He turned the knob, swung her door wide. Her bed was unused. Her room undisturbed.

Fright traveled up his spine. Had she flown from him?

No, she wouldn't. Not out into the London night. She might take her time coming to certain actions, but she would not do something foolhardy, nor would she leave here without telling him. She was honorable, her sense of right and wrong untouched. And she wouldn't leave without Amanda.

He walked through to the nursery door, knocked gently, and when no answer came, he pushed that door open. Amanda slept, hands up in the pose of a child exhausted.

He closed the door and in a flash of a lover's innate

understanding of his beloved, he knew where Jess had gone.

He took the stairs down to the first floor and the drawing room. The door stood ajar.

He stepped inside.

Jess sat on the piano bench, a silhouette of sorrow. Gracefully bent over the keyboard, she did not play but rested her hands in her lap. When she raised her face to him, he saw no features except the glitter of her eyes.

"Jess, darling."

She made no move.

"I came to apologize. I was rash this morning."

"I don't want to talk about this!" She shot from the bench.

"I know and I wanted to tell you I will respect your wishes and not make demands of you as I did this morning." He took a tentative step forward and thanked God she did not retreat from him, but stood her ground. "I ache for you, sweetheart. I wish I could take your problems from you, but I can't. I can only stand beside you, be with you through long years filled with more challenges, more issues. Children. Illnesses. Disappointments. Victories in my business and your school. Laughter with friends and relatives. Christmases and birthdays and anniversaries."

He watched her as her tears dried, her hands relaxed, and her expression was transformed from desperation to what he hoped was relief.

He felt his own. "I'm trying to show you this newly tempered man, darling." She made no response, and he took that as a good sign. He didn't need immediate gratification. Not from her. She would come to him in her own time with hands and heart open to him. In the meantime, he would be nearby, always. For the minutes of a lifetime when nothing mattered so much as the mere presence of the one person on earth whom he loved and who loved him.

"I thought I'd make some cocoa. I need it to court sleep. You are welcome to join me if you like."

She shook her head.

"Very well. If you change your mind, let me know." He made for the door.

Her whisper stopped him. "You are so good to me, and I do not, as the good doctor says, return to you those things I can."

"I'm yours, Jess. Without conditions, time limits, or expectations. Just here and forever in love with you."

He made his cocoa, drank it in the kitchen, and returned to his bed. If she remained in the drawing room, he could not see her as he passed by.

He closed his door, turned the gas wicks lower, and discarded his robe. He climbed into his cold and lonely bed.

He closed his eyes, and a vision of Jess swam before them. She whispered to him.

His eyes opened wide.

She would have disappeared like a phantom if he hadn't reached out a hand and stopped her. She was crying. Silently.

He drew her down to him and beseeched her not to go. "Come here. I told you once that you could come to me, run to me for everything—and then I did the unpardonable thing and put conditions on it, didn't

I?" He kissed tears from her cheeks. "I told you I would wait for answers, and then I pushed you to give them. That was unfair, love. Jess darling, forgive me."

She sobbed as she twined her arms about him. "I can't stay away from you," she confessed between sobs. "I told myself I was unfair to make you hostage to my own fears of revealing terrible things about myself . . ."

He silenced her with a finger to her lips. "I only want to know why you're here right now."

"I wanted you to hold me," she whispered.

"So easy," he crooned as he enfolded her and placed his lips in the crown of her curls. "So necessary. No requirements. Just love, Jess. Given for its own sake. That I can do."

He drew her forward, and rolled her beneath him. The bed, which last night had heard a prelude to new love, would know a symphony of ripe desire tonight.

He helped her remove her robe and in one smooth gesture lifted her gown away.

He took handfuls of her hair. "I wanted to do this that first day I came to Farrell Hall to tutor Amanda." He seized long strands and rubbed them over his cheek, his throat and chest, then made her moan as he did the same to her own lush body. He sank lower, trailing little kisses and caresses and opening her slim legs to him. He saw her crimson readiness and placed himself at the door to their ecstasy.

She hummed an erotic tune. "Do that. Do anything. Just love me." She urged him on with hungry hands and legs that sought to surround him.

"I won't stop."

This time you'll make all things right. You'll marry

her soon and in the eyes of man and God. Before anyone, alive or dead, tears you both asunder.

Jess whimpered and clutched at him, her tenseness shouting to him that her climax would slam into her fast and hard. "I know what you're doing."

"Making you come to me, for me, with me, in every way I can find." He gave her long sure evidence of how much he cared, and when she gripped him in the first throes of her completion, he sank as far inside her as flesh allowed and let the pulse of their consummation rage.

He pulled his body from hers, and she objected.

He put his hands on her slim white thighs and pressed them to the bed. She was glistening red ardor, full, fragrant with their mating, and ready for him—but totally unable to predict his ultimate intent.

When he lowered his mouth to her, she groaned deep in her throat.

At first sip, she tasted like cream and slick candy. Words, intent, all forgotten in his famine for her, he needed to feast. Thumbing open her thick lips, he plumped her to protrude the morsel he desired and licked and nibbled with a precision that had her bucking from the bed. He held her with a gentle reverence he'd given her each time they loved.

"Moan all you want, my woman. This is what you were meant for—*me. Us,* like this."

She sang his name in a nocturne of need. He smiled and took her all the more slowly, reveling in the rich expressions of her body's appreciation. She stilled and tilted her hips up for more. And when she cried out for no more delay, he moaned, stripped off his clothes, and immersed himself in the pulsating heaven of her body.

She repeated how she loved him.

Her declaration had him smiling and her meeting him with her never-ending tremors that gratified them both. In the minutes afterward, he sank to the bed, still rigidly joined to her while her body trembled in repeated joy.

He held her, stroked her, kissed her eyes and perspiring body. "Can you sleep now?"

She ran a finger down his chest. "You, my love, are more powerful than any cocoa."

He grinned. "You taste better, too."

When she flushed down to her nipples, he traced a hand below. "I wonder how far this modesty extends." He slipped two fingers inside her and caught his breath at the way her tiny muscles gripped him. "Mmmm. As far as that. I never knew how wet a blush could be, darling."

She cuffed him, but he caught her wrist and pressed it back to the mattress.

"I adore you." He dipped his tongue inside her ear.

She giggled. "I love you, too." Then she rose.

"Where are you going?" he asked, stunned. "I'm not asking anything of you."

"I know that. I'm going to my room."

"Not back to your bed?"

"No. I thought I'd sleep with you."

"I always did like the way you think"—his mouth watered at the sight of her naked—"and the way you look. *Hurry.*"

She threw him a quick smile. "I will. I want to get

something." She dashed off, a nymph in the moonlight. When she returned, she snuggled up to him, silken skin to his. His hand slid down her hip. "What did you get?"

"Your ring," she told him and held up her hand.

"Hmm, looks very nice. Fits, too. Must have been meant for you."

"I think so," she said with intense satisfaction in her sultry voice.

He'd measured the joy by two languid kisses when the first shriek of terror cut the darkness.

Screams rattled the rafters of the house.

Chapter Thirteen

BY THE TIME THEY GOT TO AMANDA, SHE HAD SHREDDED the sheets on her bed with a letter opener and burst a pillow so that the room was a shambles of cloth and feathers.

She lay sobbing, beating the floor with a weary fist.

Jess secured her robe around herself and knelt beside the child. "Sweetheart, sweetheart," she crooned and rocked the girl. "What can be so wrong? Tell me, tell me. I must know how to help you."

She froze, understanding how natural it was to want answers, as Rand did. Yet, for her, he had curbed his curiosity. Was she pushing Amanda too hard? But how was she to know how to proceed if she failed to question the child?

Frantic pounding on the door made Rand stride over and open it. His butler, Reynolds, and the man's young wife, who was the housekeeper, stood there, aghast.

"My lord, what's wrong? What can I do?"

Reynolds's wife wrapped her robe around her considerable middle and craned her neck to peer into the room. "We like t' think the banshees were inta the house!"

"The child had a nightmare."

"Faith an' she did. Lor', what a mess it made, too. Ring for me when you want me to clean up, milord."

"We could do with cocoa for Amanda, Mrs. Reynolds. A large pot, I think," Rand said kindly and closed the door.

Jess stroked Amanda's hair. "What happened?"

The child trembled for a second and then blurted, "Oh, Miss Curtis, I had a terrible dream. And I . . . I was seeing it again. This time I was *inside* it."

"Can you describe it?"

"It was the day she died."

Jess looked up at Rand, who was as breathless and confused as she. He cocked his head at her, then sank into a chair.

"I dreamed that she and I fought. We did, you know. I realized it yesterday when I was playing the piano. My vision was the truth. And now I can't sleep without seeing it! The doctor was right. I didn't want to admit that I remembered. He made me angry that he knew so much."

Jess shut her eyes and brought the child closer. So many similarities to her own life. Even the puzzled pattern of Amanda's return of memory.

Would she ever stop comparing the two accidents?

"In my dream tonight, we argued as we did that day. I don't . . . don't remember the exact words."

I do.

"I know what her eyes looked like, though."

Insanity wears a feral face.

"She was not like herself. She was laughing and crying at the same time. She told me she had not been good and that I mustn't grow up to be like her."

I must be stronger, wiser, loving myself first—and a man only after I discovered my *passion,* my *desire.*

"I told her I would do anything she wanted."

If only she would stay with me.

"Just stay with me."

Because I couldn't stay with him. He was so cold. So utterly . . . passionless.

"I didn't want to be alone with him. My father is . . . can be frightful, especially when he's angry."

And he was constantly angry with her.

"I think— Oh, Miss Curtis, this is horrible to say, but I think my father hated my mother!"

Jess smoothed Amanda's hair away from her brow. "Perhaps 'hate' is a stronger word than you really mean."

"No, he hated her."

"Sometimes love goes wrong and—"

"He said he never loved her."

"When? In your dream?"

"No. One day when they fought. I heard him. He said he married her for her money and . . ."

Jess waited, a snake of apprehension slithering up her spine.

"Her body." Amanda screwed up her face in a child's disgust at such topics. "That's awful, Miss Curtis." She hid her face in Jess's throat.

"I understand." Jess's eyes were veiled with tears as she focused on Rand and all the wonderful gifts this man had brought her. His honor and humor and passion. The many treasures she had long ago told herself did not exist and that she had now found in his presence, in his arms, and even—oh, especially—in his bed.

"I want to go home."

Jess pulled away to peer at the child. It was the last thing she'd expected her to say.

"I do. Please."

"But your father . . . It will take me a while to find him. I don't know where he is, and—"

"No, I mean I want to go back to school. To Farrell Hall. With you. I don't want to go with my father."

Was this wise? "Before we go anywhere, I think we need to tell Dr. Steineke of your dream tonight."

"I will if you'll come with me."

"He might not agree to let you return to school. He might think you need to come see him more often. If you have more memories that frighten you, then you'll need help overcoming the terror." *I know. It took me years . . . but I did it alone. I had no one in whom to confide. No one I wanted to tell.*

Until now.

Amanda gathered Jess's robe into her fist. "Doctors tell me I shouldn't even remember what I do."

Jess could barely whisper, "It's true that most don't remember their accidents and many things before they occurred."

"Even you said you don't remember what happened to you just before or after your riding accident."

Jess's heart stopped. She felt Rand's dark blue eyes shoot to her and drill into her brain. He knew she recalled many details. "That's what I said."

"After my mother ran out and I followed her, I don't recall anything else. Those other doctors said I never will. They told my father, but he insists that I can or should. *He's* the one who thinks if I remember I won't miss her, that I'll be cured and happy. How can I be happy when my mother is dead?"

"We mourn those we have loved and lost for a time. But eventually the pain passes and we recall the good things about them."

"I . . . I have felt as though . . . I killed her."

Jess felt bile rise in her throat. This was so reminiscent of her own feelings. "That's a guilt you must not bear. You did not kill her. She died in a fall from her horse."

"If I hadn't fallen, I might have been able to help her."

"I doubt it, my dear. Her neck was broken."

"I wish this had never happened. I look at my friends and ask why I am the one who no longer has a mother, why *I* am the one who's different."

"Life often seems unfair."

"So much gets taken away. Your mother . . . friends . . ."

Jess let her eyes drift to Rand's. "Other gifts hide among the ruins, though. We don't see them at first, but they are there." *They come when we least expect them. We fail to see them as a saving grace. Even when we do understand their value, we are still reluctant to enjoy them.*

Later that morning the three of them entered Rand's coach as it stood inside his carriage house. The necessity to go out as soon as possible and in the light of day to Harley Street overcame any fear of discovery and scandal.

They sat, gloomy amid the Templeton luxury.

Jess felt as if she rode a tumbrel to her doom.

The revelations of the middle of the night had taken their toll on all three of them. Amanda, after hot cocoa and coaxing, had finally gone to a repaired bed and rest. The staff had returned to their upstairs lairs.

Rand had urged Jess to come to bed. "At least close your eyes, sweetheart. There is little more you can do for Amanda. We'll attempt to see Dr. Steineke in the morning."

Jess had been able only to pace her bedroom until breakfast. Recognizing that Rand was right and she could do little for Amanda, she had confined her thoughts to herself.

Going in circles, she recognized what her next steps must be with Rand. She would summon courage and tell Rand what she had seen her father do the day her mother died. She'd also recount how he himself had died. In a few sentences, she would blast the wall she had erected to protect her from curiosity-seekers and—why not admit it?—from her own grief and self-criticism.

She was wildly in love with Rand, and he deserved the very best she could give him. Although old habits whispered that, despite the glory of their passion, she must not destroy the wall, she feared she would in the telling break apart. Become little pieces of her self.

The way she had been for so long after her mother died, after her father learned that she remembered not only her mother's accident but what he had done to cause it. She was so appalled by it that she was brash enough to blurt it out, accuse him, confront him—and he had attacked her.

God in heaven, it required such courage to admit her failures!

She felt her stomach churn. Feeling exposed like that made one wary. Uncivil. Insane.

Like my mother. And my father.

Jess thought the air in the coach stifling. Her whole body burned with the need to fly free.

"I'll go in first," Rand said when the horses came to a stop at the doctor's door, "and request to see him, since we're not expected."

He returned within a few minutes. His face was glum. "Dr. Steineke is very ill this morning. His cough has become an infection. His own physician is with him now and prohibits any visitors."

Jess nibbled on her lip. They could not stay in London forever. She had a school to administer. Rand had a business, a social life. Amanda had a father who was known as a gadfly. He could come to call at Farrell Hall at any time and demand to see his daughter.

Rand tapped the roof of his carriage, and the coachman turned back toward Grosvenor Square.

Silence shrouded the carriage.

Minutes later Reynolds admitted them to Rand's foyer with a forced smile. "A word with you, milord?"

"Yes, certainly." He followed his butler behind the closed door of his study.

As Jess and Amanda climbed the stairs for their rooms, Jess instructed her they should begin to pack.

When Rand emerged from his discussion with his butler, he called to Jess to come down and talk with him. Jess paused on the landing to see that he held in his hand a balled-up scrap of paper.

Jess sent Amanda on her way and sailed toward Rand, who inclined his head toward his study.

"What's wrong?" she asked when he shut the door behind her. "You look awful."

"Reynolds received a telegram this morning while we were out. It's from Pool. Emory visited my house in Kent in the middle of the night, then barged into Farrell Hall. He was quite drunk. Pool put him to bed with a jigger of laudanum for a chaser. I think we have just enough time to get you and Amanda home before Emory comes to himself."

Jess spun around. She had her hand on the doorknob when she halted. Now was not the best time to begin offering Rand long explanations of the last bitter truth about her accident and the subsequent events. But she could give him portions of it. She faced him.

"Amanda's accident and recovery have brought us together—and the parallels between her experience and mine have created memories and tensions in me that I find extremely difficult to deal with.

"Now Amanda thinks she remembers what happened to her and her mother that day. It is extraordinary that she does. Unusual. Not too many do. I did, and it created problems for me. Problems with my father, who did know that I understood he did not love my mother as much as he could have. I resented him, hated him, for that. I wanted him to love her as I think any child wishes her father to care for her mother. When I began to recover and memories came to me, as they do now to Amanda, they came in the same scrambled way. Because these puzzle pieces do not seem to fit, the mind . . . cannot cope with them. Outbursts are a natural result."

He had not moved. True to his promise to accept her as she was, he waited for whatever else she wished to offer.

"I remember my mother's riding accident. I remember, yet it was the scene of my own accident. But what happened afterward is what I have a terrible time relating. You see, my dear love, it takes quite a lot of courage to admit to the honorable man you adore that you have made," she whispered, "enormous mistakes."

She'd frozen him in time.

"But unconditional love accepts the human capacity for error, doesn't it?"

Fear crept into his expression and she knew its cause, its cure.

"I am going to marry you, Rand Templeton. Within weeks, I think. A day in June in the Tuttle church sounds wonderful. I can't run from you and the happiness I want so badly with you. Besides, my memories will follow.

"I have tried to shut you out of my future, Rand. I've failed. The day fast approaches when I will no longer be able to shut you out of my past."

Chapter Fourteen

"I HOPE HE'S NOT AWAKE YET," JESS SAID AS SHE STRODE through the kitchen door with Amanda and Pool right behind her. Her butler had gone over to the Temple hours earlier to await their arrival and handed them day clothes, two bows, full quivers, finger guards, and arm bracers—in other words, an alibi.

"I doubt it, my lady." Pool lifted his head to the cook. "What do you say, Mrs. Ludd?"

The white-haired lady chuckled and surveyed the blue cotton dress the maid and Pool had pulled from Jess's wardrobe and smuggled over to the Temple for her imminent arrival. "No, mum. Lord Emory's out, right clean, I'd say till teatime. Perhaps he won't get to see you in your finery." She widened her eyes playfully.

Jess was in no mood to laugh. The ride from London had been too tense. Besides, for the first time in days, she was without Rand. "We shall wear our finery all afternoon, in case we need evidence of our whereabouts." She held aloft her right hand with its leather finger guard.

She glanced at Amanda who had been so concerned her father might find her missing from Farrell Hall that she had chattered about nothing else during the whole journey south.

To lighten the child's mood, Jess commented on her dirty attire. "You look as if you've been rolling in the hay rather than practicing archery."

Amanda made a clown's face. "I am a terrible shot and have to fish my arrows from all manner of places."

"You'll get better. With practice." Jess bent over the mixture of scraps her housekeeper had prepared. "Oh, my. What is that?"

Cook smirked. "Dog food."

"That's an awful lot for Bones. He doesn't eat that heartily anymore. Is he suddenly famished?"

"No, mum. It's that bird Lord Templeton bought."

"The parrot?"

"God*damn!*" The kitchen door swung open. There stood a wild-haired, bleary-eyed Harrison Emory, shirt open and shoeless, shouting at the cook. "Chrissakes, don't you people answer your bells? I've been upstairs pulling the friggin' thing since last Christmas! Uh . . . Amanda dearest." He suddenly flushed at his disheveled condition, embarrassed his daughter should see him so. "Dreadfully sorry. Well, here—" He strode over and squeezed her in a ferocious hug. "I came to see you. Glad, aren't you?" he asked with watery eyes.

She screwed up her face, and in the look Jess noted an objectivity. She also saw a lack of the affection that

Amanda had shown her father in the past. Was her changed attitude the result of what she saw in her visions?

Amanda sniffed at him. "Sir, you smell rather sour."

He flicked a few glances at Jess and the servants. "I've been ill," he explained lamely.

"I can see that," Amanda said, running her eyes down his clothes.

"It's because of you. My worry, my efforts and pain."

She frowned and, in the look, told him he had not persuaded her to accept his excuse.

He stepped away from her. The veneer of authority dropped over his features. "You have always been an ungrateful child. So like your mother."

"If you mean I should be pleased that you come before my teachers and friends smelling like a brewery, you're right. I am not grateful." She stepped around him.

He sneered, shot out a hand.

Jess interjected her body. "I think it best if we let Amanda go to her room and freshen up. She'll join us for tea in half an hour in the music room, won't you, dear?"

Emory breathed very deeply through flared nostrils. Even at that, Jess could detect the unmistakable odor of stale liquor, cigars, and cold sweat.

Amanda said yes and hurried away.

Jess did not move.

He frowned. "You should understand my circumstances."

"I do not."

"Hard duck, aren't you?"

She would not take the bait.

"Now I see why you run this school."

She would not let him goad her.

"All right!" He raked one hand through his disheveled hair. "I had a bit more to drink than I should have!"

A lot more.

"I have troubles."

Not an excuse.

"Oh, you are so smug."

"Lord Emory, if you wish to insult me, I will have to insist that you do it with your shirt buttoned and your shoes on. I believe the room my butler gave you has a large tub, sir. Please avail yourself of it and meet me in the music room. I have a thing or two to say about how you will present yourself before me, your daughter, and my other students. We run a respectable school here. Even you must abide by my rules."

Jess made for the door. "Twenty minutes, my lord. Please be prompt, as I am a busy woman, and you, I assume, must be on your way."

Jess took the hall at a brisk pace.

The vision of Emory spurred her on.

He was no more than a pitiful example of mankind. She could do without him—and *would* do so.

The music room was where she had longed to be since this morning when she'd told Rand she would marry him.

She needed to play as she had never needed to eat or breathe or bask in the sunshine.

She had to feel the hard satin of the ivory keys. Wanted to pour out her frustrations—and, oh, God, yes—her hopes onto the instrument. To elicit from it the assurance that she could create beautiful things. Bright things. Hope and joy and love for Rand and maybe, please heaven, even for children. Children of her own. Rand's children.

She pulled the stool toward the piano. She sat down, tore off the finger guard and arm bracer, then held her hands high, arched, ready.

No Moonlight Sonata today.

No "Für Elise."

No Chopin.

Only Leighton.

"Serenade to Spring" by Elise Leighton.

She took up the first position and played her mother's only serenade. Her mother's sweetest work.

The notes came like a waterfall. The composition was serenity incarnate in sound alone. Her mother had written this in Vienna. Jess knew it was Vienna, not so much because she remembered her mother composing it there in their *pension,* but because she had read the notation on the score sheet. "Happy, for a little time" was the only other scribbling that told Jess this piece was loved by her very unhappy mother.

Why Elise had been happy in Vienna Jess would never know. She had given up trying to decipher why, along with so much else she'd been unable to reconstruct over the past eleven years.

But knowing didn't seem so crucial now. She had Rand. His love and acceptance of all she was and did. For what did she need the past?

Not for anything, really.

Only to disturb her.

Only to discard.

She halted.

Was the past *only* to discard?

Her mouth curved up in a weak, then wonderful smile.

Her hands sank to the keys, to the notes, to the music her mother had created . . . and Jess knew the tune was a lullaby to her fears.

She had only to reveal the hideous portions of her past. Say those parts aloud. Then dismiss them. Forget them.

For what had they brought her?

Oh, she knew. She understood.

Each element of her past, combined like a symphony of instruments to constitute her character, had brought her step by step to her present. And now her future.

She needed only to reach out to Rand and take it. Enjoy it. Nurture it.

Emory's shadow fell across the keyboard as she neared the end of the piece. She did not stop, but finished the work. He was not worthy of interrupting a work of art.

He seemed to understand that she would not acknowledge his presence, and so he took a chair near the fire.

From the corner of her eye, Jess saw what he did.

Bones, who had followed him in, lumbered to a spot before the grate. With a canine sigh, the old fellow curled up for a nap. The cat appeared and gingerly took up her post on the settee. She sniffed and waited, her tail marking cadence with her curiosity. Where Darwin was, Jess had no idea. The monkey usually traveled in the company of the other two, so it was odd that he was missing. The question wrinkled her brow but did not distract her from her duty to the composition her mother had created.

At its end, she sat in full flush at the stirring quality of the music. Then she spun to face Emory.

The dog sat at his feet. The cat monitored the sight. But a flurry of feathers and a squawk made Jess gape.

She sat, marveling at the sight of the parrot Rand had purchased at the fair. The bird ambled over to Bones, and settled like a rooster, but blinked slowly, clearly an avian attempt to imitate the watchfulness of the dog.

Under other circumstances, she could have laughed.

But her menagerie was too serious, her visitor too furious.

"I dislike too much civility, Lady Curtis. It obscures reality. Let me state my purpose: I came here to take Amanda away."

The blow was softened by her expectation of it. "Really? Is that why you went to the marquess of Ashford's home first and in the middle of the night?"

Emory pushed his mouth around his face. "I was intoxicated."

"In your state, what illogic drove you to the Temple?"

"I thought you'd be there. I suspect that you and the marquess are more than friends."

"And you thought you'd barge in and find us in a compromising situation. Really, Lord Emory, what good would that do for you?" She knew the obvious horrid answer, but she wanted to make him say it.

"I thought I might find evidence to discredit you."

"And justify your own actions?"

He pursed his mouth. "That's none of your business."

"This school is. So are its students. I protect them. One of them is a girl named Amanda Emory."

"I can and will protect her from *you,* Miss Curtis. And from what I saw when I was last here, I had reason to conclude you and Lord Templeton were quite *close.*"

"What you saw the last time was a man who was departing after taking tea in my music room with me and a few students." She swept a hand out to indicate their surroundings. "What *I* saw was my neighbor, who safeguarded me from the ravings of a madman. Still, I have not made assumptions about your character. I have gone on only facts."

"Fact, bah! You women are all alike. Gallivanting about with any man who suits your fancy and then justifying your behavior with any available excuse. Facts? I'll give you facts." Emory leaned forward, so self-possessed. "I have learned that Randall Templeton comes here daily; the entire countryside knows it. In London, word has it that your marquess says he will soon marry. I pray God, for your sake, the one he marries will be you, and quickly, too."

The threat of scandal shook Jess to the marrow of her bones, but she would never allow Emory to catch a glimpse of her apprehensiveness. "Your intimations are perversions of the truth. I have made no secret of Lord Templeton's visits."

"You should have."

"That is your opinion. And your misfortune. Randall Templeton came here to help your daughter, and more than you or I, *he* has been successful."

Emory grunted. "I mean to have Amanda examined to see exactly how successful he has been."

"Father! That is *disgusting!*" Amanda stood at the door, bright tears in her eyes.

Jess shot from her seat to take the girl in her arms. Amanda took comfort, but not permanent shelter as she tore away from Jess's embrace to stand before the man who had sired her.

"How could you even think of doing that?" Amanda seethed.

Emory was perspiring. "Now, Amanda, it's for the best. I am your father and I know—"

"You know nothing. *Nothing!*"

"I don't want any man hurting you."

"*You* did! You hit me the day she died!"

"What? *What?*" Attacked, he tried to regroup his thoughts.

His daughter wouldn't let him.

Rooted to her spot, Jess watched the room fade to red. She swayed with the force of the revelation, quaked at the mention of a scene so similar to her own experience.

"I remember how you yelled at her and me when you saw that I had overheard you," Amanda said.

"*What?*" Emory was groping. "What did you say?"

"I remember how you treated her." She advanced, taunting him.

Her father didn't like it. Cursing, he slapped the arms of his chair and stood. As a consequence of his alcohol consumption, he reeled on his feet. Stripped of his authority, he plunked back into his chair. "I thought you didn't recall anything!" He turned to Jess. "This is fantasy."

"No, it isn't, Papa. I *know* how you and she fought. You didn't like her going to tea parties or to at-home gatherings without you, how you suspected her of nasty things—riding out at noon without a maid, promenading in Hyde Park on Sundays to show herself to men, you said."

Emory raked his fingers through his hair. "Your mother was flighty. She liked parties and—"

"She liked to laugh. You made her cry."

"I couldn't often be with her."

"Because you were seeing another woman."

He groaned. "How do you know that?" He simmered with outrage.

"I heard you argue. She accused you of infidelity, and you told her it was true."

He clamped his eyes shut.

Amanda grew very still. "She said she hadn't taken any man to her bed except you but you had taken many women, so she needed one man to gain a little fun in her life."

"I loved your mother."

"You loved her money."

"Ridicu—"

"And her body."

He gaped.

"Those were your words. When she said it was not enough to love a woman's body, that you had to love her soul as well, you could not understand."

Jess caught a sob. This was the mirror image of her own parents' dilemma. *But not mine.*

"Amanda, I cared for your mother. I married her. We had you. I was a good husband and father. Better than most. As good as I could be."

"I don't think so."

"Now you listen to me!" He stood and grabbed her arm.

"No." She shook him off and stared him in the eye. "I am not leaving Farrell Hall. And I won't go to any doctor for anything unless I want to."

"You have no choice!"

"I do."

"You are a child. By law, my—"

"Your *possession?* That's what you said to Mother. But she laughed at you. I won't laugh. I can't. I will instead tell you that if you try to take me, I'll run away."

"You are twelve years old!"

"I am *not* witless."

"You are sick."

"A blight to you? A burden?"

"What? What nonsense is this, now?"

"I shall tell my friends about my memories."

Astounded, Emory gaped like a fish. "You wouldn't."

"And they'll tell their parents, of course."

"You'll be a laughingstock."

"Oh, I think I'll survive. But you, sir, will wonder about the whispers, won't you?"

"No, I— *No.*"

"That's what you told her, too. It was perfectly fine to have the world know a man used his—what did you call it?—your virility to his advantage. But a woman must be chaste. Stay in her place."

"She aspired to—"

"Have a little fun. Be herself. That was all. And in her sorrow that you would not allow it, she withered like a cut flower. No wonder she died the way she did."

Tears made hot tracks down Jess's cheeks. She dashed them away. *No wonder she died the way she did.*

"It was an accident," he whispered. "A dreadful accident. And you must accept that."

"How can I?"

How could I? I saw with my own eyes the proof that it was not an accident.

Emory faltered, licked his lips. "You remember the accident, too?"

"You said you wanted me to, and I tried, but I don't."

He remained motionless. "Perhaps now that you recall these things, other incidents will come to mind."

This touched the tender core of Jess's own fearful memories. Empathy for Amanda had her walking toward the child and putting her hands on her shoulders.

"Amanda cannot endure much more emotion to-day, sir. I think it best if you leave us." At his reticence, Jess knew he wanted more words with her. She would not permit Amanda to hear them. "Go, my dear. Find Darwin for me, would you? I think he's still dancing in the stables for Dahlia, and I miss him from our little group."

Amanda objected to leaving with tears in her eyes. "I'm going, but only because I suddenly don't have the energy to fight anymore." Without a look of good-bye to her father, the child departed.

Like duelists, Emory and Jess faced each other.

"I will return," he promised.

"I expect you will. When you do, come in the light of day with a clear head and an open mind."

"Amanda's mind is what I am concerned about now. She has delusions."

"When you heard them, you did not appear to think they were fabrications."

"Well, she takes them to extremes! I think the injury to her head has made her insane."

"You mean to lock her away!" Shock gave way to fury. "I won't let you."

"I'll get doctors."

"So will I."

"The law is on my side, Miss Curtis. I am her *father.*"

"A true perversion."

"You bitch."

She raised her chin, her smile rabid. "You have not seen me at my most feral, my lord."

"I'll go. But I will return with doctors and commitment papers. Then afterward, I will ruin you."

He would not be the first man who had tried. Jess's own father had tried to kill her, but she'd survived. She would do so again.

She flicked her head toward the door. "Get out."

Chapter Fifteen

"COME IN. SO GOOD OF YOU TO JOIN US FOR THIS lecture!" Mrs. Winslow, the vicar's wife, wound her arm through Jess's and led her into the medieval guildhall, its linenfold oak walls shining tawny in the gaslight. "So wonderful of you to bring a few of your staff, too."

"They wanted to come," Jess said and introduced the school's French teacher, Mademoiselle Dumont, and the mathematics teacher, Freddy Bremer, to her. They strolled forward to chairs midway down the aisle.

It was no fantasy of hers that the Ashford and Tuttle villagers muttered and stared in surprise that she had come out to such an event. Never in her five years in Kent had she attended any gathering other than Sunday service in the Tuttle church and an occasional strawberry festival or Christmas Eve tea. So some townspeople—those who could manage to snap shut their mouths—smiled, nodded, and spoke of the weather, the school, and their joy that the child who had run away a few weeks ago had returned unharmed to Farrell Hall.

When they drifted away, Jess took up the subject that the vicar's wife had begun. "All of the Farrell School's instructors are interested, as you might well imagine, in the public perception of abnormal and normal behaviors. This man who speaks tonight draws my curiosity, I must say."

Jess did not add that since this morning's encounter with Harrison Emory, she needed to quench a particular thirst to meet this man who was to speak tonight. This was Professor Andretti, whom Lady Mellwyn admired.

Andretti was billed as one who believed that criminals were born predisposed to antisocial behavior, and were therefore irredeemable. For one who knew the importance of environment—injured, as she had been, or born overly active, as Cat and she and their students were, Jess thought Andretti's thesis held little validity. Jess had learned, lived, and benefited from those who loved her, were patient with her, and tried to understand her.

Like a person too long besieged by forces she could not control, Jess girded herself for a battle if he spouted inanities. Yet she knew she arrived here tonight not so much shielded by her old armor of fear as fortified by valor more intrinsic, by the courage that pulsed through her blood.

Welcoming the adventure of it, she smiled.

Mrs. Winslow took it as a pleasantry and continued with her thoughts about the speaker. "I myself am eager to see if he sounds at all rational. His approach sounds . . . well, shall we be polite and say he sounds less than Christian . . . and rather *odd?"* Mrs. Winslow patted Jess's hand. "Cat and I often had discussions about the human mind and soul. As a minister's wife, I have a certain interest in how people view human nature." She wiggled her eyebrows merrily. "Jerome does, too."

"Is he here?"

"He will come later if he can. He had an unexpected caller. A parishioner in need of comfort."

"I hope it's nothing serious."

"One is never certain with this particular person. She stands in need of such help often. I myself have listened to her woes upon occasion."

Speaking of woes made Jess glance about for the woman who would undoubtedly gloat that she had come. "I wonder where Patricia Mellwyn is. She was very insistent about my attending this lecture."

"Hmm, well . . ." Mrs. Winslow's brown eyes went from mellow to glazed. "Patricia sits in Jerome's study as we speak. She has had second thoughts about her activities."

"I don't understand."

"She heads the Women's Society, and it was her idea to invite this lecturer. I might say she insisted we have him."

"Interesting—but good heavens, *why?"*

Mrs. Winslow cocked her head. "Like many of us, Patricia has foibles. Oh, I know that is a polite word for her . . . eccentricities, shall we call them? She dislikes to disclose an element in her past, which she fears makes her less than human."

"I understand the problem. I feel sorry for her."

"You are a compassionate soul, my dear. That's the first thing a person notices about you."

"I thought the first thing one noticed was how cold I am."

Mrs. Winslow threw back her head and chuckled lightly. "Dearest, that is a mask. We know it. We have all known it ever since you came to Farrell Hall. No one could do what you do with these children—lead, control, and inspire them—without a heart of pure gold. You do yourself an injustice—and you deprive us of your good advice and company—by hiding yourself away."

"I have only lately begun to see that. I do want to change."

"Jessica, you want to *grow.* So come spread your wings, my dear. So many of us fail to see beyond the terror of change and the challenge of setbacks. There is a joy in change and growth. It can bring us freedom. You will seize yours."

Jess grinned and turned around. There, at the back of the hall conversing with the town tobacconist, stood the one man who had called forth her courage to change and grow. Rand.

He inclined his head in a polite nod.

She returned it.

He remained talking to the man before him, but Jess could feel his concentration flow across the hall to her.

When can I see you? She could hear his words now in imitation of his written reply to her note of this afternoon. Hand-delivered by trusty Pool, her little missive was the most she could manage in the seconds after the row with Harrison Emory in her music room. With Amanda collapsing and nigh to hysterical, Jess had dashed off a few words to Rand, letting him know that Emory had gone and that she would come to see him when she could to describe their encounter. Amanda had cried the afternoon away, heartbroken at what she had remembered and what she and her father had said to each other.

Jessica had not left her side until supper, when the child finally grew quiet enough to eat and fall into a deep sleep. It was then that Freddy Bremer and Mademoiselle Dumont had come to Jess and reminded her of this guildhall presentation. Soon after, the three of them had piled into the Farrell brougham for the jaunt into Ashford.

Jess thought of making her way toward Rand, to be close to him, to feel his tender gaze upon her skin, to hear his rousing voice—but then thought it bold. To those in Kent, they were friends. Until they announced their engagement, their demeanor must fit the protocol of two unmarried people. So for the next quarter hour, Jess devoted herself to greeting Ashford and Tuttle villagers while she gleefully devised a plan to make that announcement tomorrow.

When the local chemist walked toward the dais to introduce the lecturer, Jess settled into her seat with her teachers and friend. She had come here tonight as much to hear the speaker as to proclaim to one and all that she could come out into society and be accepted as one of them. Obviously none of them had thought her an odd duck. She had kept herself secluded during the past years. Now she realized she need not have done so.

So many years wasted, she concluded. She wouldn't spend her time secluded anymore.

Suddenly Professor Andretti took the podium.

He looked like no one she had ever met. He was tall—exceedingly so—and ascetically thin. Broodingly dark, with bushy brows and beard, a hook nose and curly hair that sprung like wire from his scalp, he looked more like a monk possessed of the devil than a physician with the knowledge to heal.

His pronunciation of English was not Harrow or Cambridge, but tinged with a Continental flavor, and yet understandable to those assembled here. What his higher purpose was, beyond lecturing in towns and villages, Jess could only surmise. Perhaps he used the meager honorarium to fund more lectures or his writings. Over the years, as she met many doctors and those who called themselves such, she had learned that physicians often sounded more impressive than they were.

This man's credentials were formidable. He had studied at one of those small Rhineland universities that specialized in romance languages and petty dueling. But afterward he had graduated to graver studies with an anatomist, Cesare Lombroso of Pavia and Turin. This Lombroso Jess had heard of years ago. He had published a paper on the connection between madness and genius, then only last year issued another which declared that criminals were born genetically predisposed to antisocial activities. Lombroso's ideas had spread across Europe. By his infamous conclusions had she herself been judged.

At her father's request, two of Lombroso's disciples had come to examine her after her accident. They had prescribed a mix of hydrotherapy and electrotherapy combined with regular doses of cocaine. The two doctors had proclaimed her an hysteric; she had proclaimed them comatose.

Knowing that her mother had suffered at the hands of such treatments, Jess had enough wits about her not only to object but also to throw tantrums. Her wildness kept the men at bay long enough for her to save herself from their restraining ropes. But her fits also encouraged them in their belief that they were right to seek her permanent commitment to an asylum. Her father agreed. When she confronted him—as Amanda had stood up to her father today—and told him that she remembered how he had cut the girth strap on her mother's saddle minutes before she fell to her death, he had thought her mad. Her details were so profuse and so exact, however, that he felt he had no means to protect himself other than to try to kill his own daughter.

Jess swallowed at the last memory—the worst—which she had hidden behind the highest, widest wall.

She felt blue eyes on her. She glanced to one side, and across the aisle she saw Rand smile.

Rand.

Who had inspired her to overcome the first obstacles. Who had continued to support her. Now, for him and for herself, she would tear down this last wall stone by stone.

She lifted her eyes to this physician, hoping he might impart more true knowledge to these people than those other fellows she had met years ago.

And despite what she had been told about him and his theories, she was not disappointed.

Fighting the popular perception that Charles Darwin's ideas made monkeys of men, this professor claimed each human was born with different levels of intelligence, but possessed three abilities or saving graces, that no other animals possessed: the ability to make choices, to love, and to experience pleasure. The lecturer's message was neither Darwin's nor Lombroso's, nor was it precisely what Jerome Winslow would have preached from his Anglican pulpit. Nor was it what Patricia Mellwyn might have expected when she invited Jess to come hear this man's speech. But the man's message rang true with these people.

It became a hymn in Jess's heart.

And by the time the professor finished, the nods of approval had become applause and Jess rose with the others to go home. Weeks ago, when Patricia Mellwyn suggested she attend this presentation, Jess had thought she would come here to face or even argue with this man and those in the shire, like Patricia Mellwyn, who had long opposed the presence of the Farrell School's overactive children. Instead, she found herself affirmed in her own positive approach to life, its rewards and hardships. She also accepted an invitation by two local ladies to address the townfolk at the next lecture session on ways to deal with stubborn children.

Jess sailed for the door with a smile. Rand stood there bidding good night to a few of his friends, and in the flow, Jess naturally came abreast of him.

"Good evening, Lady Curtis," he said brightly and took her hand, squeezing the huge ring between her fingers. His touch may have appeared polite, but Jess felt the electric sizzle of his skin through her glove. "Did you enjoy the presentation?"

"Immensely." She let her eyes tell him how much she wanted to enjoy other delights.

His grin anointed her with a fresh desire to kiss his lips. "I'm glad you came. So are the others."

"Thank you. I think I'll come again."

He inched closer. "Soon, dare I hope?"

She gulped. What did they speak of here? "Sooner than you think."

"I count the days."

"Tomorrow will dawn brightly, sir," she said nonchalantly, waving the gloved hand which bore his ring. He ground his teeth. Then she tapped a finger against his waistcoat and smiled secretly. "I'll see you soon. Wait up for me," she instructed on a whisper, and went toward her retinue, her carriage, and her last challenge.

When was she coming?

It was getting late, and he was tired of waiting.

Rand considered the silent piano in his drawing room, tossed back the rest of his brandy, and slammed the glass down on the cabinet top.

He felt like a man on fire. He missed her! He needed her! For laughter—and bed.

He strode to the terrace doors and flung them wide. A sweet moon hung in the mist of a late May midnight. Aromas of roses and gardenias and jessamine wafted his way, stirring memories of musky minutes entwined with another flower.

He shook his head. But it was no use.

Upon the ebon canvas lit with stars, glimpses of last night and the night before, with her spread across his bed, played before him. Like fairies who teased him and then blithely disappeared, his erotic recollections of Jess obliterated his day-long obsession with Harrison Emory. To look at Jess tonight, resplendent in apple green sicilienne, eyes sparkling, he would never have guessed that a raving man had staggered into her house this morning.

He had, of course, assumed that Emory had raved at her. What else did such a sort do?

Harrison had long been regarded as intense, erratic at best. It was the gentlemen's convention, naturally, not to speak of such assessments. But Rand knew. He could read the signs. The way Emory's acquaintances turned from him when his greetings were too obsequious and his discourse too descriptive to be pertinent or useful—only showy.

Thank God, children did not inherit every characteristic of their parents. In Amanda's case, Rand thought the inheritance of traits came more from the mother than the father.

As for him, God help him, he cared not one whit if a child of his inherited any trait from him, as long as his baby had Jessica Curtis for a mother.

If that happened—if it *had* happened last night or the one before—and Rand was fortunate enough to give Jess his child, by God, he'd keep her happy. Hell, he'd make them all happy. Every day of his life.

If he could only now douse the need to feel her whole and safe beneath his hands, he would be ecstatic. If he could know how Amanda fared, and hear Jess recount what had happened with Emory, he'd ask little more of life.

But just as he had learned nothing in this long day, he could divine no clues now.

Meanwhile the night tantalized him. The breeze stirred his hair, brushed his skin. The trees rustled, whispering tales of what he wanted—and had to wait to enjoy again. That possibility made him grind his teeth and clench his hands.

And he cursed.

He had done what he could. He had helped Jess, tried to help Amanda. But he had fallen in love with Jess—and no emotion he had ever felt matched it for power, not even what he had felt for Susannah. But unlike what had occurred with Susannah, he could not let Jess slip away from him. He felt secure that he had proven how deeply he loved her, and he would never push her to do anything again. But with her acting in her own good time, he was enormously anxious for Jess to take action on this wedding of theirs. He wanted her to set a date. Soon.

Heaven knows, he had done what he could to facilitate that before they left London. After he had taken her innocence and given her the family betrothal ring, he had obtained a marriage license. On the afternoon of the second day he had gone to the *Times* and drafted the announcement of their engagement. It would run only upon receipt of a telegram from him approving its release. He had later done the same for the local papers.

But according to etiquette, that was the only action

he could take. Jess needed to move forward of her own accord. She had to write to Cat, tell her staff, set a date, and see the vicar. But how to motivate her? Before Emory's vile rumors took on a credibility unsquelched by positive action, Jess *must* marry him.

He had to wait until she was ready.

He paced the terrace.

He'd go to Farrell Hall tomorrow. He would tell her about the official newspaper announcement, then tell her about the need to move forward. That wasn't pushing her; that was reasoning with her.

Hell, he'd go there at dawn.

Despite what anyone might say.

Dawn was acceptable. It was daylight—and, Christ, he longed to make love to her while the sun rose and rouged her pearly skin with the rays of morning.

He growled.

Frustration made him return inside.

For the piano.

For solace. And a healthy dose of diversion.

What came forth was every damn piece that had ever satisfied his soul.

But the Brahms was too sweet for his mood and he stopped, then rushed into a Chopin, which salved his loneliness. But only for minutes. In mid-bar he halted and began his rendition of the first piano concerto by a young Russian named Tchaikovsky. The carnal emotion of it only amplified his hunger for the taste of lush pink lips and succulent breasts, the shimmer of satin skin beneath his fingertips, and the pressure of long legs around his hips.

As if he'd conjured substance from sheer air, a zephyr floated in from the terrace, wound itself around him with arms of desire, and sighed his name against his cheek.

He paused, a disbeliever in a land of enchantment, as the froth of his imagination took the form of woman—the only woman he could ever want beside him.

She sat next to him. Hair cascading over her shoulders in pale moon-kissed arabesques, she wore a simple skirt and a canezou of flowing gauze. Translucent as it was, the filmy garment revealed her ripe intent by two hardening nipples that peaked the cloth and his body's rigid appreciation. He leaned near, inhaling the essence of a lilac soap with which she'd recently bathed, and he searched her appearance for what else she had not worn, the easier to tempt him. No earrings, no cloak, no artifice. Just Jess. His beloved, come to him across the grounds that separated them—and would no more.

He wrestled with the impulse to sweep her from the bench, up the stairs, into his chamber and his fantasies. He understood he must not, for she had come by her own design to free herself to him and everything they could become together. Impatient, ravenous to reward her for her boldness, he let his eyes feast on her.

In profile, her hands poised over the keyboard, she offered up a few bars with a self-satisfied smile, and when he did not move, she lifted her eyes to him. With one languid look of longing she told him how much she wanted him—and that she wanted him to accompany her, play with her.

This, above all else, he had desired. This, he would give till he died.

Beatific—absolutely glowing—she lowered her lashes to gaze at his hands, and the two of them began afresh the concerto that he had so swiftly abandoned.

Sharing the keyboard as they were, the composition became a pastiche of the work, a collage of sound in four octaves, a creation in new dimensions, the more inventive for the enthusiasm of the artists.

What he played, she complemented. What they could not perform together, one accomplished alone until the other could return. With regard for the integrity of the music, they offered up this innovative example to each other of their dedication to their future. And by the time they traversed the last bars of the work, they had traveled far from the wishes of yesterday to the reality of true union.

Only then, as their hands lifted from the last notes, did he spy the ring, still securely on her finger.

The exhilaration of it had him turning to her. She met his gaze, her serenity equal to anticipation.

And she twirled around on the bench and stood.

Panic shot along his spine at the thought that she meant to leave, but it subsided when her mouth curved in a secret smile—and her hands went to the shell buttons on her blouse.

What she revealed, by pooling blouse and skirt on the carpet, were the wonders he had spent his lonely hours today recalling with hard need: parted mouth, elegant neck, sumptuous breasts, gracefully curved belly, angel hair, and the shapeliest legs God ever granted woman. And these she had enhanced by wearing ordinary black lisle stockings caught around her firm thighs by serviceable red satin garters.

On anyone else, those stockings and garters might

have looked dowdy. But Jess looked like the siren he knew her to be, only with him, for him.

His blood pounded so madly he swore he heard nothing except its roaring need.

She heard it too, her long lashes drifting closed while she let him drink his fill of the gifts she offered so freely.

He rose, desire flaring his nostrils and sending his hands to her waist.

She stepped backward, a move that confused him, though he followed. She tilted her head, a devil-may-care grin on her lips as she cupped the nape of his neck and led him back another step. And then she sank into a wide wing chair, her hand in his hair, urging him down to her.

There on one knee, he narrowed his gaze at her while in his burning brain he tried to divine her intent.

Then her fingers went to the buttons of his shirt and his trousers, and the movement brought crystal clarity to her plan.

He shrugged from his shirt, drove his fingers into her curls, and held her still while he kissed her as if he had never tasted her mouth before. And he was right. He hadn't. Not like this. Not in the fullness of her liberty.

She sighed, her eyes still closed, and her tongue traced the essence of their love from her lips.

He glanced down at her, hot naked woman, legs wide to welcome him, and he took himself in hand to give her what she wanted.

He slid into her with such sure ease that the two of them paused, clung, suspended in the euphoria. As to how long he loved her there like that, he could not have said whether it was seconds or centuries. He only knew he gave her everything and she returned it in kind.

They drifted back in time together, pressed skin to skin, hand to heart, soul to soul.

He saw the richness of her love in her dancing eyes and her smiling mouth as she tossed him a saucy look and kissed him once more, soundly. Then she chuckled, a mirthful sound he noted for its novelty.

With a moan, he took himself from her, secured his trousers, and went in search of brandy.

But when he turned back, she was gone.

His heart dropped to his feet. *Where . . . ?*

He saw her through the doors beyond his terrace, in his garden. Fully dressed, she lifted her face to the sky. Thoughts of brandy discarded, he went to her.

She'd been waiting for him. He could tell by the way she sank against him, exposed her throat for his kiss, and covered his hands as one circled her waist and the other caressed the generous globe of one breast.

"Come back inside. Let me love you in my bed," he rasped, feeling her smile run through every sinew of his body.

"Rand." His name on her lips was a rhapsody on the night air. "I came out here to talk with the stars and trees and all the creatures of the forest."

He savored the skin beneath her ear. "Do you speak to them often?"

"This is the first time," she breathed and rested her head against his shoulder.

Understanding that she implied more, he hugged her closer. "And what do they say?"

"They approve."

His heart soared and he had to ask, "Of what?"

"You. They love you." She spun in his arms, ecstasy alight in every feature of her face as she raised a palm to his cheek. "I told them that I adore you, that I am going to marry you. *Yes.*" She trilled a laugh when he arched an amused and rueful brow. "No secrets anymore, my sweet man."

"The first one I wish to know is the date," he growled with wry humor.

She disengaged herself from him, tossing him an imp's grin. "Come see me tomorrow," she invited, as she hoisted her skirt from the dewy grass and pirouetted around a rosebush. "I promise you, darling, even more satisfaction." And with that she winked and ran down the path toward home.

For an indeterminate time, he stood there like a simpleton, wearing a damn silly expression he knew was a mix of repletion and insatiable longing.

Chapter Sixteen

"What do you think of this barege, Lady Curtis?" The petite dressmaker splayed her fingers beneath the corner of a bolt of transparent bisque silk. "I think it would be a good choice for a petticoat beneath the satin."

"It won't be too hot?" Jess had to ask, but had known the moment she set foot in this shop where her venture would lead. By teatime, not only would the villagers of Tuttle know she had picked out a trousseau, but so would every man, woman, and child in Kent in the bargain.

"When do you intend to wear it?"

When, indeed? She had decided early this morning, when she returned home at one o'clock, and she had cast her intention in stone by nine, encountered butterflies in her stomach by ten, then let them all fly away. With freedom singing through her blood, she strolled the village lanes, contemplated this shop, which she and Cat had patronized whenever money and occasion merited the dressmaker's expertise—and followed her whimsy to open the door.

She smiled slowly at the wrenlike lady with the beak nose. Ever since she'd thrown Emory out yesterday, the world had seemed to dance to her tune. "I will want the gown, the veil, and the underslip in three weeks. Is it possible, Mrs. Brundage?"

"If you needed it tomorrow, Lady Curtis, I am so delighted for you that I would deliver it if the Great Flood occurred." Her gaunt face crinkled like crushed organdy. "Even more, I am honored you came to me. My assistant and I can do this. I promise you."

"Thank you. I hope you can be discreet about the date. I've just come from the vicar and have not had occasion to inform anyone of my choice. So you see why I would appreciate your cooperation."

"Of course, milady. I am in the business of keeping such matters to myself. But you really need not be too concerned. So many of us have thought you might come to me soon that when we saw the item in the newspaper this morning—"

"What item in the newspaper?"

The bell above the shop door rang out.

"Good morning, Cyrene! I am so pleased you are open promptly."

Jess and Mrs. Brundage turned toward Patricia Mellwyn, who sailed forth in a flurry of plum-colored surah ruffles and a poppy-red straw bonnet. "Hello, Lady Curtis. I saw your carriage outside. I'm so delighted to see you again."

"Good morning." Jess nodded to the woman who had once been able to squeeze the delight from her day like juice from a lemon. But such a sour event would only have been possible aeons ago, in some other lifetime, when Jess permitted such abominations to occur. However, last night after the lecture, her visit to Rand, and her receipt of Spence's telegram about Cat's safe delivery of two girls, Jess had affirmed that her march toward total control of her life would proceed. Nothing, no one, would bar her. Not Harrison Emory. Not even Patricia Mellwyn.

"Thank you, Lady Mellwyn. I—"

"Having Cyrene create something special for you?" Patricia Mellwyn forced a smile beneath her copious red veil, too chipper for her ordinary hauteur. "She is a marvelous seamstress. I know firsthand. Ball gowns, wedding gowns"—her lace-gloved fingers rubbed together a bit of the snowdrop satin that Jess had chosen minutes before and that still floated over the edge of the cutting table—"even christening outfits."

Jess stared her down.

The woman flushed bright enough to match her hat. "I didn't mean it *that* way! I swear to you! But it's not a secret, you know. Everyone has seen how Lord Templeton dotes on you." She was trying to recover some dignity by retreating to polite language.

But Jess would not allow it. She had had her fill of those who would gossip about her or ridicule her to their own satisfaction. She ignored the woman and whirled to face the chagrined dressmaker.

"Mrs. Brundage, you have been very helpful to me this morning and I am grateful. May I return tomorrow at a convenient time for measurements?"

"Certainly, Lady Curtis. What time is best for you?"

"Two o'clock?"

"Wonderful. I look forward to it."

"Thank you. So do I."

Jess picked up her gloves, chatelaine, and parasol and headed for the sunlight.

Outside, Jess paused to close her eyes, catch her breath, and give in to the impulse to visit the confectioner. Pushing open her parasol, she realized too late she'd brought the broken one she'd taken to the fair. Just as she collapsed it and muttered a few unladylike words about its reliability, the ting-a-ling of the dressmaker's shop bell sent a shiver up her spine.

Jess walked away.

Patricia Mellwyn fell in beside her. "Lady Curtis, wait, please. I—I wish to apologize."

"I don't wish to hear it, Patricia."

"I came into Tuttle this morning to see you."

"Really. Why not call at my home, as most people would? And how could you know to find me here?"

"Your butler. I begged him to reveal your whereabouts."

"Odd." Jess remembered the time when Cat had disappeared. Only Pool had known her destination, and he had disclosed nothing until she pleaded with him for a clue. Of course, she had had good reasons to find Cat, and Pool had understood her frenzy. "My butler has no need to impart to you any such information."

"I know, but I . . . I gave him good cause."

Jess huffed, "How surprising," and twirled away.

Patricia Mellwyn reached out a hand. "I told Pool that I needed to explain to you why I invited that professor to speak at the guildhall last night."

That stalled Jess in her tracks. She spun to nail the woman with rabid eyes. *"Why?"*

Patricia glanced about to see if anyone could overhear their words.

Her interest in appearances, despite her proclamation of repentance, sent Jess sailing past her.

"No, wait! I realize how I've hurt you, and I—"

"Do remove your hand from my sleeve, Patricia. Now, I will be utterly blunt and tell you that you have hurt so many people for so many years, you have no idea of the destruction your tongue has caused. My cousin Cat remembers how you gave her the cut direct for years after Spence left her at the altar for his own good reasons. But you make assumptions, draw conclusions, never give people the benefit of the doubt, or even take the time to try to learn how people are different or unique."

Jess stepped closer to the confectioner's shop door, the scents of sugar and spice luring her toward sweetness. "You are bitter, Patricia. You brush everyone with it. Your husband, his acquaintances. But most of all, you hurt yourself. Only you know why. Ultimately, only you will be left to care."

"I see that now. My husband has warned me, he says, for the last time. Inviting this professor was intended to be an insult to you and your school. I thought he'd speak about his studies of abnormal behavior and how people cannot be changed. . . ."

"Whatever you thought the lecturer might have said is certainly more important to you than what he did say," Jess told her. Since Patricia had sat in the vicar's study baring her soul about whatever troubled her, she had not heard the professor. If she had, she might not have been so apologetic today. The flaws in Patricia's remorse rubbed Jess's nerves raw. "The professor," Jess elaborated, "offered a few illuminating ideas. He said not one word about physical conditions or types of behavior that signify whether one is destined to be a thief or a murderer. Believe me, no one was offended by his lecture."

"I am so glad," Patricia gushed like a schoolgirl. "Afterward I heard as much from Mrs. Winslow, but I wanted to hear it from you."

"I have never had such power before," Jess mused, drawn by the woman's persistence in the face of her own unforgiving stance. "How is it you apologize to me now?"

"I have seen what you and your cousin have accomplished with your students. You have taken children who were overly active, unusual . . . imperfect." She swallowed hard on her impertinent words—and caused sparks of hatred to rocket like Chinese fireworks in Jess's heart. "You even took in that Emory girl who had the riding accident and who looked so . . ."

"Forlorn? Impaired? Intellectually defi—"

"No! Don't say it!" Patricia's hands shot up to cover her ears. "That's what I cannot bear. Could not . . . Ever. I was mortified." She removed her hands. Her eyes were glazed. "I did not want your school to open, and I could not bear the sight of imperfect children because I . . . I had two of my own! They were born that way. Frail, fey little creatures who did not live beyond a few weeks because they were so malformed that I—"

Jess melted in sympathy and touched Patricia's gloved hand. "Oh, the heartache you must have—"

"No!" She stepped backward, tears trailing down her cheeks beneath her veil. "I don't want your pity. I only now have learned that I can't expect it because to want it is to wallow in it. And I must accept that I can't have children. I am horrified to admit that if the two of mine had lived, I might have been as cruel to them as I have been to you and Cat for bringing your girls here. What kind of mother abandons her own?"

Jess advanced, hands open. "Patricia, I know first-hand what it is to have a parent attempt to hurt you. But it is because"—*oh, my Lord, is this true?*—"that person can behave no other way at that time, in that place."

"Small justification for indifference."

"If that's what you showed your babies, it was your method of protecting yourself from hurt. At least you've admitted it, accepted it."

She snorted. "I never was kind enough to you to merit your coddling."

"I agree. But I'm not coddling you. I'm trying to tell you that you have two assets that many parents lack: you recognize the error of your ways, and you never let your feelings turn into brutality."

Truly appalled at that, Patricia trembled. "Oh, Jessica, I would never do that! I let them die, though, without my attention or comfort or help. I'll spend my life knowing that I ran from them, and I tried to make others turn their backs on you and Cat for the help you two tried to give. For many years I was shortsighted and hateful, and I must make it up to you."

"That you have come to me this morning to tell me this is a good start, Patricia."

The woman suppressed a sob. "On the contrary, Jessica, this is an ending to my opposition to you and your school. I won't bother you anymore."

"Perhaps we can make a new beginning. Together."

"I don't know what you mean." Patricia secured her veil about her collar, self-conscious in her surrender.

Jess noted that passersby found this little discussion a curiosity that made them pause or point and hurry off. "Why not come to Farrell Hall for tea tomorrow and I'll explain—"

A male voice interrupted her.

"Can I be of some assistance?"

Jess and Patricia looked up to find Rand Templeton.

"Good morning, Jess," he greeted her with warmth in his lambent blue eyes. "Hello, Patricia," he said in concerned contrast. "Should we three retire to the tearoom so that you two can have your discussion in one of the private alcoves?"

His suggestion was just as heartwarming as the rest of him. Jess beamed at him and opened her mouth to say—

"No." Patricia sniffled. *"No."* She hauled herself up into her old shroud of dignity, pivoted, and repaired to her waiting carriage.

"What in blasted hell happened here?" Rand said, watching her leave, while his expression remained placid for public benefit.

"Would you believe Patricia Mellwyn invited that

lecturer to the hall last night to see if she could cast aspersions on Farrell School and have us closed by public demand?"

"My God, she said that?"

"Not in those words. But she did plainly apologize to me for engaging him."

"Extraordinary."

"That's what I thought. And you won't believe how she bared her soul to me about her reasons for opposing the Farrell School."

"I daresay I won't." His eyes shifted to hers in joy.

"Nor will you believe that she confided in me an old secret from which she thinks she cannot set herself free. *Oh, Rand,"* she moaned, a hand going to her own mouth while tears sprang to her eyes. "Patricia Mellwyn and I are very much alike."

"Not anymore, darling." He stepped near, his voice a warm spun-sugar delight. "I saw the proof last night."

She smiled up at him, her sorrow banished by his ardor. An imp emerged. "I rather hoped you *felt* it."

He growled. "If you look at me like that for another second, I'll scandalize half of Kent by making you *touch* what you do to me."

"Only half?" she tossed back. A gush of desire flooded her body. "I would like to stroke your best intentions"—she ran her eyes down his molded torso as he sucked in air—"but I came here to buy candy." Her gaze locked with his.

Rand seized her arm and, in the gentlemanly move, told her with clamping fingers how he meant to bind her to him in any way he could, whenever and wherever he might. "I'll give you sweet things, you witch."

"Ooooh." She pursed her lips as she allowed him to turn her toward the shop. "I hoped you might—for nights and days without end."

He grunted, then flung open the door. "Pick the day when we can start."

"I did so this morning." She glided past him.

She bent over the counter, salivating over French truffles when the confectioner popped in from the kitchen and oozed his delight at their appearance in his shop.

"I must commend you, darling," Rand whispered when the burly man disappeared to the back room to fetch a sample of this morning's buttercreams for Jess to try. "In full blossom, you are the damnedest tease I have ever met."

"I'll make it up to you."

"In ways I am listing beyond number."

She chuckled. "Are you here in Tuttle by chance?"

"Pool told me you had come here."

"My butler and I must have a talk. He told Patricia I was here. Now he has told you."

"At midnight, dear lady, you instructed me to call on you today. I did at the first decent hour, only to find you not at home. Now, I have no idea what Patricia's threat to Pool was, but mine was extremely simple."

"Oh?"

"I told him I'd grind him up for haggis if he didn't."

She shook with silent laughter. "What is so urgent?"

"That is *my* question, sweetheart. What are you

doing in town so early in the morning?" He cocked a black brow, his expression a riot of hope mixed with exasperation.

"Choosing fabrics." She graced the burly confectioner with a joyous thank-you when he reappeared and offered dark chocolate buttercreams on a doily-covered plate.

"I made these this morning, Lady Curtis, with Cadbury's pure cream chocolate. Lord Templeton, would you care to try one, sir?"

"No, thank you, I—"

"You don't like chocolate?" Jess paused, appalled, her glove instantly off to take the tidbit halfway to her mouth. "*How* can you not?"

He gritted his teeth, but grinned at the solicitous confectioner. "Thank you, Mr. Soames. I have always said you make the best delights west of Vienna."

"I have bonbons today, fresh from Paris. Would you like to try them, too?"

"We'll take a pound, sir," Rand said.

The chubby man disappeared with a clap of his hands while Rand popped a chocolate into his mouth. She watched, mesmerized by the way his lips moved as he ate the candy.

He stopped. His eyes locked on hers. He began again slowly, languidly enjoying the chocolate until the tip of his tongue emerged to slide along the rise of his lower lip.

Her eyelashes fluttered. Her throat grew thick. She gulped as he swallowed.

"Eat yours," he crooned.

The inferno of her mind consumed everything before her, except the nearness of him. She tipped her chin up in a coquette's challenge, raised a candy, and took it on her tongue while the man before her turned to stone.

His gaze memorized her every move. In the glow of the fires he set as he examined her lips and throat and hardening nipples, she would create more fantasies like the ones she had devised last night.

She finished her chocolate, grinned, then pivoted toward a display of cakes on glass-enclosed shelves. She pointed to a two-tiered creation when Soames reappeared. "Do you make taller cakes? With more layers?"

"Yes, ma'am." Was it her imagination that the man contemplated them both like a gleeful cat? "How many layers would you like?"

"Ten!" she shot back as Rand came to stand so close that his body heat roasted her reason.

"Ten?"

"Yes." She nodded, while she felt Rand's hand on her elbow and wished it were on her frantically beating heart. "Make it a veritable *tower.*"

"A tower. I see. And when would you want it?"

"Three weeks from now."

"Which day?"

"Saturday. Send it up to Farrell Hall by ten in the morning. And I want marzipan roses and baby's breath on top."

The confectioner practically burst his straining gussets with satisfaction. "Am I to assume that is the day you've both chosen?"

"Both?" Jess asked Soames, but frowned up at Rand.

He looked as surprised as she. "What have you

done?" Rand asked, hovering over her, a giant all too smug.

"*Me?* Only what I was supposed to do!" This was not the way she had planned to tell him. "What have *you* done?"

Rand faced Soames, while his fingers dug into Jess's elbow. "Might we ask you for a pot of tea, sir? We shall sit at that corner table."

Soames waved a hand. "Absolutely, sir. Fast as taffy hardening. I'll just go make it myself . . . now . . . right now," he said, wide-eyed but shaking with laughter as he scurried off.

"I have tons of preparations to attend to, Rand. I don't have time to sit and have tea." She toyed with her gloves and a grin.

He lifted her chin. "Why do you need a ten-layer cake, darling?"

"To cut! To eat! To celebrate! To give each unmarried guest a slice to take one home and dream of finding his or her beloved as I have found you."

The shock of love professed washed over his sharp features.

"I adore it when you look at me like this," she whispered.

He was so close that beneath their myriad layers of clothing, she could detect his long, hard intent. "And I, my charming minx, adore it when you talk to me. So tell me more. Will I find myself at this event where this castle of icing is distributed to half the world?"

"I think you will be the first to arrive," she said solemnly, though one fingertip scrolled down his waistcoat. "I'll be the last." She grinned.

He groaned.

She frowned. "Why would Soames think we have both chosen this date?" She hooked her finger in the chain of Rand's pocket watch. "What have you done, my love?"

He arched. "Nothing extraordinary—"

"Rand?"

"—for a man who craves you."

"Tell me."

"If I do, what do I win?"

"Insufferable man. What makes you think I'll wager? I am not fond of losing and choose my bets wisely. How do I tame you quickly for the eternity ahead of us?"

"I have a few sensational ideas. One begins with vicars and cakes."

"Hmm, should the cake be chocolate?"

"Make it any flavor you like as long as I get to lick the crumbs from your fingers, sweetheart."

She leaned over like a conspirator. "Tradition says it must be *virgin* vanilla."

He hooted in laughter. "But I will be extremely gratified . . . at least until I get you alone and am rewarded with other sweets for my labors." At the sizzle of her body's appreciation for his rhetoric, she held him off with a hand to his heart while he tempted her with "Why would I not? I've already become addicted to the delicate pastry of your skin."

"Rand—"

"And the bites I had of the tasty apples of your cheeks made me want other savories—"

She screeched.

His eyes dropped to circle her breasts. "Your melons—"

She eeked.

"And cherry . . ."

She choked.

"Fondant with slick slices of peach"—he glanced about as if he owned the world—"covered in cream."

She dissolved.

But Soames entered and she seized her sense of time and place, then suppressed a giggle at Rand's uncomfortable flex of his torso. She waited until the shopkeeper had set down the accoutrements for their tea before she knew if she would ever breathe again.

"I am so delighted," the confectioner said effusively as Jess tore herself away from succulent dreams, "that the two of you have come to me this morning. Imagine. You buy your wedding dress at Mrs. Brundage's—"

Jess's mouth dropped open at Soames's words.

"And then you come to me for the wedding cake."

She gaped at Rand, who looked less startled but definitely cockier than she ever could.

"But to think that you'll be married in our village church, too. Well! That is an honor."

Long after Mr. Soames had once more disappeared into his kitchen, Jess watched the terribly satisfied gentleman who sat before her.

"How could Mr. Soames know? I never realized that news traveled so fast!"

One corner of Rand's mouth hitched up in a lopsided smile. "I think he had fair notice."

She smelled a rat. "He watched me enter the vicarage at nine?"

"Is that where you were, my love?"

She scolded him with a sideways look. "You didn't know I went there?"

"I suspected. Hoped."

"Then how can Soames know barely after I do that I mean to marry you in the Tuttle church, hmmm?"

"Do you really want to know?" He scorched her with cobalt-blue eyes.

"Absolutely." She leaned forward. "How?"

Rand crossed his arms. "It seems our betrothal announcement was in the Tuttle and Ashford newspapers this morning."

She recalled the dressmaker's remark about newspapers. "You scoundrel."

"I put it in the London papers, too," he said in earnest. "After you reconfirmed it last night, I couldn't wait. You did agree to marry me, my love. I was only moving things along in the right direction, and I went to Farrell Hall this morning to tell you. But there has been no time for talk."

"Nor is there now," she warned as villagers opened the shop door and set the bell ajingle.

Instead of purchasing candies, however, the populace of Tuttle village had come to bill and coo over the betrothal of the marquess in their midst and the lady who ran the school for girls. Their congratulations meant that the tea grew cold before Jess and Rand got to drink it. It also made conversation about Harrison Emory impossible.

When it appeared that no time would be found unless she scheduled it, Jess rose from her chair. "I must go. We must keep up appearances, mustn't we, love? And I do have classes to teach this afternoon.

Don't trouble yourself to come over for Amanda's lessons until I tell you she is up to it. She slept last night, but she was awake early. I left her with Darwin dancing for her as she tried to play an accordion. She was laughing, which was a boon. The cat does more to soothe her, though. Animals can do that for the sick and the old. I'm not certain why, but I knew it when I was young. Thank God something helps. . . ." Her concentration drifted to her duties and her worries.

"Come along, sweetheart." Rand rose, left a ten-pound note on the table and took his bonbons and her arm. "I'll see you to your carriage."

When they were outside, he asked her to describe the confrontation with Harrison.

"He was the worse for an encounter with liquor. That worked to my advantage. I took it. He's gone, Rand." Some other time she'd tell him of Emory's intentions. Not on the street. Not now. Today she wanted to enjoy the delirium of being in love and betrothed and adored. "He's left and now, my love, I want only to look to the future."

Rand opened the door of her brougham. "Three weeks Saturday. What time?"

"Eleven o'clock."

"All of Tuttle and Ashford will cram themselves into that church . . . which means you can't change your mind."

She waggled her hand, which beneath her glove bulged with his ring. "Never."

"God, I want to kiss you."

"You look like a schoolboy." She laughed softly.

"I feel rather like a *green* boy," he corrected, his

meaning shining in his eyes. "I hope you are engaging an orchestra for the reception. I want to dance with you."

She clenched her jaw, the past rising before her to obscure the brightness of her future. "I am not a very good dancer. I've never danced very much in public, and—"

"You should. Grace like yours was meant to be admired."

"I've had no practice, Rand. I never made a debut. Never had beaux. I am not—"

"You are perfect. And you are mine. Look into my eyes. Yours are such a wondrous aqua. I look at you and see the beauty of a sun-blessed grotto. I love you so. Tell me, dearest woman, do *you* want to waltz at our wedding?"

"With you, I would do anything."

"Then you shall." He tapped a finger to her nose. "In the interminable weeks before this wedding, I will come to Farrell Hall to give lessons." He wiggled his brows. "Piano for Belle and perhaps Amanda. But dancing lessons for you, headmistress."

"What if I am a slow learner?"

"Sweetheart," he said gruffly, "if you get any faster or any more proficient, before my next birthday I'll have apoplexy!"

"Oh, but my dear Lord Templeton, I do want you very healthy, lest you spend your days and nights . . . in bed."

"Unable to get up? I guarantee that, with you, darling, I will be perpetually *up.* Yes, well . . ." He made a terrible effort to clear his throat and glanced about. "In the meantime, I will content myself by booking passage for our wedding trip. Is there any special place you'd like to visit, my love?"

She tingled with excitement. Her voice dropped an octave. "I will go anywhere with you."

His blue eyes narrowed on her mouth. "I have a place or two I wish to show you."

"You have shown me the most important."

He touched his thumb to her lower lip, the way he had that first day when she asked for the gift of his time and his talent.

She kissed the tip briefly and said, "From a pulpit, heaven always sounded far away and fragile, but in your embrace, it feels like paradise."

He stopped breathing. "Thank God you set the date only three weeks away." He thrust the box of bonbons into her hand. "Take these home, eat them, and call them a small substitute for what I soon will give you to make everything complete. In fact, there is only one more thing I can think of to make this final. Have you written to Cat to tell her any of this?"

She beamed at him. "I received a telegram from Spence last night before you and I played our duet. Cat delivered two baby girls yesterday morning. She's in superb health. So are the twins. Spence is ecstatic. I sent a return telegram this morning to tell them to recuperate quickly. They have a family wedding to attend."

Chapter Seventeen

THE DAY BEFORE THE WEDDING THE LYONNS FAMILY arrived in a coach bursting with baggage. Among relatives, kisses and hugs went around with congratulations for betrothals and babies and good health. Farrell Hall's staff stepped in to fly about the old manse, fussing over Cat and cooing over the two newborn girls. Spence had his hands full with rambunctious two-year-old Vic.

"No, you don't, old man." Spence caught his son by the suspenders. Vic had been waddling his way toward his mother, who was climbing the stairs to their suite. "Let those three get settled first. You and I shall go greet the Triumvirate."

Jess chuckled at Spence's term of endearment for Precious, Darwin, and Bones. "Come along, Vic." She crooked a finger at the towheaded little boy who resembled his father in every way but the iris-blue eyes of his mother. The chubby darling grinned so broadly it lit up the hall. "This time we have more than three lovely animals to show you. Your father will have to make the trio a quartet."

Spence groaned. "Good God, what sort of creature have you added?"

"A parrot."

"Of course. Just what you needed to round things out," he teased as he draped an arm over Jess's shoulder and they made their way toward the music room with the promise of tea and cake for Vic. "What species? Where'd you get him?"

"Rand bought him at the village fair a few weeks ago, rather as a joke. I have no idea what he is or where he came from, but he is—*if* he is a *he*—a rather odd duck."

Spence chortled. "Then he'll fit right in with the Triumvirate."

"I'm afraid he wants to fit in with Bones more than any other."

"I don't understand," said the man who had left the army to become a research scientist. In the past three years, Spence had experimented, classified, and published numerous studies on plant and animal life. In the process, the name of Spencer Caldmore Lyonns, earl of Dartmoor, sparkled with a meticulous reputation.

"You will. You need only watch him a bit." She thrust open the doors and there, like royalty waiting to receive their subjects, stood the quartet, precisely where Jess had told them to remain until the flurry of moving in the Lyonnses subsided and they could hold their audience.

Assembled before the double doors to the garden,

the quartet blinked at the sight of Spence and Vic Lyonns. Then all hell broke loose.

The monkey in short pants began to dance, rather like a whirling dervish, Jess thought. The cat, true to form, rose like a fairy from her cloud and sauntered forward. Bones, never one to change his greeting to this man, shot to his feet and came over to clamp his mouth around Spence's ankle.

The gentleman in question tolerantly rolled his eyes to the ceiling. "Someday I hope this fellow gets his fill of my trousers. This ankle-biting gets damn boring."

Tears of laughter cascaded down Jess's cheeks while the dog growled, Spence crooned to him, and Vic clapped his hands.

Meanwhile the parrot became indignant, screeching loud enough to make Vic gape. Then, in imitation of the dog, the parrot flapped its wings and skittered across the carpet toward Spence's other ankle, which became this bird's trophy.

"Wonderful," Spence mused. "Now there are two of them." He glanced at his son. "I shall soon take up short pants, like you, Vic. My long ones are fast becoming tattered. I say," Spence said as he sat down with Vic squirming to be free, "what have we here? A bluebird from paradise. Rare, rare. Come here, old man."

The bird flew up to perch on his knee. The two creatures studied each other, eyes blinking, heads cocking, examining each detail. Spence held his curious son's hand in one of his huge ones while he reached out to offer his forearm to the huge parrot.

"Very fine specimen. From the jungles of Brazil. *Anodorhynchus hyacinthus.* To us, the hyacinth macaw. Rand chose well. These birds love familiar people but hate strangers, and therefore are very good house pets."

"Yes, well . . . the girls like him. So does Pool."

Spence beamed at the bird. "Quite a test of your mettle, old man. Pool likes no animal, vegetable, or mineral mucking up his orderly domain. He retired me and my laboratory to the room off the stables right smartly three years ago."

The bird tipped back his head and cawed. Repeatedly.

Jess tittered, then coughed to keep back the chuckles.

"Good God," Spence muttered, "what's the matter with him? He sounds like—"

"He's barking?" Jess asked, innocence personified.

"Actually, yes."

"He is."

"Pardon me?"

"He is. He befriended Bones immediately upon arrival. He eats from the dog's dish, sleeps near his bed, and supervises him on his hunts. The bird even sounds like Bones. I've no idea why or how, but he does. He *is* a comedy of errors. And I . . ." She toyed with a grin. "I adore him. For his eloquence—and his antics."

"So you should. He is remarkable. In good health, which is no mean feat for having been transported all the way from South America. But also because I rather think that *he* is a *she,* my dear."

"How can you tell?"

"As a specimen, she seems the right size. I have a friend in London who is an ornithologist. He owns a pair of hyacinths. The female of the duo is smaller than her mate. About the size of this beauty. Was it she who brought those in?" Spence nodded toward a set of twigs by the garden door.

"Ah, yes. Every day. Pool quickly sweeps them right out again."

"I'll have a talk with him. This bird is trying to build a nest of rose and yew and privet, I see." He examined the creature's long, graceful tail and wings and then her powerful black bill rimmed in bright yellow. "These jaws can do worse damage than our Bones ever could, even when he had teeth! I am grateful," he said, addressing the macaw, "that you merely took a chunk out of my pants and not my hide."

"Thank you!" cawed the bird.

"You're very welcome."

"Birdie! Birdie!" called Vic.

"Birdie! Birdie!" the hyacinth echoed.

"Oh, precisely what we needed," muttered Spence, "a bird who thinks she's a dog and talks like a human!"

"Down! Let Vic down!" yelped the boy.

"Very well, but be gentle with them, son. They haven't seen you in so long, they may be a bit rusty and need to relearn how to keep up with you."

"Tea?" asked Jess as Vic scrambled away with the Quartet.

"Cake?" queried the macaw.

"Yes, please," replied Spence to Jess, but to the bird he said, "Would you like cake?"

"Thank you!"

"You're welcome." He shook his head at Jess while

his wife came to stand behind him, hands on his shoulders.

"Who is this?" asked Cat in her melodious contralto.

"Our latest addition at Farrell Hall," Jess filled in as she passed Spence his tea and admired her cousin's healthy apricot cheeks and glistening brandy-colored hair.

"Hmm, it seems we have had so many new pets these past few years," Cat mused as she came around to sit in the chair nearest Spence and admire the plumage of the bird. "You are lovely, madam. How did you come here?"

Jess filled Cat in on how the bad bird arrived, but asked, "How did you know the parrot was a female?"

Cat rolled a shoulder as she accepted her tea. "Oh, one knows these things." She winked at her husband.

The macaw took that as a cue to sing, *"Pretty lady, pretty lady,"* until the three humans shook their heads in exasperation.

"Quiet!" roared Spence.

And the bird, cowed, shut up.

Cat leaned toward the macaw and offered sweetly, "Not to worry. His roar is worse than his bite."

"Only to some," Spence corrected.

"Those who require it." Cat pinned the bird with a look. "So you must learn, madam, not to ruffle the feathers of a lion."

"Mixed metaphor, my love."

"But apt. See, the macaw understands. Don't you, dearest?"

"Thank you!"

"You're welcome. Now do remain quiet while the

other animals talk, will you? That's good." She smiled at Jess. "I want to know about Rand. Where is he? I thought he'd be here to greet us."

"He will be as soon as he's able. Last-minute wedding trip plans, he said."

"I see. Paris, I hope?"

"To begin. There is another destination, which he keeps a mystery."

"A puzzle will keep you on your toes," he'd said. "It's a way to ensure that you come to the church." Bah. As if she'd fail to go.

Cat took in Jess's hair and eyes and hands. "You look extremely calm for a woman who is to be married in less than twenty-four hours."

"I am," Jess replied. "I feel as though I have a hive of bees living in my stomach, but that has absolutely nothing to do with the ceremony, you realize." *Only with the fact that I am determined to tell the last of my secrets to my new husband tomorrow night when we're alone and when we belong to each other in the sight of God and man.*

"And you thought you'd never marry," said Spence. "I find it extremely gratifying that you have chosen Rand Templeton. He's been the best of friends, and he is undoubtedly the most honorable fellow I've ever met. I'll be happy to welcome him to the family."

Jess flushed with the warmth of her own appreciation for her fiancé. "I'm thrilled you approve."

Cat grinned. "And to think that this entire time Rand's home was down the lane, just next door. I must know how this happened. Your letters were fine but not informative. I want to hear every detail, Jess."

Spence grunted. "In that case, my dears, I'm off to see how Pool has taken care of my new hybrid lima beans. I'll take this menagerie with me. What do you say, Vic? We'll leave Mommy and Aunt Jessie to their wedding plans."

With that, the little boy took his father's giant hand and giggled at the single-file procession of monkey, cat, dog, and parrot as they ambled out the door.

"Cake?" Jess asked politely, knowing this part of the conversation would not be light. She owed Cat an explanation and an apology before she left on her wedding trip. She wanted to begin her marriage on a clear note of truth—with Cat, to whom she had lied for so many years, and with Rand, to whom she had never told tales but had been honest more in the breach than in the full observance.

Certainly if she'd had the opportunity to tell him in the past weeks, she would have. But being betrothed had meant social engagements where private conversation was impossible. Then whenever Rand was here, it seemed Pool or the students or her staff flocked around with never-ending questions and needs. Even those moments when Rand tried to teach her to waltz had been fleeting and more tantalizing physically than productive of rational discussion. Finally she had nearly given up hope of telling him before the ceremony. And she knew he understood. He always had. He always would.

Satisfied her relief would come soon, she focused on her cousin, who sat here in the blossom of maternal flower and shook her head.

"No, Jess, no sweets for me, thank you. I'm trying to eat for three but not too much. When I finish nursing I'd like to be able to fit into some of my dresses. Frugal to the end, you know. But I will have a scone with some orange marmalade." Silently Cat contemplated Jess as she served her. She accepted her plate, nibbled on the scone, then put it aside. "I am simply ecstatic for you, you realize."

"I knew you would be."

"I did always claim that there was no reason on this earth why you shouldn't marry, sweetheart."

Jess shrugged. "I never found a reason to consider it until I got to know Rand."

"One doesn't think of marriage unless it is to the right man."

"In your case, there was only one man despite those things and people that kept you apart." Jess paused, knowing the truth of what she said also applied to her—and her shortcomings. "Rand accepts me as I am."

"True love." Cat beamed.

"I have never felt like this. So utterly . . ." She waved a hand.

"Free?"

"Yes! Adored, too!"

"Definitely true love, sweetheart."

"And to think none of it would have occurred if Amanda Emory had not come to the Farrell School."

"Life can be capricious," Cat mused. "Spence reentered my life because of extraordinary circumstances. It is important to take what you are given in these instances and make the most of them."

"I have learned that lesson well, Cat. When Amanda came here in January, I thought I could train her myself. Such folly to think I knew enough. I didn't, of course, and when I grew frustrated, I went to the only person I could think of who could help me. Rand." Jess smiled at her cousin.

"Over the past few months I saw Amanda grow from a sorely beset child to one who was healthier, happier, and able to study longer. One who remembered how to play the piano. Heavens, now she even sings! Yesterday when Rand came to give her her last piano lesson before we go off tomorrow, she even waltzed with him!"

Cat widened her eyes. "Ah, but the one who should learn to dance is you, my dear. Has your intended groom taught you?"

"I'm afraid there hasn't been much time, and I am not so accomplished as he."

"Practice makes perfect. And soon you and he will have as much time together as you want!"

"You know," Jess whispered in awe, "before I met him, I could not imagine being this happy for so long, minute after minute—hours and days of it."

"You deserve years of happiness. It looks marvelous on you, too, sweetheart."

One of Jess's hands went to her hot cheek. "The undying blush?"

"The eternal joy."

"Oh, Cat." Her face fell, and she kneaded her hands. "I'm so afraid this is a dream, that it will all go away like a puff of smoke. I wake up and pinch myself."

"Sweetheart, it is real. And please don't pinch too much. We want no black-and-blue marks on your wedding day." Cat tossed her dark amber curls and gave Jess a saucy look. "I am dying to see your wedding gown. I'll bet Mrs. Brundage preened her feathers for days when you asked her to make it."

"When word went around that I had asked her to sew my trousseau, too, even Patricia Mellwyn was mollified."

"Patricia Mellwyn? The woman hasn't had a kind word to say of anyone in years."

"She does now." Jess sipped her own tea.

"Oh?" One of Cat's fine brown brows rose. "I detect a story behind that comment. Do tell."

Jess told her of the lady's efforts to get the professor to lecture at the guildhall and Patricia's subsequent confession and apology. "Her remorse was real. I understood it immediately and have insisted she come here for tea. She has—four times now. She teaches a group of girls embroidery."

"I *don't* believe it!"

"Do. She and her husband will attend the ceremony and the reception here tomorrow. You will see that Lady Mellwyn is very much reformed."

"My hat is off to you, Jess. No one has made the woman come to heel for years."

"I did nothing except be myself, and perhaps circumstances combined so that Patricia realized the error of her assumptions. This business with Amanda has changed so many of us. Most, for the better."

"With the exception of whom?"

"Harrison Emory."

"I see. I met him years ago with his wife. Timid little thing, she was afraid of him, I thought. Yet the aspect of him which struck me most was that he is rather . . . pompous."

"Among other things."

"Such as?"

"Self-centered."

"A malady of many."

"But in his case, detrimental to his daughter."

"How?"

Jess found her throat clogged. In the past three weeks she had not talked about this, and in the crush of wedding plans she had not thought about Emory and his threat. Besides, he hadn't returned, nor had he written to Amanda.

"Emory fails to understand the nature of head injury. He thinks it a scrape of the knee that can be made better with time, or as a disease that can be cured with a simple potion."

"I am certain you have instructed him otherwise."

"Ah, yes, but to no avail."

"I thought you wrote to me that Emory seemed committed to Amanda's recovery."

"He is . . . and he isn't. He told me he wanted her to regain her memory to see if she could and then to learn how much she could recall."

From the terrace, Rand entered the room. Though he lifted a hand and grinned to greet Jess, he paused as Cat went on in an uncharacteristic huff.

"Well," Cat scoffed, "I know you told Emory that recovery of memory to head-injured patients was nigh to impossible."

"Yes . . ."

"Yes, but what?"

Jess met her cousin's concerned eyes. "The impossible has occurred."

"*My God.* How can that be?"

"I don't know. The mind is a mysterious place."

"What does Amanda recall?"

"Amanda remembers that Harrison and his wife argued. She told him so, and he didn't deny it. Amanda also said he struck her during that argument. God knows why."

"You are certain, Jess, that this is no delusion. No vision?" Cat persisted.

Rand came forward.

"Perhaps in her fall from her horse, she was not struck terribly hard."

"Or not as hard as you."

Jess shifted in her chair. Staring into her teacup, she sensed Rand had not moved a muscle. "Or not in the same way."

"No, of course not. No two head injuries are alike. They are— Why are you looking at me like that, Jess?"

"Because I—I have a confession to make to you. I've kept it from you through the years. I hated the idea of telling you, and every time I tried, I could only think of how you'd hate me, loathe me for years of falsehood."

"My dearest Jess, how could you think I would ever hate you?"

"For this you might. The lie caused a lot of damage."

"I know of none. What possible damage—"

"I always knew how my mother died."

"Yes, of course, we did. She broke her neck when her horse failed to clear a privet hedge."

Jess shuddered with what else she knew of the tragedy. "I was right behind her. I too tried to clear the hedge."

Rand stepped nearer, right next to Cat, who greeted him with a brief glowing smile but returned her attention to this subject that had her rapt.

"Yes, Jess, but you couldn't take the hedge," Cat continued. "There was no clearance. Your horse stumbled on the tangle of your mother and her mount."

"And I was thrown into a nearly thicket, which evidently cushioned some of the blow."

"You were in a coma for so long afterward."

"But eventually I remembered much of what had happened immediately *before* my mother was thrown."

Though Jess could not look into Rand's face, she saw him clench his hands.

Cat grew suddenly very still. "Since when have you remembered?"

"Since the day my father died. In fact, hours before he died."

"Six months or more, wasn't it, after your accident and your mother's?"

"Yes."

"Well." Cat sat back. "I am amazed. I always thought you couldn't recall a thing."

"I lied. For years."

Cat examined her like a specimen under glass, and Jess braced herself for the next obvious question: why?

"I see." Cat swallowed while tears filled her eyes. "It must have been terrible for you to have to lie."

"I want to tell you why."

Cat bit her lip.

Rand came even closer.

"My father killed my mother."

Rand stood right in front of her, and Jess knew she could walk into his embrace to say this if she wanted, but she needed to do this standing alone.

"He cut the girth strap on her saddle. I saw him do it minutes before he came inside to argue with her about . . . about her latest lover and her indiscretions. At first I did not believe what I saw him doing, and when he came through the garden doors, I asked him about it. He hit me across the mouth before I could finish. I tried to tell my mother, but she would not listen. She was intent on defending me and yelling at him.

"He fueled her rage with crude words"—Jess met Rand's compassionate eyes—"and the vilest insults. Even my mother was shocked. That's when she charged through the garden doors. I ran out behind her. She mounted, even though I told her not to go. She was crying and laughing. She jabbed her heels into the horse and went off. I had to stop her! I followed her but couldn't catch her, and then we both went over that hedge. . . .

"No one else ever knew what my father did. I guess no one looked at the strap. No one suspected him of murder. I don't know why, especially since Aunt Mary told me that my mother was notorious by then and my father was a well-known cuckold. I was in a coma and couldn't tell anyone what I'd seen, even if I had remembered. My father must have reached a point where he went mad and couldn't cope with her any longer. He was so ashamed of her that day. He cried, but she only laughed at him, reveling in his agony. I often wonder if she knew she might drive him to kill her. If she planned it . . ."

Rand swallowed repeatedly.

"Oh, Jess," Cat said from her chair, tears falling freely. "My father told me your parents had their problems. He worried about you and offered to have you come stay with us while they . . . lived in the fashion to which they had become accustomed."

"For those times when I was here, I was always grateful, Cat. They were, until recently, a few of the happy times of my life." She girded herself for the last tale of horror. "But that is not the end of my story."

She moved around the room, reaching for any convenient object. "I must tell you about the way my father died."

Cat rose. "No, my dear Jessica, you needn't. My father suspected that he died under hideous circumstances. What my father did not know was that yours had committed the premeditated murder of your mother. So horrid . . . Oh, Jess, my father conjectured that the man had some awful reason to come to your room that night. Now that I know it was his fear of your revelations about the murder of your mother, I need hear no more of this."

Cat sniffled, barely recovered as she looked at Rand. "I will leave you to tell your future husband the one remaining fact about your past that blocks you from total joy with him."

Perceptive Cat. Jess watched her cousin turn and calmly gaze into Rand Templeton's eyes. "She is yours, my dear. What she is about to tell you, I already know—and clearly, you do not." She rose.

"I'll see to my family. You see to your future," she told Jess and, with a swish of her skirts, left them to a silent room.

"I didn't mean to intrude," Rand said finally into the vacuum. "I saw Spence by the stable block, and he told me the two of you were in here. . . . Look, Jessie, I'm willing to wait for this, darling."

She went to stand in front of him. "I want to tell you. Now is better than tomorrow night. Infinitely better."

He stared at her, waiting as ever with the gift of patience, and his love.

"Months after my accident when my father heard me recount my visions, he feared I would tell everyone about them. I did, of course. Like Amanda, I didn't think they were real. Not at first. But then I began to *know,* deep in my soul, that my mind did not play tricks. One night he came to me. I still slept a lot, recovering. My governess slept in the same room, in case I had problems in the night. He came. He was drunk. And worse, he had a pistol."

Rand reached for her.

"No. Let me . . . let me say this."

She caught back a sob and forced herself to say words she'd never uttered since that shocking night her father attacked her. "He came in, shouting, waking us up. He wanted me to repeat what I had told him that morning about what I had seen him do to my mother's girth strap. I sensed enough rage in him not to repeat it. My governess grew terrified. She pleaded with him to leave. He prodded me on. Finally, when I would say nothing, he drew the pistol on me.

" 'Tell me again!' he shouted over and over, until he

was crying along with me. He grew so enraged that he pressed the gun to my temple and told me to repeat the story. Terrified, I got it out. My governess was aghast and sprang at him, but he turned and . . . he shot her. Simply killed her. I screamed. He dropped the gun, and I scrambled to get it. I pointed it at him, fired once, and then stopped—horrified at what I'd done, but more appalled that I had missed him. And he was bigger, stronger. He gained it back with little effort, then pointed it at me. The room was so deathly silent, I swear to this day I can hear his finger squeeze the trigger . . . but at the last moment before firing, he cursed and cried, then put the barrel to his head. He shot himself. He died instantly. I never told a soul. I never had to. The room, the bodies, told the tale. I did not need to elaborate.

"I went to Aunt Mary's after that. For years, until she died five years ago and Uncle Walter and Cat brought me here to live, I tried to build a new life. To forget. But of course I didn't entirely. And it kept me from you for so long."

She took the one step toward him she had longed to take for months. Running one hand up his cheek, she whispered, "Tomorrow can't come too soon for me, darling."

He crushed her to him then, and with his lips to hers, he vowed that bliss was already theirs. Today and always.

Chapter Eighteen

"I LOVE IT!" CAT CRIED AS SHE CIRCLED JESS AND FLUFFED the alençon trim of her floor-length veil. "You are gorgeous. Now, enough of this. We're already ten minutes late! Take up that garden of lilies and jessamine Rand sent over from his greenhouse and let's *go!*"

"Hmm, the gown *is* rather nice, isn't it?" Jess moved this way and that before her mirror to admire the article of clothing she never thought she'd wear.

"Sweetheart, admire yourself at the reception, will you? From the way Rand looked last night at supper, if you keep him waiting one minute more than necessary, we could all be pâté before luncheon!"

"Or *for* luncheon!"

"Jessie."

"I know, I know. It's just that you don't get married more than once, do you?"

"You and I don't, no."

"Right you are." She spun and the snowy satin skirt twirled out over her endless crinolines.

Cat raised both arms. "I'm going down to tell Pool you're dawdling."

"Eek! Don't do that!"

Cat opened the bedroom door. "If it lights a fire under you . . ."

"Not to worry," she said, lost again in a fairy tale that for once was her story. "Rand is waiting."

"I give up," Cat muttered as she shut the door and strode away.

Jess chuckled. Then looked herself squarely in the eye. This new person before her was so serene, and all because . . . "Rand is waiting. And you are so fortunate, my dear. Can you imagine how very blessed? No, you never did, did you? But"—she scooped up the huge bouquet adorned with Queen Anne's lace and satin bows, "you will give back to him all of those things he gave you—and more. You'll bring him companionship and perhaps children. Offer him happiness."

With that, she grinned at herself and pivoted toward the stairs, then walked down the hall and outside to the waiting coach.

But when she put one foot up, only Cat sat inside. "Don't stop now, Jess! I sent Pool on, swearing you would join me in this coach within minutes. Everyone has left. All the house staff and each and every student. They're all gone to Tuttle church, darling, as you should be."

"But where's Amanda?"

"What? Why?"

"She came to me earlier this morning complaining

of a headache and said she was afraid she might not be able to go today. She was afraid of seeing all those people. But I persuaded her to attend. Or I thought I had. And now she's not here. Did she come down to you to say she wasn't going?"

"No. Would she have? After all, she doesn't know me very well. Not as well as she knows you."

"I would think she'd say something." Jess turned and put a hand to her forehead to shield her eyes from the sun as she gazed up at the second-story bedroom window. Amanda's drapes covered the panes, as if she slept. Or hid.

Jess placed her bouquet beside Cat on the velvet seat. "Take this, and when you get there tell Spence to inform Rand I'm late but I'm coming. Then send the coach back for me. I must get Amanda."

"But, Jess—"

"Please, Cat. I want this child to know some joyful minutes."

Cat surrendered. "All right, Jess. I'll go. But when this coach returns, you'd better be ready. I've a feeling that Rand Templeton will be in it, ready to fling you over his shoulder."

"I will be, Cat. I promise. Go now and do this for me." She closed the brougham's door and turned back toward Farrell Hall and the one student she could never leave behind on such a day as this.

Hoisting the voluminous train and veil of her wedding attire, she hastened inside. There the Quartet swiveled their heads as she passed, they themselves being the only creatures within miles who were exiled from Tuttle church today.

"Be good boys and girls, will you?" Jess pleaded

with them. "If Amanda comes through here, raise a ruckus, hmm?" And with that she ran up the stairs and along the second-story hall to Amanda's door.

She knocked. "Amanda dear, it's Miss Curtis. We're late. And I am eager to be off. Come along, sweetheart."

No answer came.

"Amanda, please. I—"

Jess paused to peer at the oak door. What if Amanda had run away again? What if she'd had another vision this morning and that was why she didn't want to appear in public? What if—

Jess rapped loudly on the door. "Amanda, listen to me. If you're upset and want to talk, I can. I will. Lord Templeton is a patient man, but it won't be too long before he grows rather wild, you know. Can you just let me in for now, and I promise you we'll talk right after the wedding. . . . What do you say?"

Nothing.

"Amanda!"

Jess took hold of the doorknob—but it did not turn.

She stared at it, hurt and yet understanding perfectly. "You've locked the door. Oh, but why? Haven't I always helped you before? Why do this? . . . Amanda, if you don't unlock this door, I will have to go get the master key from Pool's cupboard. . . . Very well. So shall it be."

Under full sail, she hurried down to the servants' quarters, in two flashes found Pool's huge ring of keys, and marched herself back up the stairs. Without so much as a knock or a word, she inserted the master key in the lock, twisted the knob, thrust open the door, and found herself staring at a seated, bound, and gagged Amanda . . . while she herself was hauled backward in the stranglehold of someone who held a gun to her head.

Jess closed her eyes.

No, not like this. Not again.

"You should have gone to your wedding, Miss Curtis."

You should never have remembered I cut the girth strap, Jessica.

Jess expected to tremble, to grope for words. But time and love—oh, most especially love—had changed her. If years ago she had recovered her memory, she had also now recovered her dignity, her courage. More important, over the years since last a man had held a pistol to her temple, she had developed a maturity, an integrity he could not conquer.

"Emory, don't be foolish."

"I was foolish to send my daughter here!"

I was mad to think those doctors were right! You recalled it all along, you little liar.

"No, Emory. You weren't foolish."

And to think I fed you, spent money on you, time.

"Emory, you sent Amanda here because you loved her. You still do."

"Yes, by God." He shoved the cold circle of the barrel harder against her temple. "Enough to take her where she'll do no harm. Where she won't betray me."

But she betrayed me. Went with any man who showed half an interest in her. I couldn't let her bare herself to the skin and make me a laughingstock!

"The witch had an affair with another man! Had his child! The thing died, as well it should have!"

Jess felt her stomach roll.

Amanda was whimpering at the revelation that the baby sibling she had mourned so much and loved so dearly was a bastard, who her father thought should die.

"Don't do this to your daughter, Emory. Let her recover. She will be a credit to you. She loves you. That is so clear to see." *Though why I might never know and never need to. Only Amanda can find the words . . . words I never found for my own father.* "Don't destroy her love. Don't take her away like this."

"I must."

"So you couldn't get any doctor to sign papers to commit her without an examination. Is that right? And you came here to spirit her away while we were all at church. This is loathsome, Emory. It's beneath you. And look what you've done to Amanda. See in her eyes what she thinks of you now."

"Shut up! Shut up! *You* turned her against me. *You* put those ideas into her head about me hurting her mother."

"No, Emory, I never—"

"Of course you did. Everyone knows about your mother and her infinite number of lovers. Then, to cover his shame, your father shot your governess and committed suicide."

Amanda's eyes were as round as Roman coins. Sitting in her boudoir chair, she could not move for the torn sheets that were cordons on her hands and feet. But the child could hear—and cry.

"Emory, please. My story is old. Forgotten by all

except by you. But Amanda's is just beginning. Would you hurt her after all she's been through?"

"She thinks I killed her mother!"

Jess shifted enough in his arms to smell the aroma of liquor on his breath and to hear remorse in his words. "Did you?"

"No! No! Why would I? I loved her! She just didn't love me!"

"Weren't you to blame for that as well? Amanda says that you had other lovers. Is infidelity a sign of devotion? Have I missed something in the definition of married love?"

"You bitch," he seethed and hauled her to the matching boudoir chair. "Sit here and be still! So much as flinch while I do this and you are dead."

Visions of other threats, another scuffle so long ago, appeared before Jess. "Where will you take her?" she whispered to him.

He wrenched her arms back behind the chair. In the process, he fumbled with the pistol and had to lay it on the table beside her. Jess considered the weapon, cold and gray and shining, while he busied himself tearing sheets into strips with which to bind her.

Touch it, part of her commanded.

I can't! the child in her replied.

Use it and live!

But if I miss—

You must not.

"It doesn't matter," Emory was rambling on, huffing angrily and rending the sheets. "Wherever she goes, no one will listen to her. I'll see to that."

"I'll find you, Emory."

He laughed like the demented. "Not likely, lady." And then he gagged her so tightly that Jess felt she might vomit—and die choking.

This time you must not act out of anger—or fear. But turn to him she did, and in a flash she clenched her hands and hit him so hard in the face that he stumbled to the floor.

She lunged for his pistol.

He saw her, shot out his hand, and enclosed hers.

They struggled.

The gun went off.

Once.

Twice.

The reports knocked Jess senseless—only for a moment, but long enough for him to pick Amanda up like a sack and run for the door, leaving the pistol—miraculously, hellishly—within Jess's reach.

Within one beat of her heart, she snatched it up and scrambled to her feet.

My God, I'll have to kill him.

The thought staggered her.

But with the cold metal in her hand, she followed him—clear-eyed, determined, unforgiving.

She tore the gag off and called to him from the top of the stairs. *"Emory!"* He could not run too quickly with a squirming young woman in his arms.

He looked up at her, backing toward the front door.

"Emory!" Jess descended in measured steps, her intent crystal clear to her as him, especially since she held the pistol outstretched, her hand as steady as a rock. "Put her down or I'll shoot you."

"At this distance? You'd probably hit her." He laughed, all nerves. "You'd never take the chance."

"You don't know my skill."

"Don't waste your breath. Amanda and I will flee like a nightmare. You'll never find her."

"I guarantee you I will haunt you until the day you die, Emory."

She stepped down into the hall, level with him, though he approached the open portal—and an unseen cadre who stood like four sentinels—teeth bared, claws poised, hands clenched, bill open.

Jess dared to hope she might not have to pull the trigger. "Amanda belongs with those who love her for all she is and can be. Leave her to us, Emory."

"Never!" he boomed, and blindly turned.

That was the cue the Quartet needed.

Bones tore at Emory's ankle, bringing him to his knees. The cat sprang onto his shoulder, hissed, and raked his cheeks. The monkey pummeled him about the head and neck. The bird grabbed his hand, which had once imprisoned his daughter, and in one crunch tore a chunk of bone and flesh with her powerful bill.

Emory howled in bright pain.

Amanda rolled away and, wide-eyed, watched the horror of her father in bleeding, broken agony.

Jess dropped the pistol and ran to her quickly, removing her bonds and holding her close. "My darling," she crooned, "you are safe now. He won't ever take you away, Amanda. I'll see to that."

"Good God, Jess!" Rand bellowed from the open doorway, four animals and Emory before him while Spence stood agape close behind. "What in hell happened here?"

Though Jess could at first find no words to summarize it, Rand knew. A commanding figure in his dove-gray morning attire, he stepped across the mélange before him. Spence took the pistol and trained it on a writhing Harrison Emory.

"Darling." Rand took her in his arms and rocked her while she herself hugged Amanda close.

"Amanda and I are fine, Rand," Jess managed finally over a sob of delayed terror when he pushed her hair from her cheeks and examined her for wounds. "If you'll just give me a few minutes more to collect myself and summon a doctor for Emory, I would very much like to get married today—especially today when I can enjoy my future, free of my past."

Epilogue

THE CHRISTMAS SEASON ARRIVED THAT YEAR HERALDED by a blanket of snow. Soft and silent as a snowfall, Jess's anticipation of this particular night grew like an avalanche within her breast.

She gazed at her husband from across the crowded church reception hall and admired the man who was hers, heart and hope and all. Imposing as he had ever been, he spoke with Patricia Mellwyn who had flowered in these last months into a wise and helpful friend.

Rand Templeton, however, was the one who exuded the brightest élan. He chuckled instead of smiled. His magnificent blue eyes danced instead of considered. His hands reached, possessed, and freed. As they always had and would.

Jess sipped her punch, leaned back against the wooden pilaster, and smiled to herself. Oh, he was still as revered as ever, by friend and cohort alike. But now he was enjoyed all the more for his warmth, his gaiety, his love of life.

For these refinements, he credited her, his wife. "My life, my love, my everything," he often proclaimed in the hushed aftermath of their minds' and souls' union. But Jess felt she had so much more to give him—and she had long feared she might not be able.

For these past six months, in fact.

While he had given her everything a woman could want.

That day of their marriage he had given her time to recover. Far from the few minutes she had claimed she needed to recuperate from Emory's attack, she took over an hour. Amanda, too, resilient with the security of Jess's arms about her, had insisted on going to the church. Emory had been taken away by the constable soon after the Tuttle village apothecary declared him able to endure incarceration. After being released under the promise that he would stay far from Farrell Hall and his daughter for at least a year, Harrison Emory darkened their door no more.

Before the Tuttle church altar, Rand and she had exchanged vows with grins upon their lips and kisses uncounted afterward. She had even waltzed—and not too badly, she might add—at the reception hours later.

As the sun set upon that remarkable day, he had taken her to London, to Grosvenor Square, to the massive bed of the marquesses of Ashford—and to paradise once more.

Paris, in the following two weeks, rivaled it for pleasure. They saw the sights, but most of them were the wondrous ones inside the lavish blur of gold and ivory in the suite they occupied at the Hôtel Fontaine. But she did meet a few artists, and she and Rand did take in an opera and enjoy a day-long boat trip down the Seine. She knew ecstasy when she felt it, and, God, had she reveled in it, as she had never imagined she could.

She called herself a glutton. She called her husband a wizard.

He termed her his. Simply his. For the universe to witness how he loved her.

If in his eagerness to show her unique delights he exposed her to the infinite joys of conjugal bliss, she did not object. Not when he bought her sultry Parisian lingerie that could steal the blush off one of Spence's hybrid roses. Not when he bought them two novel conveyances called bi-cycles and they pedaled off to an abandoned château in the French countryside with wine and cheese for an afternoon of love in the grass.

And especially not when one morning he announced that they would leave Paris that afternoon for another destination, which—with a teasing light in his eyes—he refused to reveal. But as they stood upon the quay, the sign above the platform proclaimed their destination.

"Vienna," she had marveled. "Vienna." And then she'd thrown her arms about him, there in front of everyone, and kissed him as if she'd never have enough of him.

They had climbed aboard the Orient Express and settled in a private car outfitted for a sultan.

"You're going to indulge me too much," she had

told her chuckling mate as she collapsed naked against the voluminous red velvet cushions less than an hour later.

Rand followed her down, his body a vibrant testament to his intent. "Tell me," he whispered, his lips caressing her intimate ones, "when you've had enough."

She arched, her hands fluttering to his hair. "You'll stop?"

"Only to have more of you in inventive ways," he told her as he turned her and brought her up on her knees. One thumb inside her, two fingers finding her point of delight, he prepared her.

"Ohh!" she moaned as he replaced his fingers with the part of him she craved minute by minute. "I think I must have married the right man."

"The only man," he corrected and nipped her ear. "Ever."

Vienna seemed as much a whirl as Paris now, months later. Rand had promised when they left that any time she wanted to return, they could. All the reasons she remembered Vienna for being wonderful as a child were magnified by the presence of this man whom she adored.

But then, of course, the two gifts he had given her in Vienna were beyond compare. And he, in his modesty, had never claimed them as his doing entirely.

"Chance can often work to one's benefit," he mused, with a telltale laugh in his blue eyes late one night after he had taken her to supper at a café on the Ringstrasse and they had sat down next to a group of physicians who studied the psychology of man.

As serendipity permitted in the casual atmosphere

among violinists and accordionists, the Viennese doctors had struck up a conversation with the Templetons. In the discussion, Jess learned that Rand knew a few of these gentlemen well and that they had heard of her and her school from him.

"You planned that meeting," she persisted as they undressed that night for bed. "Tell me it isn't so and I'll eat that box of chocolates all by myself." She nodded to the two-pound box of sinful sugar-coated fruits and nuts Rand had bought that afternoon from a confectioner.

"Eat all of them, darling." He had swung her up in his arms and headed for the frothy expanse of their eiderdown bed. "I myself have developed a hunger for a particular milky dessert."

"You are outrageous!" She couldn't stop her laughter as he settled her on the sheets. "You expect me to believe you didn't know they ate together there each week, hmmm?"

He went quite still. "I knew." He thumbed her hair from her cheeks. "I also knew they needed to meet you, hear you speak about your success with overly active students—and with Amanda."

They had dinner with those doctors and professors repeatedly during the following two weeks. Next spring one of them would come for two months to Farrell Hall to study their behavioral techniques with the girls. Another professor, interested in following the footsteps of the late Dr. Johann Steineke, had already published a paper after a visit to the school in October.

But what had happened on the final night of their Vienna idyll put more gratitude and adoration into her soul than she could have measured in ten lifetimes of loving Rand.

That evening, Rand hired an open barouche and ordered the driver to have his horses clop across the charming cobbles to a different café. Garlanded in roses and enough baroque gilding to please the worst libertine, the restaurant claimed, Rand said, not only the best Wiener schnitzel and the greatest selection of schnapps but also an orchestra so renowned that the heir to the Hapsburgs, the archduke Rudolf, often caroused there with mistresses and hangers-on until the sun came up.

What he had not told her was that this place was patronized by musicians, singers, and producers of operas, concerts, music-hall entertainments, and theatrical plays. What's more, the tone was impromptu. Whatever the mood, the artists here learned to respond to the call of their muse. When, after supper, the orchestra played the latest favorites, the patrons waltzed or polkaed. Soon the joie de vivre led many to perform.

Thus it was, quite without forethought, but in the spirit of freedom, that Jess found herself seated at the piano. Stunned at the very idea of a public performance, which she had never before attempted or been asked to do, she knew that she sat here because she had come so far from her inhibiting past.

And in that spirit, she performed the work that epitomized her progress: "Serenade to Spring" by Elise Leighton.

One publisher had asked to print the score. When Jess had revealed there were more like this one, the affable man had asked to hear a sample. She had sat at that piano long into the umber summer night, sharing the talent of her mother, who was never praised while she drew breath but who was now—next month, in fact—to be published with distribution on the Continent and, soon, in Britain as well.

And all because one morning she herself had gone to a man and asked for the gift of his time and talent, and he had multiplied the joys with his own infinite sweetness and unfailing love.

Why would she not want to present him with what she could?

She had yearned for it. Prayed for it.

But as time marched on and their carnal demonstrations of a bliss divine magnified with each touch, she had despaired of success.

Certainly a child was the only unique treasure she could bestow on him. Money he had aplenty. Connections he had already shown her to her benefit. And he had set an example of patience that no one could ever match.

Of course, she wanted to give him the ultimate incarnate expression of their love, their mating. Their marriage.

She had feared she was incapable of doing so.

She'd even been tempted to confide in Cat.

But that was last week, when she was still uncertain, hoping against hope that the signs she saw were substantive.

And now there could be no doubt.

"Darling, I repeat"—Rand had evidently stood near her long before she heard him—"are you well?"

She rested her head against the pilaster and let her eyes praise the handsome man who was her lover and her mate.

"You look rather dreamy, sweetheart." A frown furrowed his finely molded features. "I have seen you like this before. Either you are about to have one of your chills or you're just damned taken with the looks of me. Which is it, Jess? I need to know whether to call for the doctor or simply kiss you."

One hand drifted to his jaw. "Take me home."

He needed no more. Assuming the worst, he relieved her of her punch glass and, without any adieus, swept his wife into his arms, took her cape to wrap around her, and had her carry his as he strode to their waiting brougham.

Inside, he uncapped a flask of brandy, told her to take one sip, then secured her to his chest.

Shivering with the present she knew she could not wait until tomorrow to give him, she reveled in the way her husband bound her to him in the darkness.

He was so very dear. So concerned. She thought he looked rather fierce, actually, as he paraded through the foyer of the Temple with her in his arms, then dismissed her worried maid to say he would take care of her himself. And so he did.

Not stopping his ministrations to kiss her or caress her as he usually did when he stripped her to her skin, he rummaged through her lingerie drawer to produce an old flannel nightgown she had often worn in winter.

"Love of mine," she chuckled as he slipped the hideous thing over her head, "I really am not ill."

"No? Well, we won't take any chances, will we?"

"I'm very healthy."

"Yes, well, you look well, but . . . hmm, do you want the fire higher? I'll get a footman to bring more coals. And cocoa? What do—"

She put two fingers to his lips. "I need only you. In bed—skin to skin, as you once promised we would always be."

No sooner said than done, she was quite naked, flesh to his flesh, as he pulled the covers up to her chin and clamped her closer to rub her back. She sailed like that for endless minutes until she felt him relax and she found the way to say the words she knew he'd never forget.

"Very soon it will be Christmas."

"Mmm."

"Our first."

"Of countless more."

She smiled and kissed him above his heart. "I have never been so happy during Christmas. Except for one thing."

"What would you want, love? If I haven't put it beneath that tree downstairs, I will, I swear."

"No, I meant that I had such a difficult time thinking of what to give you."

"What you give me, my matchless wife, is you. Your laughter and patience, your objectivity and intelligence. You are more than enough." He pressed her back to the pillows, loomed above her, then kissed her deeply. "You are all and all to me."

Knowing that within his bounteous heart there was room for others, Jess smiled at him, and at that sign, he paid hot homage down her throat to her breasts. In her new state, his tongue felt like the silken lap of more new adventures—this time, into parenthood.

She sighed as he continued his explorations, familiar territory to them both but, oh, so eternally enchanting. And when at sweet last, he joined them as their Maker had intended, he slid into her with a sure, slow glide that had her undulating and him gripping her wrists above her head.

"You must stop now," she told him, breathlessly.

He didn't understand at first, so lost was he in the possession of the moment. "What? Why?" He closed his eyes and arched back in simple ecstasy.

"I want to give you your Christmas gift."

"Now?" His eyes popped wide, and he chuckled. "We said we'd wait for the morning and the Lyonnses! I intend to give you other things at the moment."

That wreathed a smile on her lips. "Give me your hand."

He hovered over her and dropped a suckling kiss on one appreciative nipple. "If you think I'm leaving this bed now to go downstairs to that tree—"

"Your present isn't under the tree." She laced her fingers in his and led them to her stomach. "It's here, under my heart."

He blinked.

"Where you put it."

He stilled.

"Where it lives."

His face fell and his eyes flowed into hers with a bright gleam.

"Where I'll keep it safe and warm until the day I can place him or her in your arms, and your child will see what I have seen—that no man will ever equal you."

Words paled in comparison to the expression on his face and the might of his embrace.

"Merry Christmas, my generous Rand," she managed to whisper to him long silver minutes of delight later. "No gift from God to me will ever mean more than this gift of you and your abiding love."

Author's Note

Jessica and Amanda's disability affects more people even as I write this and you read it. The National Head Injury Foundation in Washington, D.C., estimates that someone in the United States sustains a traumatic brain injury every fifteen seconds, and every five minutes one of them will die from it. Traumatic brain injury (TBI) is a leading cause of death and disability in children and young adults.

Thanks to improved paramedical procedures and the technological breakthroughs in treating shock trauma, many of those injured survive. But as many as ninety thousand of them will endure lifelong disablement. Some of that loss of function is physical, some mental, some a combination of both. Each survivor can expect to face five to ten years of intensive medical services to assist with recovery at a cost of about $4 million dollars over a lifetime.

Obviously Jess and Amanda suffered milder injuries than many. Often, in the centuries before this one, the means to save such victims was limited. After riding accidents or severe blows to the head, people simply died. Those who lived were often misunderstood and misdiagnosed as mentally deficient or ill. Such attitudes are prevalent among the general public even today.

Sad to say, for many victims, that attitude can be more deadly than the initial blow. And for the children and young adults who suffer to surmount the limitations of their disability, the burden can become a curse.

Preventive measures can help decrease the incidence of TBI. Wearing a helmet while biking and a seat belt while driving is a good rule to follow. Driving safely is just as important, since over half of all TBIs occur in motor vehicle accidents. Young men, ages fourteen to twenty-four, are the greatest segment of those injured. But accidents will happen—on sports fields and in the home, where no protective device can halt the assault of sheer happenstance.

Meanwhile, I hope you will wish to learn more about TBI and how to help those who are its victims. My work here in *Gifts* is fiction; the information used for that purpose is therefore brief and necessarily modified to suit the necessities of character and plot. Far from being an expert on TBI, I have used what layman's truths I knew from my own family's experiences with the disability. I heartily recommend that you write for more information to National Head Injury Foundation, 1776 Massachusetts Ave. N.W., Suite 100, Washington, D.C. 20036.

And in the meantime, I hope you enjoyed this book which was a labor of love for me to write.

In my next novel, I shall return to the medieval period in England when Henry IV ruled a kingdom riddled with rebels and conspirators. In my story, Henry sends his most trusted retainer—his Dragon, Lord Jordan Chandler—to negotiate a marriage of convenience and hopefully end the rebellion in one corner of his domain. But the Dragon finds himself enchanted by the lady whose hand he must give to his own nephew. When the lady takes his heart and then is accused of conspiracy, Jordan must clear her name—and give her up. Look for *In the Dragon's Keep* in the summer of 1997.

Please write to me to let me know how you enjoyed *Gifts* and my other historical romances for Pocket, including the predecessor to *Gifts, Treasures.* A self-addressed stamped envelope is helpful for a reply.

Jo-Ann Power
4319 Medical Drive
#131-298
San Antonio, TX 78229

POCKET BOOKS
PROUDLY PRESENTS

THE NIGHTINGALE'S SONG

JO-ANN POWER

Coming Soon
from
Pocket Books

The following is a preview of
The Nightingale's Song . . .

Cheshire, England
November 1403

She must be perfect.

Blond.

Blue-eyed.

Small-boned.

Hare-brained.

But very well endowed.

The ideal woman for a wife.

Pretty. Please God, deaf and dumb. But filthy rich.

Jordan chuckled, then spurred his horse. With a whicker, his black Flame objected.

He could not fault the animal. It was torture to travel blindly through any blizzard. "Though these made of snow are more easily done than those made of men's and women's folly, eh?"

What an illusion, to fashion this woman gorgeous!

"With my luck of late, I'll find myself betrothing my nephew to a harpy. No matter," he muttered to himself, "I'll do it even if she's bald, walleyed and toothless!"

Though how could he in good conscience do that when he knew the spark to this marriage's candlewick would be this issue of the bride's beauty?

But he must secure this union. He needed to

conclude the agreement to burn brightly in King Henry's sight, just as he needed the bride's agreement to come quickly to her marriage bed.

Certainly, there was little said about her to predict that outcome.

Rumor had made her legend.

Clare of Trent was the only wealthy woman along the war-torn Welsh marches who had managed to refuse all suitors since she was sixteen.

"Aged now," said one source.

Twenty-three, confirmed his own visitor to her father, the traitorous Earl of Trent.

"A hermit," declared one companion of her sire.

"Silent," clarified his own friend, "when present. But so often absent from the great hall's table that people whisper she is given to much prayer upon her knees."

Jordan harumphed to himself. "As long as she is given to much passion upon her back, she should become the model mate for a young man who values such talents."

As an older man who survived the turmoil of the past decade's civil wars, Jordan prided himself that he had learned crudely at the early age of ten to look beyond his nose. It was the trait which had forged him to his king's regard these past twenty years. As retainer. Adviser. Trusted friend.

Why should the matter of this marriage be any different from those other occasions when against all odds Henry of England's Dragon had prevailed?

It wouldn't.

Still I would like to see her before I bargain for her.

But he wasn't seeing much. Not in this storm.

He yanked his cowl closer down his helm and brought his cloak more securely across his mail tippet and breast plate. For this four-day journey, he had decided that he and his two men should don light armor and royal livery for the horses. In this territory, so near the rebellious Welsh border, he wanted to take precautions against robbers and political adventurers.

Jordan narrowed his gaze into the gloom of night and reaffirmed his three goals. Getting a wife for his nephew. Gaining money—and an unwilling but necessary ally—for his king. Obtaining his own retirement from the fray of court politics. Intrigues. Murders. Feigned love on fevered beds—

In the vacant silence of the snow-swept night, he distinctly heard the swift hiss of weapons drawn.

He flung off his hood, dropped his visor across his face, and shot up his one hand to halt his two men while his other hand slid inside his cloak for the deadly comfort of his sword.

"My lord?" croaked one of his men.

Jordan sliced the air to quiet him. He sensed his other man come abreast, his broadsword at the ready. Jordan brandished his own long blade and reined his horse into position for attack. The three, as prearranged, formed a triangle of defense, swords drawn to their challenge in right hand, lethal misericordes in the left.

The minute sifted like sultry sands as telltale hooves on slick ground whispered, picked, then churned the earth. Years of working Henry's will on far-flung fields from Ireland to bloody Shrewsbury had Jordan estimating the number, speed, and purpose of this band.

He counted.

Five.

Mounted.

Armed.

But *where?*

Two there. And there.

Two sprang upon them from the copse. The third

and fourth drove at them at an angle that pinched them toward the stream.

The fifth?

Where could he be?

Jordan met the first of the four, swords crossing until he wore his opponent down and lunged, the sharp point of death's grace delivered to the brigand's unwisely bare throat. The man fell, a heavy blot upon the earth.

Jordan spun. Where was the fifth?

Not here.

So where? *Where?*

But there was no time to ponder as one outlaw picked one of Jordan's men, the second another, while the third man bared brown teeth in invitation to advance.

Jordan took the advantage, sprang forward with a cry of righteousness, and easily buried his blade into the cur's tough gizzard. Surprise lit the fiend's eyes as he doubled, babbling in his blood, to hit the ground.

Jordan whirled about to aid his men, when from his right side, he heard the rider whom he had counted but not yet seen.

The fifth man galloped forward, but unlike his companions, this one wore armor—and he charged at Jordan with a lance firmly bracketed into his breastplate. Jordan cursed at his own lack of a shield and focused on the point of the weapon which was used only on battlefields. Not ambushes. But this point—good Christ—was *blunted!* And the fool aimed the three-pronged weapon at Jordan's left shoulder.

Scarce had the idiocy of the man's target hit Jordan than he knew his intent.

No death for me! Not clean or quick. But capture's what this heathen craves.

Why?

Instinct made him raise his sword to go for the only unprotected portion of the man's body—his thighs and manhood.

But the blunted lance slammed into Jordan before he could cut the fiend from his children.

He reeled and the world exploded.

Jordan felt the familiar pop of ball from socket. The poker of pain that seared his torso, then his brain. A soundless cry of torment left his lips while his mind, logical beyond the frustration of his weakness, asked why he fell to this well-planned attack by a phantom in the snow.

He thudded to the ground.

Dusk dimmed beyond his agony.

Trussed quick as a pig to slaughter, he cursed silently as the brigands yanked his hands behind him. Twined ropes about his wrists. Ripped his helmet from his head so fast he thought his nose went with it. When he condemned them to fire and brimstone, they shoved a rag into his mouth.

Before they could blindfold him, he craned his neck to see who his attackers were—and found no one he knew.

But he heard—

Horses?

Jordan felt the earth pound with more hooves. There were more of these knaves?

He froze.

His attackers paused. Ceased their struggles to lift his bucking body from the ground to the horse they'd drawn toward him.

"Who could that be?" spat one.

"No one goes in these woods!"

"These are fairies then?" ridiculed the other. "Christ, gain cover!"

"But Chandler—?"

"Leave him!"

They scrambled away.

Through pain-glazed eyes, Jordan peered into the graying night. Ear to the earth, he heard the buzzing of the newest swarm of hornets to this hive.

Six?

No, seven.

Mounted.

Armed?

Not upon war horses, but . . .

Oh, hell. Palfreys???

They thundered into the clearing, a phalanx on females' horses. At their helm one woman stood in her saddle, shouting orders, her posture erect, her hood gusting in the wind to unveil a copper beacon of hair and the creamy counterpoint of flushed skin.

Jordan spit out the poorly tied gag and muttered about fantasies of warrior-women while he picked at the ropes around his wrists.

In a rush, his Amazons on petite mounts circled the troop who tried to take him. He sprang to a sitting position and inched back into a thick bush for cover just as an arrow missed his cheek.

The women squeezed the circle of brigands smaller. Two of them shot arrows from horseback and even in the blur of snow, these women hit their marks. Two others sported daggers. They tossed them with a nefarious ease to prick two of his attackers like pincushions.

One brigand, scarce a foot away, chose to stand. The next second saw him sinking to his knees, face-to-face with Jordan, an arrow piercing his throat.

Jordan snatched up the man's dagger with his good right hand and vaulted to his feet. Two of the women who had sported small wood axes and dismounted now found themselves sore beset by two men who believed hand combat their best defense. But women were no match for men in blood lust, and it took three women to try to pry one man from a friend. The women clawed and gouged his eyes until one skewered him with her own dagger.

A cry caught his attention.

Jordan spun, seeing the leader yanked kicking and screaming from her horse. Her attacker shouted of how he'd rape her before he killed her. He held her with a knife to her throat, dragging her backward by her braid, a brazier in the alabaster evening. Jordan could have found her in hell for all the brilliance of her crown.

He grimaced, the taste for this man's guts filling his mouth with sour joy.

He ran bent, his left arm useless, and in one bellow, he threw himself upon him. They tumbled. In the roll, Jordan's shoulder circled in his flesh. The hot shock boiled his brain but not his warrior's perception. His right hand and arm prevailed by grasping the outlaw's and in so doing, gouging his windpipe and blocking his air. The man purpled. Frothed. Jordan pressed his jugular, while his hand lowered slowly, slowly—and his misericorde slit skin down into the brigand's heart.

Jordan's nostrils flared. The stench of death nauseated him. Would he ever be free of it? Please, God . . .

"Deliver him," the rescued woman moaned.

Jordan glanced up and forced himself to stand.

She peered down at the lifeless body, open-mouthed, hand across her chest. But he knew she saw nothing.

In that moment with anguish blazing through his shoulder and rush of victory flooding the rest of him, he, too, looked—and gazed upon a flesh-and-blood woman far more fabulous than words.

A bright, blazing flame, she glowed against the misty grays of winter's dusk. A vivid vision of yellows, reds, and whites.

He shut his eyes. He shook his head. He almost laughed! And that novelty alone staggered him.

You are a warrior, Chandler, not a poet.

He forced himself to look at her again and view her humanity in cold terms.

She was no weak blonde, no watery-eyed waif, but all those essences a troubadour would declare too lusty for any right-thinking man to desire, lest he lose his soul.

God knew, his own had fled.

But not his senses. *Nay.* His right hand itched to touch her while his gaze absorbed her.

Her eyes glowed bronze. Her hair, escaping from her thick braid, tumbled in copper curls to her cloak. Her skin had been whisked pink by wind and exertion, while snowflakes dusted russet eyelashes with intricate embroidery.

She brought forth tears, but did not shed them. Instead, she flung them from her cheeks and threw back her head in defiance of the circumstances.

But then she smiled at him. Hers was a splendor of which bards dared not write for the madness they'd incite.

A sunbeam of a woman.

Through pain, confusion, and the rush of victory over greater odds, Jordan felt a shiver of premonition about who she was. Certainly, in this clime few women could afford as many handmaids. Fewer still had the independence, the strength of will or skill at arms to lead retainers in an assault such as he witnessed here. Nary a woman would be so bold as to even leave her solar, yet here stood this beauty. . . .

He felt his heart drop to his feet when he admitted the truth to himself.

She might be perfect. To him.

But this was Clare of Trent . . . and she was meant for his nephew, Geoffrey, who would gauge his wife's perfection as he had his paramours'—by how pale she looked, how docile she remained, and how aggressively she performed, not in her horse's saddle, but in her husband's.

Jordan sighed. She was as far from perfect as the sun from the moon.

"Sir, I repeat you are not well. Your shoulder hangs at an odd angle . . . Sir?" She placed a palm to his chest, and through his layers of breastplate and tunic he felt her concern.

"Aye," he found his tongue, his eyes falling to her hand. For blithe seconds he had forgotten everything except what it would be like to hold such glory in his arms. "This is an old injury."

"And a recurring one, I take it from your nonchalance."

"Unfortunately, aye." Her hand lingered. He tried to clear his head, but the sight of her—the touch of her—robbed him of pain, and that alone was worth the dalliance.

"Will you allow me to assist you and put it back in place?"

Jordan cradled the limb which hung oddly forward. About him and this bedazzling woman, her bevy of women sheathed their swords and daggers, shouting to each other of each brigand's condition. Their victory had made them proud and boisterous as men. "I assure you, my lady, after I have seen to my two men—and these who have attacked us, you may do for me."

When he strode toward Nathaniel, she kept pace beside him. "My women are quite able to truss any of these brigands still alive or—" She glanced about and discovered what destruction her women had really wrought, "pile up the bodies. They can also aid your two while I set you aright."

Jordan saw the truth of her statement as his youngest man Nathaniel hopped up to him, supported by one accommodating black-haired woman.

The lad was shaken but whole—and by his wobbly smile, well pleased by his striking assistant. "It's my ankle, my lord. I twisted it myself in my haste to do one of those fellows in."

Jordan nodded. "You did well. Put no weight on your afflicted foot lest that injury grow worse. We'll get you tightly bandaged and—"

"We can do that for you and put him atop his horse," the woman beside Jordan persisted in her own purpose. "Let me see to you, good sir, before you faint."

"I assure you, madam, this has happened to me so often that fainting—were it even tempting—would be a temporary charm against this woe. Pardon me, but I have men to care for." *And an ambush to decipher. By men who knew my name. My location. And what else, only those who employed them could say.*

Jordan swung back to consider this gorgeous creature before him. His gaze narrowed on her face—her wide brows, innocent eyes, and determined chin. A new thought—and a malicious one—crossed his mind. *I do not know how you happened to come upon us so conveniently.*

"You whiten with the pain again, sir. I say you are too stubborn for your own good." She pushed back a lock of her glowing hair and peered at him through the lace of snow. Her cheeks flushed with an indignant anger and she jammed two hands on her hips. "What ails you beside your shoulder, sir? You look at me oddly, and yet I might remind you that you are the stranger to this land. Who . . . ?"

Something about what she'd just said made her stop and think. Then she shot a glance at the green-and-white livery of his horse. "My lord," she murmured, and Jordan wondered if she were praying or cursing, "who are you?"

She took a step closer and examined his features. "These woods belong to a friendly tenant of ours. I know him and his family. But I do not know you. Why do you and your small band pass here?"

Jordan had his wounded men to aid. "I am the king's man. So you can understand my haste—and my concern for my men." He turned to see to them.

She hastened to keep up with him as he walked toward the place where he'd left his other man Edward. Jordan continued his reconnaissance through brush and gorse to find him reclining in the snow. The axe which had pierced his thigh lay on the ground near its horrendous handiwork. Jordan concluded that the pretty blond dove who cooed to him brought him as much relief with her looks as she did with her hands. Still had she done good service by Edward, stanching his blood with a bit of torn cloth. Jordan supposed it was this beauty who had also removed the axe from Edward's gaping wound.

Jordan knelt in the gore-stained snow. "Let me see him."

"He needs," insisted the lady in charge as she followed him down beside his man, "to be bathed, cauterized, set, and sewn."

Edward agreed between clenched teeth.

Jordan knew the damage such weapons could cause. They could not only cut major blood vessels so severely that the hurt man could watch his life drain from him in minutes, but also they could hack bones so badly the man prayed for death to deliver him some relief. Then, if he survived both those conditions, he had to hope no putrid matter formed to eat away his flesh. Through the long recovery, the patient needed a positive nature to bolster his efforts to once more sit, stand, and walk.

Jordan tried to give Edward some of that healing power in his words. "By the grace of God, man, I'd say this wound is not but half an inch deep and only as long as my hand."

"Agreed, my lord. These ruffians were so poor at their trade," he tried to laugh, but lost it to a grimace, "they used small weapons."

"Aye, Edward. You'll live." Though Jordan would not wager one penny sterling Edward would do so easily without a warm, dry room to welcome him—and soon. "We'll make an unexpected call upon those who live in that cottage you spied."

"We'll stop his blood first," said the lady of the bright hair and eyes. "Then we will take him to a far better place than the shepherd's cottage. To Castle Trent."

Jordan lifted both brows at her. "Then you *are* Clare de Wallys."

Her gilded eyes dashed to Flame's livery. Her expression crystallized. "And you are King Henry's Dragon."

"Aye. Always."

She shut her eyes. When she opened them again, she seemed distant, cold. Like a brilliant star burnt out. "You have come earlier than we expected. Three months sooner than planned, Baron Chandler."

He nodded slightly, observing etiquette in such a delicate situation. Telling himself he did it for protocol, he ignored the voice which whispered that he did it to see her sparkle once more. "Aye, my lady, I am pleased to meet you."

Her nostrils flared. He might be termed the Dragon, but she breathed the fire here tonight. "I cannot say the same."

Jordan sent her a look of reproof. The others were listening, trying to cover their interest by keeping busy. By such initial encounters were many judged. He would not be misperceived as weak or wily. Yet, whatever else he was, he had always been temperate in the treatment of his foes. And while it was still questionable if she shared her father's treacherous nature and therefore fully qualified as his own enemy, Jordan would not be underestimated by her. Or her father. So he engaged her in a flank attack. "Even to an emissary such as I, manners are important, my lady."

"What care I for niceties when all I wish for in this world can be snatched from me with your slightest word?"

He lowered his voice. He would not deprive her of her dignity unless she left him no other choice. "Then I bid you have a care, madam, for what you say to me."

"Aye, for I have heard the tale that when the Dragon's anger is incited," she said as she turned to pass from one of her women to another a flagon of wine down to Edward's eager lips, "people die."

Every one in the clearing froze.

But Jordan kept up his facade of indifference. "That is an old story."

"And true?"

"That depends on how you tell it." He smiled with the grim grace he'd learned from Henry's French and Viennese tutors of diplomacy. Its power caused two women before him to cower.

But not Clare. "I must hear your version sometime."

"There is no need to discuss it, madam. Not even with my friends."

His chilling tone made her vibrate with hot anger. *Good.* Her head snapped up from her ministrations.

She was shocked, he knew, at the look of objectivity he gave her. 'Twas the one he gave any and all who dared to cross swords with him.

Part of him was pleased that he had conquered her. Part of him mourned the cruelty of suppressing so worthy an opponent. "For now, I will say it matters not who I am or what my past may tell of me. I was told you agreed to this marriage to my nephew."

She shot up like an arrow, walked around him.

Jordan came up behind her. "Madam? If I have traveled four days through winter weather under false assurances by your father, Henry will be furious."

"What you mean to say is that at the slightest provocation Henry will take what's mine without benefit of marriage. He took a crown from his cousin Richard, mayhaps even his life. So what is one woman but tinder for Henry's hearth?"